THE MIRROR OF PHAROS

For Poppy

THE MIRROR
OF PHAROS

warm wishes
Enjoy!

J S LANDOR

J. S. Landor

Matador
9 Priory Business Park,
Wistow Road, Kibworth Beauchamp,
Leicestershire. LE8 0RX
Tel: 0116 279 2299
Email: books@troubador.co.uk
Web: www.troubador.co.uk/matador
Twitter: @matadorbooks

ISBN 978 1788039 208
British Library Cataloguing in Publication Data.
A catalogue record for this book is available from the British Library.

Printed and bound by CPI Group (UK) Ltd, Croydon, CR0 4YY

Matador is an imprint of Troubador Publishing Ltd

MIX
Paper from
responsible sources
FSC® C013604

For Rob and Ben

In between the doors of time
Lies a sacred space
Enter those who wish to climb
To the Magus place.

Chapter 1

The circle begins

In the hour before dawn, two amber eyes patrolled the sky over the hushed town. From their hiding place in Osmaston Wood they could see the world and when the fluttering white shape appeared, they were ready. They fastened onto it, glistening fiercely, and gave a quick blink.

Instantly, the wind stirred. Copper leaves fell from the trees and a thick seam of fog stole down the hills, wrapping the town in a ghostly shawl.

High above the rooftops a large seagull circled about, surveying the maze of streets below. He'd flown many miles through a long night to reach this place deep in the Rollright Hills. And now, at last, his journey was almost done.

In his beak he held a flat, brown parcel, not much bigger than a child's hand. All he needed was to find the right address.

But this was easier said than done. The sprawling

fog had invaded every nook and cranny and large chunks of the town were completely hidden from view. There seemed little else for it – he'd have to fly in for a closer look.

No sooner had he begun his descent than a sharp wind blew up, blasting the leaves on the pavement skywards. The seagull swerved wildly, beating his wings hard, but before he could regain his balance an even more savage gust forced him in the other direction. From the streets below, it looked like he was dodging bullets fired by a deadly enemy.

A third icy blast sent him nose-diving towards the market square. He flew dangerously close to the church spire, whistled past a line of open-mouthed gargoyles and narrowly missed a statue of the town's founding father, William Godley.

Behind the plate-glass window of the baker's shop, a wedding cake loomed nearer. The seagull gave a desperate squawk and banked steeply upwards. For one heart-stopping moment, before his wings carried him clear, he clipped the face of the town hall clock and the package glowed faintly blue.

It had been a close shave. He was a rugged bird from the weather-beaten cliffs of the Pentland coast, yet the freak wind had caught him completely off guard.

Several dizzy circles later, he swooped down to a small red-brick house on the outskirts of town. It stood on a steepish bit of road at the end of a row of terraced cottages. Number 12, Hill Rise, Morton Muxloe. This was the place!

He skidded to a halt on the gravel driveway and sat with his breath making little clouds while he studied the front door. It was yellow with an old-fashioned bell pull on one side and a brass door knocker near the top. But what interested him most was the vertical letterbox in the middle. It looked exactly the right size.

Hopping boldly forwards, he tried pushing the package through the narrow opening. It wouldn't go. Even with his head cocked on one side, he couldn't get the angle right – the parcel kept jamming. After several more attempts he shrieked in frustration. There had to be some other way to make his delivery.

He took off, climbing high over the slate roof and soon spotted the answer to his problem. At the back of the house, half overgrown by trailing ivy, another door beckoned. This one had what looked like a much larger letter box close to ground level. With a delighted cry he dived down, determined to finish the job once and for all.

Inside number 12, Jack Tideswell woke with a jolt. A moan erupted from the knot of bedding which seemed to have turned him overnight into a human sausage roll. He struggled free and yanked back the curtains. Not morning already! He felt as if he hadn't slept a wink.

Flopping back, he stared blankly at the ceiling and wondered what day it was. *Saturday? Sunday?* The answer came to him like a stab in the stomach. 'Noooo!' he groaned. *Monday.*

In the kitchen below, the clanking of cups and plates competed with the news on the radio. 'Give me a break!'

he yelled, pulling the duvet over his head. Instantly, the radio volume turned to full blast. His fist thumped the mattress. 'Not fair!' Nan could blame her hearing all she liked, but her tactics for getting him up were just plain sneaky.

'Storm-force winds and torrential rain are expected by this evening,' blared the weatherman. 'As deepening lows sweep in from the Atlantic, the Met Office has issued flood warnings ... Take extra care on the roads tonight ...'

The seagull glided silently past Jack's window and came to rest on the garden wall, folding his wings like a cape around his large body. In the kitchen, he could see a small thin woman in a multicoloured dressing gown, buttering a slice of bread. His belly rumbled and he let out a hungry cry.

Nan looked up. Her corkscrew hair stuck out at odd angles and the expression on her face suggested she'd got out of bed on the wrong side.

'What do *you* want?' she said, jabbing the butter knife at the gull. He was staring at her with such intensity it looked as if he might actually speak. She pulled her dressing gown tightly around her. 'It's no good. There's nothing here for you.'

The bird gave another plaintive cry.

Nan put down the knife and banged on the window. 'You're not wanted. Go on. Push off – shoo!'

The seagull ruffled his feathers but made no attempt to move, and when she looked back a few minutes later he was still there, his head drooping with exhaustion into the pillow of his chest. Behind him, the mist had cleared to reveal an angry sky flushed with red. The light seemed to give his body a strange, luminous quality. Nan shivered. Her mother had told her once that seagulls were the ghosts of drowned people.

'Oh … all right,' she said, opening the window at last. She flung some crusts of bread on the garden path and the big bird hopped after them, flapping his wings and shrieking his appreciation.

Nan watched him and, for a moment, a giddy, faraway feeling took hold of her. An icy breeze lifted her hair and she reached out to steady herself.

To her relief, a furry head met her hand.

'Odin! For heaven's sake, where've you been? Get in, will you.'

With a yowl, a large black and white cat leapt down from the windowsill and wound himself jealously around her ankles.

'That's quite enough of that.' Nudging the cat with her foot, Nan hastily shut the window.

'Time to get up!' she bellowed at the ceiling. 'Bacon sandwich on the table – twenty minutes and counting!' She knew Jack's routine: five minutes to wash and dress, five minutes to eat breakfast, five minutes to pack his school bag and five minutes to spare. Except there never was any time to spare.

Jack didn't feel like breakfast, not this morning. He had a tight knot in his stomach which felt like an iron fist squeezing his guts. Swinging his legs out of bed, he dragged himself to the bathroom and stared sternly into the mirror. *Come on, get a grip,* he told himself. *It's not as bad as you think.*

The round face beneath the mop of black hair looked unconvinced. Perhaps he wouldn't be in such trouble if he appeared a little more lean and mean.

Twenty minutes later, he stood beside Nan in the hall. At twelve years old, he was already able to look down at her, although he had to admit that didn't take much doing: his grandmother was barely five feet tall.

Out of habit, she tapped the barometer. The needle twitched nervously from *Fair* to *Change*, then right around the dial to *Stormy*. She pulled out a red anorak from the coat rack under the stairs.

'I don't need it,' mumbled Jack.

'What is it with boys and coats? You can't be "cool" when you're wet and freezing.' Nan unzipped the anorak and held it out with a flourish, like a matador tempting a bull.

Jack rolled his eyes. Reluctantly, he pulled the coat on.

'And don't take it off the minute you get to the corner,' Nan called after him.

Jack set off at a run, the bacon sandwich he'd forced down churning in his stomach. When he reached the bottom of the hill, he took the coat off and bundled it into his school bag.

Back in the kitchen Nan sighed, knowing he would. *Stop fussing,* she told herself. If she wasn't careful, she'd worry herself into an early grave. After all, there were far worse things in the world than catching a cold …

Outside, while the clouds bulked together in the stormy sky, two amber eyes watched Jack sprint into the distance. A wolf sat at the corner of Hill Rise, his head lowered between his broad shoulders. When Jack finally disappeared from view, he lifted his nose to sniff the air. As if responding to a signal, a fierce wind began to blow once more.

CHAPTER 2

The traders were busy setting up their stalls in the market square. Rows of brightly striped canopies billowed like balloons, tugging at the metal frames that held them. 'Batten down the hatches, lads,' someone cried out.

A flock of pigeons took off, their wings producing a clap-clap-clapping as Jack raced towards them across the cobbles. Several heads turned to watch.

'What's his hurry, then? Seen a ghost or summat?'

'Nah, late for school more like. Look at 'im go. Aye aye, watch out … Ow! Bet that 'urt!'

In his haste, Jack had skidded on the uneven stones. Face down, arms outstretched, he lay sprawled beneath the statue of William Godley like a slave paying homage.

For a moment he didn't move. His eyes closed and briefly the flapping of the canopies grew louder. Then it faded and what he heard next made him wonder if he was about to pass out. Blowing in his ears like a whispered message came the distant roar of the sea.

He shook his head, trying to chase the sensation away. Seagulls! He could hear them gabbling. He must be imagining it. Morton Muxloe was in the middle of England, more than a hundred miles from the coast.

'You all right, mate?' someone shouted.

Jack sat up, spitting the grit from his mouth. The town hall with its imposing clock tower loomed over him and, above that, great fleecy clouds rolled across the sky. He felt small as a speck of dust.

'Oi! I *said*, are you okay?' The fishmonger, a burly man in a brown apron, lumbered towards him.

'Fine.' Feeling like an idiot, he scrambled to his feet, grabbed the books and pens which had spilled from his bag and tore off through the broad arches at the end of the square.

Despite the stitch in his side, he kept going. 'You can do this,' he muttered. Not so long ago, when he'd swum for the Dolphins, he could run the mile to school in under ten minutes. Those were the days. He pictured the bright yellow caps of his club mates slicing through the water. By now, morning training would be over and they'd be having breakfast in the canteen, laughing and bragging about lap times.

He crossed the bridge over the River Churn. He'd never told anyone why he'd quit the sport he loved. He could barely admit it to himself. But it was the selfsame reason that had him running like a lunatic through the town centre. Fear. Simple as that. He was trying to avoid another ambush.

Glancing left and right, he sprinted past the black railings of St Mark's Church. Apart from an old man raking leaves, there was no one in sight.

His chest deflated in a sigh. He had to be *so* careful. They could be hiding anywhere: behind a hedge, in a shop doorway, under the stone bridge, in the churchyard ... With a shudder, he remembered how they'd pinned him to a gravestone and threatened to bury him six feet under.

Turning into School Lane, he raced for the gates of Muxloe High and for a moment he thought he'd made it. Then, above the hubbub of voices in the playground, laughter rang out – a hard, merciless sound like crows cawing. It was them.

They stood just inside the gates, their arms locked together like rugby players in a scrum: Fakes, Suttle, Gormley and Blunt, the meanest gang of thugs he'd ever known. They were having fun tormenting a first-year girl who scampered backwards and forwards like a rabbit, trying to dodge past them.

'Let me go!' she whined. 'You can't do this.'

'Whassat?' Blunt bore down on her. While the other boys sniggered, he caught hold of her ponytail and twisted it around his wrist so she was forced to dance on tiptoe. 'Gotcha by the tail,' he said, holding up the mane of hair. He produced a pair of scissors from his pocket. 'You squeal and I'll cut this off.'

Jack stepped forwards and tears of relief welled in the girl's eyes. Everyone knew he was the gang's favourite victim.

'Aaah, Tideswell!' crooned Blunt, stretching out his arms in a mock welcome. 'At last!'

The girl scurried away, tripping over Suttle's outstretched foot as she went.

'Bin jogging 'ave we?' Blunt hawked the phlegm from his throat.

Jack stared at the glob of spittle on the tarmac and said nothing. If he responded, the bully would find some way of turning it into an argument.

'Look at you, Jacko. You're sweating! Maybe you need to lie down.'

The school bell rang.

'Out of the way,' said Jack, barging past.

'Saved by the bell, eh? I don't fink so. Floor him, Fakes. Gorm, you get his feet. Suttle – 'ere, the scissors.'

Before he knew it Jack was sprawled on the tarmac. Fakes sat on his chest, a grin of anticipation on his face. 'You're gonna love this,' he said.

Gasping for breath, Jack tried to see what the others were doing. But Fakes rammed his head back down. 'No peeking. It's a surprise!'

Hands pushed down on his ankles and he realised they were removing his trainers. Struggling hard, he kicked out and one of the mob yelped. 'Hold him, dammit!'

A horrible ripping sound followed. Unable to move a muscle, Jack closed his eyes. *Will it always be like this?* he thought.

Someone's breath blew down one side of his face. 'Such a loser,' hissed Blunt in his ear.

Jack's eyes flashed open again.

'Snip!' laughed the bully, pressing the open scissors to his throat. 'Got anyfing to say?'

Jack held his breath while Blunt slowly ran the blade

11

over his Adam's apple up to his mouth.

'Nah, thought not. Sensible boy! You keep this shut, right, or we'll 'ave you. And that old bat you live with. Wouldn't take much to fix that heap of scrap she drives.'

And then it was over. Fakes' backside lifted from his chest and the boys moved away, crowing and slapping each other on the back.

Jack crawled over to the trainers which lay a few feet away. They had slashes down the sides and the laces had been chopped into pieces. With a sniff, he pulled the bits out. Then, ignoring the glances of the latecomers who hurried past, he put the trainers on and shuffled into school.

In an alleyway nearby, the wolf sat quietly watching. When the playground emptied, he padded across the road to where the shoelaces lay. With unblinking amber eyes, he stared down into the pile. The pieces began to move and within seconds a mass of fat, white worms slithered beneath him. One by one, he ate them all.

CHAPTER 3

'Mind where you're going!' said the woman with the brolly.

'Sorry,' mumbled Jack, without looking up.

The afternoon traffic honked noisily as the woman gazed after him. He kept lurching from side to side, watching his feet instead of the pavement ahead. A man with a Yorkshire terrier stepped smartly out of the way, but somehow Jack had got tangled in the dog's lead and a great deal of yapping was going on.

The woman clicked her tongue. She'd read about underage drinking and here was the proof of it – a schoolboy drunk in the middle of the afternoon! The thunder rumbled overhead. With a flurry of indignation, she opened her umbrella and hurried away.

Jack kept his eyes glued to the ground, unaware of the impression he'd created. He was too busy playing a game. It called for serious concentration, not to mention some fancy footwork: he was avoiding all the cracks in the pavement.

If you make it home without treading on a line, he told

13

himself, *they'll close school* … He jumped two squares to the right. *You'll have an amazing adventure* … He leapt three squares forwards. *Aaand* … He wobbled slightly. *Blunt will get it. Big time.*

The sky glimmered with distant lightning and the wind licked at the trees. In a garden across the road, a flowerpot crashed to the ground, leaving an untidy heap of soil and several red geraniums scattered on the lawn.

Perched on a nearby fence, a magpie, as big as a crow, let out a harsh, rattling cry: 'Tsche, tsche, tsche.' It seemed to be laughing at him.

Jack looked down to find he was standing on a crack. 'Oi! Now look what you made me do!' Without thinking, he reached for a stone and hurled it at the bird. 'Waster!'

The magpie took off, clapping its wings, and disappeared over the rooftops, screeching insults of its own.

Jack stared miserably at his feet. The ancient black plimsolls which he'd been forced to borrow from school lost property made him feel like an oversized ballerina. Sadly, the comparison had occurred to his classmates too. Everyone, except his best friend Charlie, had dissolved into hysterics when he'd turned up for registration.

Mr Marsh, his form tutor, hadn't been exactly sympathetic either. Usually a kind man, Boggy hadn't bought his story about a mad dog mauling his trainers. And since Jack couldn't tell him what had really happened, the teacher had given him a sad look and a lunchtime detention for being late.

Big splashes of rain started to fall. Turning up Hill

Rise, Jack could hear the wind chimes on the apple tree in the front garden jangling furiously.

He stopped in his tracks. Ahead, a dark cloud was moving in his direction and something about it looked very peculiar. He screwed up his eyes. It was sort of solid and appeared to be spinning. In fact, now it came closer, he could see it wasn't a cloud at all. He walked faster. Then he broke into a run. A blur of whirling shapes, like gigantic insects, swarmed towards him. They looked far too big to be bees. What else then? Locusts?

As he vaulted the garden wall at number 12, he felt a thud on his back, right between his shoulder blades. He twisted round, trying to see what it was. There was a second thud and a third. Something landed on his shoulder, then on his head. The 'thing' wriggled in his hair. Panicking, he shook his head wildly and put his hand up to extract it. Its skin felt leathery and its legs – all four of them – were scrabbling madly to escape the tangle.

Before he had time to remove the creature, a dozen more fell around him and then a deluge.

Frogs were falling from the sky like enormous green hailstones. Some of them lay stunned on the ground, others leapt in all directions. Jack pulled up the collar of his coat and bolted for the front door.

Inside, he jumped up and down. Something was wriggling down his back. He ripped the coat off and threw it on the hall floor. A tiny frog, which had been clinging to the lining, hopped into the darkness of the cupboard under the stairs.

15

'Hang it on the peg!' bellowed Nan from the sitting room.

Jack burst in on her. 'You won't believe this, but it's raining frogs!'

Nan looked over her newspaper and pushed her glasses down her nose. 'You mean "raining cats and dogs",' she said. 'I think you'll find that's the usual expression.'

'No! I mean frogs!' cried Jack. 'Come and look!' He dragged her out of the chair and propelled her towards the bay window.

A particularly large frog hit the glass with a splat. Nan took a step back. 'My word!' she said.

A mass of seething green bodies covered the front lawn. There must have been several hundred at least. Some were dead, others dying, and still more were scrabbling desperately over each other to escape. Nan's display of autumn dahlias had been completely flattened, and before their very eyes the garden was fast turning into a mud bath.

Jack gazed at the squirming bodies. Those that could still move were heading out of the garden.

'Have you ever seen anything like it?' he said.

Nan shook her head. 'Can't say I have.' Another frog hit the window and she winced. 'I read a news report once – some village in Kent, I think … The frogs got sucked up by a whirling wind, a bit like a small tornado. They were dropped nearly a mile away, poor things.'

Odin leapt onto the windowsill and sat with his ears pricked, his tail twitching furiously. The frog rain had stopped and the three of them watched in stunned silence as the survivors limped away.

At last, Nan turned to look at Jack. She was about to suggest they go outside to clear up when she noticed how exhausted he seemed. With a glance at the black plimsolls she said, 'Come and sit down. How was your day?'

'Fine,' Jack lied, flopping into a big armchair. To avoid any more questions he cut in with one of his own. 'So has it ever rained cats and dogs?'

'Not exactly. It's just a saying,' said Nan. 'But there was a time when sailors thought cats could influence the weather. They were supposed to bring heavy rain.'

Odin gave a low angry growl and the fur on his back bristled.

'Dogs, on the other hand, were connected with the wind. So "raining cats and dogs" is a way of describing strong rain and wind.'

Odin hissed angrily and fluffed out his fur.

An intruder had appeared in the front garden. It was five times bigger than him with eyes of amber that kept looking his way. And it was eating the bodies of the frogs, those that hadn't survived the downpour.

'Odin, as you know, is named after a storm-god,' Nan went on. 'Is this anything to do with you?' she joked.

More hisses issued from the windowsill, followed by another throaty growl. Finally, the cat spat explosively.

'Oh, for heaven's sake, what's the matter with you? I'm trying to talk to Jack.' Nan went to the window.

The intruder had vanished.

'Really, Odin, why don't you go out? It's no wonder you're in such a bad temper. You've been inside all day.' She turned back to Jack, who'd taken the opportunity to slip away.

'Everything all right at school?' she called.

'Yep,' he said over his shoulder. 'Tons of homework.'

Nan listened to the footsteps on the stairs. With a heavy heart, she turned back to Odin. 'Doesn't give much away, does he?'

The cat answered with a horrible yowl that sounded like a curse.

CHAPTER 4

Jack sat at his desk and stared into the dark void of his computer screen.

Next to the keyboard, Nan had left a glass of milk and a plate of homemade biscuits. They looked oddly volcanic, like lumps of lava. He nibbled warily at the edge of one. Nan was always devising strange new recipes. He never knew what to expect next.

The biscuit melted on his tongue and his eyes closed. Mmm … candyfloss! Weird, but delicious.

The taste reminded him of the funfair in Dunton where they spent their holidays. From the Ferris wheel, you could see for miles along the coast to a finger of land they called The Spike. And there on a rock, surrounded by sea, stood the Pentland lighthouse. It looked magical, a red and white candy cane engulfed by foaming waves.

The wind rattled the window, making him jump.

He gazed at the dreary heap of books. Homework: time to do some. He'd missed so many deadlines his teachers had put him 'on report'. Nan would go into orbit if she found out.

He picked up the latest assignment. 'Write about a building of historic interest that you have visited.' He laid his head on the desk. Historic interest! The two words didn't go together.

He ate another biscuit. Then he clicked his fingers. *Of course!* The lighthouse was historic. It must be at least a hundred years old. He'd never actually been inside, but so what? He'd find a website, copy and paste the text and be done with it.

He turned on the computer. A tiny cartoon duck in a bow tie waddled across the screen to a fanfare of trumpets. He waved and quacked cheerfully, performed a series of cartwheels and then crashed into the recycle bin. Jack smiled. He must have seen it a thousand times before, but Mac the Quack always amused him.

The monitor beeped and a chat box flashed up: 'Charlie Day is online'.

A message appeared. 'hey! u ok?'

'still alive,' Jack typed.

'those muppets need a brain transplant … when they gonna grow up …'

The cursor flashed while Jack's best friend waited for a response. 'they went too far ☹ we have to stop them,' Charlie added.

'yeah,' replied Jack miserably. They'd already had this conversation at school and neither of them had a solution.

'c u 2nite?'

'dunno …' he wrote. 'got to work ☹ … mebbe talk l8r.'

Somewhere in the house Odin mewed plaintively, but no one paid any attention. The radio blared in the kitchen and a delicious smell of fried onions wafted up through the floorboards.

Mac meanwhile had climbed out of the recycle bin. Wearing the lid on his head, he tapped his foot, awaiting a command. A second later he toppled over and lay flat on his back, as if he'd died of boredom.

Jack punched in the words 'Pentland Lighthouse' in the search box. Then he hit the return key. He might as well have detonated a bomb. Mac began jumping up and down, making a cutting motion across his throat, signalling shutdown.

'Whoa! What did I do?' yelled Jack.

Just before the computer crashed, a message appeared: *Fatal error: system immobilised.*

★★★

He let out a long groan. The machine appeared to be dead, and when he tried rebooting, all he got was a grey screen. He buried his head in his hands: the day couldn't get any worse.

There was a soft thud on the desk beside him and he felt Odin's delicate nose touch his ear.

'Go away,' he said, without looking up.

Odin paced backwards and forwards, butting his hands and making funny chirruping sounds.

'I said leave – me – alone!' Jack elbowed the cat onto the floor.

Odin leapt straight back up, his tail lashing from side to side, and yowled with fury.

'Okay! I'm sorry. There. Satisfied?'

The caterwauling continued louder and louder.

'What *is* the matter with you today?'

Odin went to the door. It was clear he wanted to be followed.

Reluctantly, Jack got up and trailed after him, thumping down the stairs, along the hall and into a small dark room at the back of the house. He felt for the light switch and flicked it on. A mouse scurried away under the skirting board.

'You're not doing your job properly,' he grumbled.

The cat gave him a long hard stare. This room was so untidy it would defeat even the toughest mouser. Piles of books and papers lay everywhere – on the mantelpiece, the window ledge, the chairs, the top of an old piano, all over the floor. It was Nan's study. She'd once joked that it resembled the state of her mind. Jack was inclined to agree.

Odin had disappeared beneath a half-moon table which served as Nan's writing desk. Now that he had Jack's full attention, he seemed a little calmer.

The table was pushed up against an old door which hadn't been used for years. A heavy, faded, green curtain hung over it to keep out the draught. At the bottom, however, the material was pinned back to reveal a large hinged cat flap. This was Odin's exit to the outside world. And it was blocked. A small brown parcel had somehow got jammed diagonally across the opening.

'Oh, I see! You can't get out,' said Jack.

Odin's yellow eyes glinted.

Jack leant forwards to remove the obstruction and, without wasting a second, Odin leapt out, leaving the cat flap banging to and fro. An icy blast of wind whistled into the room, blowing Nan's papers everywhere.

Jack crawled out from under the table and sat cross-legged among the towers of dusty books, turning the parcel over. To his surprise it was addressed to him:

Jack Tideswell

12 Hill Rise

Morton Muxloe

Somershire

There was no stamp or postmark, just his name and address. He stared at the bold, spiky letters. They had obviously been written in a hurry. But something about them made him catch his breath – the handwriting looked strangely familiar, like his own.

Outside, Odin paused briefly to sharpen his claws on a fence post before plunging into the long wet grass. The trees creaked and groaned and somewhere close by, a garden gate banged shut. The pungent scent of wolf was everywhere.

CHAPTER 5

The wrapping around the parcel was actually a small paper bag, the kind Nan used to put sandwiches in. It had been rolled over at the top, rather than fastened with sticky tape, and was covered in splodges of mud.

Jack's nose wrinkled. A slimy trail glistened in one corner where some creature, a snail probably, had crawled over it. He ripped the paper off and threw it aside.

In his hand, he held a round piece of metal about the size and shape of a compact disc. It was heavier than a normal CD and bronze-ish rather than aluminium, but he couldn't think what else it might be.

On one side, engraved near the edge, he noticed a shape that looked like a fish, the kind a small child might draw.

He shrugged. He hadn't ordered any games recently, though it might be a demo. Sometimes companies sent him free software to tempt him into buying stuff. Yet there was no label, nothing to identify it. And why had the postman delivered it to the back of the house – through the cat flap of all places? It made no sense.

He slowly climbed the stairs back to his room, running his fingers over the metal surface. It was pockmarked in places and had a bluish tinge, which gave it a kind of antique quality. If this was a game, the designers had gone to a lot of trouble. He'd never seen anything like it before.

As he entered the room, the computer screen flickered. A second later it turned black and a small blinking cursor appeared in the top left-hand corner.

Jack stood still, listening to the gentle whirr of the hard drive. Strange, when only ten minutes ago the machine had been completely dead. The disc felt slightly warm in his hand. He walked to his desk, put it next to the keyboard and sat down, bemused.

Not only had the computer woken itself up, but a series of equations had begun rolling down the screen. It was nothing like the normal startup. It looked more like some nightmare maths test.

Line after line of letters, numbers and calculations scrolled by, until eventually he couldn't focus on any of them. Half-mesmerised, he gazed through the storm of writing to the blackness beyond. There was his room in reverse: the unmade bed, the wardrobe with one door open, the rattling window and the piles of homework.

At least we're up and running, he told his pale reflection.

Finally, the equations came to an abrupt halt and the screen filled with an intense blue. With a smile of relief, he laced his fingers together and flexed them, waiting for his homepage to appear.

But it never did.

Instead, a low thrumming came from the machine, so strong it made the whole desk vibrate. A pen rolled onto the floor, books and paper shifted, and the glass of milk wobbled. His hand shot out to steady it, but the liquid continued to tremble. He could feel the vibration running up his arms and down his spine until it seemed to pass through his flesh into the marrow of his bones.

'No!' He stood up in alarm. An intense blue-white light had flared around the desk, enveloping him. For a second he found himself fighting for breath as something powerful tugged at his very core. Then, without warning, a plummeting sensation took over and his room and everything in it seemed to fall away.

It was worse than any rollercoaster ride; his stomach lurched into his chest, his heart pounded in his throat and his head felt dangerously light. He flung his arms wide, grabbing at non-existent handholds. What had he done? What the hell was happening to him? He opened his mouth to scream, but nothing came out.

CHAPTER 6

The rumble of a huge engine reverberated all around. Jack remained curled in a tight ball, every muscle of his body braced for impact. But nothing happened – no bone-crunching landing, no unbearable pain. Instead, a soft springy mattress bounced gently beneath him.

He sat bolt upright, checking his arms and legs. No blood, nothing broken … where was he? Heavy curtains enclosed him on every side and when he reached up, he found he could easily touch the ceiling. It felt like a coffin. With a sharp intake of breath, he whisked one of the curtains aside.

Below him, he saw a dimly lit, wood-panelled room. Though small, it was extremely luxurious, with oil paintings on the walls, a rich red carpet on the floor and furniture of polished mahogany. A stag stared out from a tapestry and, beside it, the night sky was visible through a round window.

A heavy sigh escaped him. At least the curtains were nothing sinister. They'd been drawn for privacy around a sort of grand bunk bed. Instead of a ladder, it had a miniature staircase at one end with a carved banister. He wriggled towards it, climbed down and went over to the window.

It was hard to see anything much. Directly beneath him, a vertical wall dropped away like the side of a building, and in the blackness far below swirls of white came and went. His vision adjusted slightly. No … it couldn't be … the wall didn't belong to a building. It was an enormous hull: a ship!

Understanding came and with it a terrifying jolt. An instant later, the throbbing of the engine died.

'What the devil was that?' said a voice.

A light came on and a small, balding man in striped pyjamas heaved himself out of the bottom bunk, a black sleep mask pushed high on his forehead. 'Dammit!' he muttered, fumbling about on the bedside table. 'Where are they?'

A pair of glasses lay on the floor, one of the lenses smashed. Jack hurried forwards to pick them up.

'Are you looking for these?'

The man stepped back in fright. 'Who the blazes are you?'

'Jack … Jack Tideswell … sir.' Despite the pyjamas, the man looked important. There were two monogrammed letters on his breast pocket: HL.

Jack held out the glasses and HL put them on.

'Wait a minute!' he exclaimed, peering at Jack through his one good lens. His bald head turned scarlet and his eyes bulged. 'I know you! Why, you little villain! What are you doing here? In *my* cabin?'

'I … I don't know …' Jack had never met this angry man in his life before and he had no idea how or why he came to be there.

An ominous creak made them both jump. Then the whole cabin began to vibrate.

'Dear God! What was that?' said HL, growing hysterical. 'I hate boats – I hate water! I knew I should never have come …'

Someone banged on the door. Glad of the distraction, Jack rushed to open it.

'What's wrong with you? Didn't you hear the alarm?' A steward in a white uniform stood sweating beneath his peaked cap. Behind him, crowds of people moved along a narrow corridor. 'Get your life jackets, go to deck five. You *do* remember the muster drill?'

'What in heaven's name is going on?' said HL, hastily pulling on his trousers over his pyjamas.

'We have a situation, sir.' The steward stepped into the cabin as several people barged past. 'The Pentland light is out – we've hit a sandbank. Everything is under control, but you and your son must go to the Muster Station. At once, please.'

'My son!' spluttered HL. 'That good-for-nothing little thief is *NOT* my son! He's a stowaway – arrest him! Good grief, man! Don't just stand there!'

But by then Jack had spotted his chance. He'd already slipped past the steward and disappeared into the crowd.

★★★

29

Swept along in a crush of bodies and unable to see anything over the heads in front, he tried to stay calm. But every time the lights flickered a cry of alarm went up and very soon what had begun as an orderly evacuation turned into chaos.

Shoved and squashed till he could hardly breathe, he arrived in a hallway where scores of angry people swarmed around an ornate staircase.

'What's the hold-up?' yelled a man in a red checked shirt. He hoisted a wide-eyed toddler on his shoulders. 'I've got kids here. They're getting trampled!'

From halfway up the stairs, a stout woman shouted back, 'One of the doors is jammed. It's single file!'

Heart thumping, Jack looked around. On the wall nearby he spotted a diagram of the ship's layout. He traced a trembling finger across it and found he was on deck three, two whole floors below the deck the steward had mentioned. To reach the next staircase he'd have to double back.

It took ages to push his way into the corridor again. With his back to the wall, he squeezed past the oncoming passengers and broke into a stumbling run. It was hard to keep his balance and when he realised why, he felt sick. The ship had begun to tilt.

An elderly man lurched towards him, grabbing him by the arm. 'What are you doing? Turn round! It's a dead end that way.'

'It's worse back there!' cried Jack. 'Let me go!'

'Listen, lad, I'm telling you, it's no good. The front end's cut off. You shouldn't be on your own anyhow. Where are your parents?'

Jack stared at him. It was such an absurd and pointless question. 'They're dead,' he yelled. 'Dead!'

Appalled, the man backed away. 'But – how?'

Before he could say any more Jack fled, turning left, then right and on down another corridor.

In a deserted lobby, he paused between a pair of lifts. He knew others must have tried but he punched the buttons anyway. Overhead, the tear-shaped pendants of a chandelier jangled and swung. 'Come on, come on!' he yelled at the doors. They remained firmly shut, the panel of lights above them no longer functioning.

With a groan he tore on, passing one cabin after another until he thought the maze of rooms would never end. Then finally, turning a corner, he saw what he was looking for. It brought him skidding to a halt. Beneath the dim glow of a fire escape sign, torrents of water poured down a broad staircase.

Now he understood what the man had meant. At least three-quarters of the steps were engulfed in a murky, black pool. To get to the next deck he'd have to swim. He approached the water's edge. There was no going back. He took a deep breath and waded in.

The cold hit him like a hammer blow and an involuntary scream exploded out of him. His body couldn't take much of this; he had to move quickly. Wading deeper, he kicked against a door frame, using it to propel himself along. In a moment he would dive under. Three or four big strokes should be enough …

And that was when he heard it – barely audible above the creaking of the ship – a muffled cry. He stopped to listen. Had he imagined it? He pressed his ear to the wall. Nothing. And then – yes, there it was again: the whimper of a child. 'Mum? Dad?'

Freezing water swirled around his ears, nose and eyes, sucking the energy out of him. For a moment he was torn in two, unable to abandon the frightened voice, yet driven by a desperate desire to save himself. What on earth should he do? He had to decide fast. He took a great gulp of air. If he hesitated now, he knew he would change his mind.

★ ★ ★

He surfaced with a splash, his head pounding and his hands numb. This was a *bad* idea. The cabin was dark as a dungeon and more than half of it was submerged. What if he was already too late? Ahead, something pale glimmered underwater. It seemed to confirm his fear. But when he paddled closer, he heard a sharp gasp.

'Jack?'

Strands of blonde hair streamed towards him like silvery grass. A small girl with the most frightened eyes he'd ever seen clung to a porthole.

'Jack! It *is* you! Oh please, you have to help me. Mum, Dad … I don't know where they are.'

Jack gazed at her, his brain fogged by fatigue. 'What's your name?' he spluttered.

A look of misery swept over the girl's face. 'You know who I am!'

He shook his head.

'You do! You helped me with the picture, remember? On the quay. It's Lily!'

Jack had no idea what she meant. 'Look – I'm sorry – we can't afford to waste time. How old are you, Lily?'

'Seven!' she wailed. 'It was my birthday yesterday!'

'So can you swim?'

'Only with my water wings. And I don't know where they are!'

'It's okay. You're going to be fine. Here, put your arms round my neck. You mustn't let go, understand?'

Lily nodded vigorously.

'Can you hold your breath? For a *long* time?'

Her eyes glistened. 'Like a mermaid, you mean?'

Jack forced a smile. 'Yes, that's it!' Somehow her belief in magic made him stronger. 'Try counting to a hundred. Shut your eyes. Ready? Big breath. One, two, three …'

As he dived again, Lily's fingers dug into his neck. He was glad he'd told her to close her eyes, because through the gloom the floating forms of two adult bodies were visible.

'Twenty-eight!' she announced proudly when they surfaced.

'Brilliant!' said Jack, struggling to keep them afloat. He could only just see the top of the staircase. 'Think you can do it again? Bet you can count even higher.'

He pulled forwards with giant strokes as darkness closed in. This time he had to feel his way, clawing up the metal steps, one by one, like an astronaut in slow motion. It seemed to take for ever and when at last he reached the landing, he found the next flight was engulfed too. He had to keep going.

His lungs were at bursting point. How long had he been underwater? Perhaps only a minute or so, yet it seemed like a dozen. Then, just as his own strength began to fade, the little hands around his neck relaxed their grip. He lunged down. In desperation, he grabbed a handful of long hair, dragging Lily after him like a doll.

Almost there, he told himself. But he'd used every last ounce of effort. He *had* to open his mouth and breathe. Water rather than air rushed down his throat and his feet kicked wildly. Then blackness and confusion filled his mind.

CHAPTER 7

'Come on, lad, don't give up now. Yer done well to get this far. Yer got guts, I'll give yer that.' A big man, with bushy eyebrows and an even bushier beard, crouched over Jack, pounding his back.

Jack retched. 'What happened? Where am I?'

'Fifth deck. Carried yer 'ere meself,' said the man. His overalls smelled of oil and hard work. 'You was lucky. Got 'ere in the nick of time. If I hadn't seen yer …'

He stopped short, his eyes widening as if he'd seen an apparition. 'Well I never!' he said. He peered into Jack's face. 'Seems there's no "if" about it. Mouse! Yer back, after all these years! This ent luck or chance. Somethin' else is goin' on.'

'Lily – the girl – where is she?' cried Jack in confusion.

'Never you worry. She's all right! Look, 'ere she is, poor little mite. Gave me a proper surprise. Pulled you out, then up she pops, like the ghost of a Christmas angel! Yer saved her life, mate, no doubt about it. Her hair was caught in yer hand!'

A shivering figure in a white nightdress huddled

against a ventilation shaft nearby, coughing, sobbing and trying to speak all at the same time. 'I got to f-f-fifty-nine,' said Lily. 'Then I couldn't think. I ... I just couldn't think ...'

The ship gave a lurch, leaning further on its side towards the ink-black sea. A wall of water exploded over them and all at once they found themselves sliding down the deck towards the railings. Lily screamed, digging her heels into the floor.

'Hold on!' roared the sailor, grabbing her outstretched hand.

Jack was certain they would slip right over the edge, but the rolling waves seemed to have another plan. An enormous swell lifted the ship so it was on a more even keel, and though it lasted only a few seconds, they managed to scramble to the railings.

Cries for help filled the night air. Everywhere people struggled for handholds before the deck dipped back down. Above them, an enormous neck-shaped funnel groaned. It had the ship's name emblazoned across it: *The Empress*. Jack closed his eyes as a great jagged crack ripped downwards through the letters.

'This ent no good,' muttered the sailor. He scooped Lily into his arms. '*The Empress* has a date with destiny, I'm afraid. Come on, Jack! We ent got long!'

Jack didn't move. The sound of his own name had him rooted to the spot. First HL, then Lily and now this man – they all knew him. 'Wait!' he called. 'I don't understand. Who are you?'

'Why,' said the sailor, 'it's Bill, of course. Bill

Armitage. First engineer. Ent 'ardly surprising you don't recognise me. I'm older now – and hairier!' He tugged at his beard. 'But you … well, you ent changed a bit, Mouse. Look at yer, still wearing them old pumps!'

Jack glanced down at the black plimsolls. He'd only borrowed them today. 'You're mistaking me for someone else.'

'Oh no I ent!' Bill's eyes sparkled with emotion. 'You're Jack Tideswell, that's who you are – a piece of bloomin' magic! And I was put 'ere to save you. I only just realised that!'

'Magic? What do you mean?'

'I dunno. It's a puzzle beyond my reckonin'! But yer 'ere for a reason. And so's she.' He gave Lily a wink. 'Proper important this one, sittin' all posh at the captain's table. You best look after her, Mouse.'

There was another ear-splitting groan. Lily grabbed Bill's hand in fright. He looked up at the funnel, then at the ship's stern which had risen out of the water. 'Come on, we gotta get higher up!'

'What about the lifeboats?' Jack could see crowds of people on the boat deck above.

'They won't be able to launch 'em. She's listin' too 'eavily. Reckon she's gonna roll.'

'So what do we do?'

But Jack's words were lost in a roar of groaning metal. The deck heaved as if *The Empress* was shrugging. There was nothing they *could* do, she seemed to say.

Slowly, they climbed back along the ship. Bill made them put on lifejackets that he found in a stowage container. He seemed lost in his own world, rambling on about the ship's misfortune.

'My old dad would be ashamed,' he cried. 'The lighthouse never went out in his time. He was a good keeper.' He steadied Lily against his knees as he fastened the lifejacket around her tiny waist. 'Wanted me to follow 'im, but I 'ad me own plans. Dreams don't always work out, do they?' He brushed away a tear and turned to Jack. 'All set?'

'What are we going to do?' asked Jack again.

'Yer gonna jump.'

'What!'

'We ent far from the coast and the rescue boats'll be 'ere afore long. It's yer only chance.'

'But you're coming with us – aren't you?'

Bill shook his head.

'Why not? The ship's sinking, you said so yourself!'

'There's others what need my 'elp, Mouse.'

Jack stared at him.

'Don't stand there gawking. Go on! Make sure you jump clear. Then swim, hard as you can. I know yer can do it. I seen yer, remember?'

'No!' sobbed Jack.

'Have you forgotten our little bet?' Bill gave his cheek an affectionate cuff. 'Won fair and square, yer did. And I still owe yer! Now go on! There'll be such a pull when she goes.'

Jack climbed the railings first, hardly daring to look down. Walls of water smacked against the hull and rocketed skywards, plucking at him like giant fingers.

It felt like standing on the edge of the world.

'No! I – I can't!' protested Lily when it was her turn.

'You have to!' urged Jack. 'Come on. Think, Lily. What comes after fifty-nine?'

'Sixty.'

'See. You knew the answer all along! You're halfway to being a mermaid already.'

Lily held out her hand. 'Promise not to let go?'

Jack fought against the terror that was making his whole body shake. 'Promise,' he said.

★★★

As the two children jumped, a blinding white light illuminated them, sweeping like a laser beam over the sorry hulk of the capsized ship. The Pentland lighthouse, cause of the disaster, had come back on.

Jack closed his eyes tight. The wind whistled in his ears and the waves rose to greet him. Only somehow he never reached them. He just kept falling – down, down, down through the light – until eventually the tiny hand that held his simply melted away.

CHAPTER 8

He came to with a jolt, bright points of light dancing in his eyes. Six high-pitched bleeps, time pips on a radio, sounded somewhere far below and a newsreader started talking. A hand touched his shoulder and he jumped.

'Hey! Your message sounded kinda miserable. I came straight over.'

An impish face covered in freckles beamed down at him.

'Charlie!' The smell of chewing gum battled with the overpowering aroma of Nan's cooking. He was home, back in his room! He threw his arms around his best friend.

'Blimey, you okay? You look completely out of it!' Charlie Day patted Jack on the back, her cheeks blossoming bright red. With her other hand, she pulled on the black beanie which had almost fallen off her head. 'What's up? Don't tell me Blunt sent one of his messages.'

'No … he didn't. W-what time is it?'

'Six o'clock. Why?'

Jack plunged his face in his hands. Impossible. Either he was going mad or the events he'd just experienced had taken place in no time at all. He glanced down at his clothes and the black gym shoes. They were bone dry.

'Jack, what's the matter?'

'I was on a ship …' He spoke slowly, as if trying to convince himself. 'An ocean liner.'

'What?'

'I was trapped, it was sinking … Charlie, it was terrible. I nearly drowned!'

'Hey, you were dreaming, that's all.' Charlie patted his arm. 'You fell asleep. When I came in you were slumped over the desk like you'd been shot.'

'No way! I was there. I remember every detail. There was a cabin full of antique stuff. And a bloke with broken glasses … he called me a thief! And then … well, then I rescued this girl. Only when we jumped ship we got separated.'

'Yeah? What was she like?' asked Charlie, casually.

'I dunno. Small, lost … she wouldn't last a minute in the sea!' Jack stared at the carpet, blinking back tears. What if Charlie was right? He must sound like a complete idiot. He tried not to picture a tiny white form sucked under the waves.

'Dreams do make sense when you're in 'em,' said Charlie. 'It's only afterwards you think "What the hell was that about?".'

Jack said nothing.

'Maybe it was to do with your mum and dad.'

'Meaning what?'

'You know …' Charlie's voice grew uncertain. Jack never talked about his parents. All she knew was that they'd died in some kind of diving accident.

'That was completely different,' snapped Jack. 'There was no ship for a start. Or loads of other people.'

'True. But think about it. You were trying to save someone – that girl. What was her name?'

'Lily!'

'All I'm saying is, maybe in your unconscious you wish you could have saved –'

'You're talking rubbish! Quit the psychology.'

'Okay, okay.' Charlie raised her hands in surrender. 'Hey!' she said, quickly changing the subject. 'Brilliant screensaver. Looks like a lighthouse.'

Jack followed the direction of her gaze. On his monitor an extraordinary image had appeared: a dome-shaped building floating on a turquoise sea. It *was* a lighthouse. Charlie at least had that right. Except he'd never seen anything like it before.

The structure was covered in a canopy of blue glass which looked almost part of the ocean itself as it moved across the screen. Twelve feet protruded below it like the points of a dial, and a tall spire, thin as a needle, rose to the light on top. The last rays of a fabulous sunset made everything glint until, gradually, the screen darkened and the thin spire lit up. Then, every so often, a word materialised from the beam on top:

P h a r o s

'Cool! It's solar-powered,' said Charlie. 'Pharos. That must be the name.'

'Hmmm?' For once Charlie's habit of stating the obvious didn't bother Jack. Something about the graphic had him mesmerised.

Stop it! he told himself. The tugging sensation he'd experienced earlier had begun to return. His hand shot out and closed on the disc which lay half buried by books and paper next to the keyboard.

'What's that?' asked Charlie.

'Nothing.'

He opened the middle drawer of the desk, threw the disc in and slammed it shut. The ship was a figment of his imagination. None of it was real.

He stood up, straightening his crumpled shirt. 'Let's see what's for dinner. Coming?'

The beam from the lighthouse flickered. Though neither of them noticed, something delicate as gossamer glimmered on Jack's sleeve. Spooled around one white cuff button was a single strand of blonde hair, so fine a piece of reality it was almost invisible.

CHAPTER 9

Charlie did most of the talking at dinner, entertaining Nan with impressions of teachers at school. Jack was relieved to let her get on with it. He felt tired beyond words.

He sat contemplating his best friend while she gossiped on, barely drawing breath between forkfuls of Nan's toad-in-the-hole. Her hair, all apart from one unruly wisp of ginger, was still crammed under the black beanie which she rarely removed. And her baggy T-shirt, easily three sizes too big, looked like a hand-me-down from her brother. Sometimes it was easy to forget she was a girl.

The thing he liked about her most was her directness. With Charlie, you always knew what she was thinking because she invariably told you so. Sadly, it wasn't always what you wanted to hear. The moment Nan went to fetch the dessert, she started in on the subject of Blunt.

'It's time to teach those morons a lesson,' she said. 'If you don't stand up to them, they'll keep walking all over you.'

'Charlie, there's four of them, one of me. What do you expect me to do? I'm not Superman.'

A smile played at the corner of Charlie's mouth.

'What's so funny?'

'You! In tights and a cape, jumping off a skyscraper.'

Jack gave her a stony look, praying she would get the message and shut up.

'Does Nan know about Blunt?' asked Charlie.

'No!'

In the kitchen, Nan whistled tunelessly to the radio.

'So are you gonna tell her?'

'Course not! She worries enough.'

'Oh come on, Jack. She's tougher than you think.'

'She's sixty-three. I need to look after her. You know what she's like. A bit, well …' He was going to say 'batty', but the whistling in the kitchen had stopped. 'She's tuned in to a completely different channel to the rest of us.'

'Nan *is* different, but she's smart,' said Charlie in a hushed whisper. 'She'll talk to the school.'

'Exactly. And that'll make things a million times worse. If the school tries to sort it, Blunt will definitely get his own back.' Jack could feel himself getting irritated. Of course Nan was smart. He didn't need Charlie to tell him that.

'Well, you can't go on avoiding them for ever. I mean, you don't come to the skate park any more, you've given up swimming *and* cycling. I never know where to find you at break times –'

'Oh, I get it. You think I'm running away. Is that it? You think I'm a coward.'

'No! I know you're not a coward but –'

'I'm just trying to get through it the best I can, okay?' Jack kicked the table hard, making Charlie jump. 'You're supposed to be my friend! You should back me up, not run me down.' He stood up, scraping his chair across the tiled floor. Then before Charlie could say another word, he stormed out of the room.

The entire house reverberated to the thud of footsteps on the stairs and a door slamming.

Charlie's fork dropped with a clatter. She'd never seen Jack in such a mood before. She'd only been trying to help. How dare he accuse her of not being a friend? She got up to leave too.

'What was all that about?' Nan arrived with a steaming treacle pudding.

Charlie shrugged. She couldn't let on. Jack would hate her for it.

'Just like his dad,' said Nan. 'Cool as a cucumber most of the time, my Ed. Then just when you least expected it: Boom!'

She put the pudding on the table with a dramatic thud. Thick sauce oozed down the sides and a pool of what looked and smelled like molten toffee formed at its base.

Without another word, Charlie sat down. A moment later she was tucking into a large helping, her eyes shut tight. 'Yum!' Nan's recipes always had a hint of something unusual. What was it this time? … Hot tarmac on a summer's day and bike races outside Jack's house. A-mazing.

A tiny smile lifted the corners of Nan's mouth. No one could scrape a bowl clean like Charlie. The delicate blue pattern on the crockery probably wouldn't last until the washing up. But at least the angry creases in the child's brow had gone.

'You know …' Charlie wiped the back of her hand across her mouth. 'Jack never talks about his parents.'

'No.'

'They were divers, right?'

'Marine archaeologists.'

'Wow!'

'Clever people, always travelling.'

'So …' Charlie straightened her spoon awkwardly.

'You want to know what happened?'

'Yeah.'

'They went to Egypt.' Though Jack never discussed his parents' deaths with anyone, not even her, Nan saw no point in hiding the details. 'Jack was only five and about to start school, so he stayed with me. Didn't like that very much …' Her fingers flicked at a crumb. The tantrums had been spectacular.

'Anyhow, soon after they arrived, his mum called. Typical Alice, talking so fast you could hardly keep up. They'd found some ruins in the harbour at Alexandria, part of the Pharos lighthouse – the seventh wonder of the world!'

'Pharos!' The image on Jack's computer flashed into Charlie's mind.

'Impressive, eh? It was going to be a huge project. She even talked about finding Jack a school out there.

She was so happy, so full of plans …' Nan's voice faltered. She cleared her throat. 'A week later, their boat was found abandoned at the site. People saw them go off the side but – I'm afraid that was that.'

'Oh.' Charlie didn't know what to say. 'I'm sorry.'

'It's all right, dear. It was seven years ago.'

'But it must have been terrible for you. Jack was so little.'

'Yes. He refused to believe it at first. He was so sure they'd come home. They never found them, you see. Right up until his sixth birthday he kept hoping and then … well, he didn't want the cake I made. Wouldn't even blow out the candles. He lost his appetite for a long time.'

Charlie stared glumly into her bowl.

Nan banged her hands on the table. 'Thank goodness for the famous Hill Rise bike races!'

Charlie looked up, puzzled.

'When you moved here you challenged him to a race, remember? Then half the neighbourhood joined in. You were organising competitions all summer long.'

'Funny, I was just thinking of that. He was surprised a girl could ride so fast!'

'And that day he came in hungry as a wolf!'

Outside, the wind rattled under the eaves, making them both jump.

'Come on, let's drive you home,' said Nan. 'The weather's filthy. It was raining frogs earlier. I'll fetch my boots.'

Charlie nodded grimly and set about clearing the

table. But halfway to the kitchen, her cheeks bulging with a leftover roast potato, she stopped munching. Raining frogs? Her nose wrinkled. Surely the expression was 'raining cats and dogs'. Jack was right about one thing. His grandmother *was* on a different wavelength.

★★★

Upstairs, a bluish glow from the screensaver fell across the bed where Jack lay fully clothed, fast asleep, one arm drooping down to the floor, the other flung across his eyes. When the front door clicked shut, he stirred uncomfortably. 'A promise is a promise,' he mumbled. He hadn't meant to let her go. He had to keep looking or she'd drown.

In his dream he dived deeper in the murky sea, conscious of something powerful which kept on tugging him forwards. What was it? He felt like he was on some kind of quest.

Out of the gloom, a small figure floated towards him, her white clothes ballooning. 'I like the picture,' she whispered. A gleam, very like the thin spire on the screensaver, appeared in her eye.

'Lily!' he yelled. But before he could discover what she meant, her spindly legs turned into a mermaid's tail and she finned away, vanishing in an instant.

CHAPTER 10

Nan pulled out of Charlie's driveway with the windscreen wipers working at double speed. The water ran in torrents down the side of the road and the car wheels produced a spray that rose on either side like an enormous pair of bat wings.

A gale was roaring in from the east and even the high hedges gave no protection. With every gust, her battered blue Beetle rocked unsteadily.

Inside, two fluffy dice swung violently beneath the rearview mirror. Nan reached up to stop them. She'd bought them as a little joke to herself. 'No such thing as chance,' she'd told Jack. 'There's a reason for everything. And reasons for the reasons.'

A large branch smashed on the road where the car had passed a moment before. She drove on without noticing. An unpleasant drowsiness had crept over her and tiny lights were popping in her eyes – the first signs of a blinding headache.

She squinted at the white line in the middle of the road. It kept jumping from side to side like a charmed snake. Her hand rummaged in the glove box. A collection of maps, sweet wrappers and an old apple core spilled onto the floor, but no painkillers.

'Damn that seagull,' she groaned. She shut the glove box with a snap. If only she'd trusted her instincts and chased the bird away. But no, she had to go and open the window, didn't she? Silly fool!

Nan recalled the moment with a shiver. A sea of voices had swept into the kitchen, almost knocking her off her feet. Hundreds of them, all talking at the same time, like a flock of jabbering birds on a beach.

She rubbed her aching temples. The voices had been with her all day. She could hear them even now, though she had no idea what they were saying. There were so many they drowned each other out.

'Shut up!' she bellowed.

Briefly, the hubbub subsided. Then she heard a word she recognised. For a few seconds, no more, the voices seemed to work together to produce something she could understand – a name, repeated over and over in a kind of chant.

She listened closely. Yes, there it was again, faint but unmistakeable, like waves breaking on a shore: 'Tide … swell, Tide … swell.'

What did it mean? The voices sounded so sorrowful. Was Jack in some kind of trouble? She sensed danger all around, a terrible and sinister kind, but she couldn't put her finger on the cause.

That was the problem with her sort of magic. It was hit and miss. Sometimes it worked, sometimes it didn't.

'Half magic', she called it. She knew the seagull mattered, but she didn't know why. Infuriated, she punched the steering wheel and the car let out an angry honk.

On a good day, when her magic worked, it was … well, one hundred per cent pure magic. Like the time Jack had fallen from the tree. She'd never forget it. One minute she was watching telly, the next she was running flat out down the garden. Even before it happened, she knew he was going to fall, and she was there to catch him.

So why had her gift deserted her now? If something threatened his safety, she needed to know what it was.

She turned into Hill Rise and bounced through a pothole with a muddy splash. What a night! All she wanted was to be in bed with a steaming hot Brandy Brainstorm. Her own special remedy always did the trick.

She accelerated up the hill and was almost home when an almighty thud on the roof made her duck her head down.

'Hell's bells!' she gasped. From out of nowhere, a cat had sprung from the roof onto the front bonnet and off into the darkness. Then, before she could even begin to slow down, another more astonishing sight appeared in the headlights.

'What on earth?'

An animal stood in the road, watching her approach with great interest, its huge grey-brown head lowered between massive shoulders. Nan's heart thumped. It wasn't a dog, she knew that much. It looked much more ferocious and something in its manner suggested it had no intention of moving out of the way.

She slammed her foot on the brake. To her dismay, nothing happened. She tried again, pumping the pedal even harder. This time the car skidded sideways, its tyres squealing on the wet tarmac.

Suddenly, time itself seemed to slow down. As the car advanced, she could see everything in terrifying detail – the beads of rain dripping from the animal's ears, the cloud of hot breath that enveloped its snarling muzzle. And then, for one terrible moment, she gazed right into its piercing amber eyes. She couldn't believe it. The creature was a wolf.

An icy chill gripped her body and the next thing she knew she seemed to be standing on the road too, watching the scene unfold like a spectator. She gazed horrified as the Beetle ploughed over a ditch and took off, somersaulting through the air before landing in an adjoining field with its horn blaring. A fire ignited below it and, on the driver's side, a circle of splattered blood spread across the windscreen.

Nan let out a scream of terror. The noise brought her to her senses and she found herself gripping the steering wheel again. The crash hadn't happened – she was still on the road! She braked hard, tyres screeching, and the car spun a hundred and eighty degrees, spraying water everywhere, before coming to a standstill facing the opposite direction. Her head whipped around. Behind her the road was empty: the wolf had gone.

With a sob, she rested her forehead against the

steering wheel. Her hands trembled uncontrollably. She was in no doubt why the animal had appeared. He wasn't real, he couldn't be. He was a premonition of something yet to happen – her magic had just given her a glimpse of her own death!

She struggled out of the car and leant against the bonnet, her heart drumming in her ears. Only then did she see the bundle lying in the road.

It was Odin, his fur so drenched and matted that he looked half his normal size. Rushing over, Nan fell to her knees beside him. The cat's body was limp and still. She searched in desperation for a pulse. Nothing.

'Odin!' she wailed, her crumpled face turned hopelessly to the sky. Great tears rolled down her cheeks, mingling with the cold rain. She took off her coat and wrapped the furry corpse in it, cradling the bundle like a baby.

Moments later, the street lights in Hill Rise flickered and the whole town plunged into darkness.

CHAPTER 11

That night a ferocious Atlantic gale raged up and down the country. Roads and railways were blocked, rivers burst their banks and power lines were severed. There was no let-up … except, that is, for a brief lull close to midnight. While everywhere else fell strangely silent, the storm closed in on Morton Muxloe and unleashed its full might, roaring through the market square like a beast on the rampage.

From the shadow of the newsagent's doorway, the wolf watched the chaos unfold. An ancient chestnut tree, more than eighty feet tall, stood by the town hall, shaking its limbs wildly. His amber eyes locked on to it and within seconds a vortex of swirling air engulfed the trunk. Groaning, the tree rocked to and fro. It had stood for more than two hundred years yet, little by little, its roots began to lose their hold.

The faint midnight chimes of the town hall clock rang out. The wolf's eyes snapped towards the building and the chestnut tree gave one last deafening creak. Down it toppled, smashing into the council chamber and silencing the clock completely.

A ton of masonry and wood hit the cobbles with a crash. By some miracle, it missed the statue of William Godley. Grim-faced, he stood amidst the clouds of dust with one finger raised, as if giving the creature a stern rebuke for the damage.

The wolf blinked. A piece of loose brick teetered on the edge of the wrecked building. A second later, the wind sent it hurling at the statue. Pieces of stone exploded in every direction. Godley's lecturing arm had been removed at the elbow.

And so it went on. Wherever the wolf directed his gaze the wind gathered force. In the high street, the roof of the undertaker's rattled ominously. The wolf padded slowly towards the building and a gust lifted the entire roof. Cracks appeared in the walls, tiles flew like bats and, from the loft, an avalanche of coffins tumbled onto the road.

One of them smashed straight through the plate-glass window of the jeweller's shop, setting off an alarm. No one took any notice. Most people were huddled indoors with their heads buried under pillows. Even the police had decided to sit tight.

For an opportunist thief, it was perfect timing. A gloved hand reached furtively into the window display and removed a diamond ring worth more than a thousand pounds.

The wind softened as the wolf listened to the receding tap of heels on the pavement. Then, from somewhere over the rooftops, came the sound of a bird screeching, a harsh cry like an unnatural laugh: 'Tsche, tsche, tsche …'

CHAPTER 12

When Jack woke next morning, the house was strangely silent. A shaft of sunlight streamed through a chink in the curtains like a beam from a film projector and landed squarely on a tiny blue horse which pranced on its hind legs behind a display of model motorbikes. The ornament shone with such intensity it looked almost alive.

He pulled the duvet around his ears and turned away. The horse had been a gift from his parents, a souvenir which had arrived after the accident in a crate of their belongings. He could do without that particular memory.

He tossed and turned a while before realising he wasn't a bit sleepy. Instead of his usual grogginess, he felt oddly energised. He stared at the ceiling, trying to figure it out. Nothing major had happened. It wasn't his birthday. Or Christmas. It wasn't even the weekend. So why did he have butterflies in his stomach like he was on the brink of something special?

All night long he'd dreamt he was stuck on the ship.

Lily had been there too, tugging his hand and trying to show him the way out. But he couldn't bring himself to leave, not while he kept hearing the voice: 'Mum, Dad ...'

He cringed at the recollection. This time it hadn't been Lily calling. The voice had been his.

He got up and went over to the horse. Made of the deepest blue crystal, it seemed to paw at the air as if about to bolt. And on its back, where the saddle might have been, a tiny engraved J with two pinprick eyes smiled like a face.

Jack blew out his cheeks in a long sigh. Charlie had been right. He still missed his parents far more than he cared to admit. Why had he let himself get so angry with her? Blunt and his mob had a lot to answer for. Even when they weren't there they'd managed to stir up trouble.

He glanced at his bedside clock. *What the heck?* 'Nan!' he yelled. 'It's ten o'clock!' Why hadn't she woken him? School had started a whole hour and a half ago. He grabbed his dressing gown and thundered down the stairs, bellowing her name.

The kitchen, like the rest of the house, was silent. There was mud everywhere, wet towels on the floor and a mass of bottles, jars and books on the counter. Propped up against the kettle, a scribbled note read: 'Gone to vet, back soon. (No school today – power cuts.)'

No school? A roar filled the kitchen as Jack punched the air: *Yes!* One of his wishes had actually come true. He thought of the magpie ruining his game. Tsche, tsche, tsche ... Now it was his turn to laugh. For the time being, at least, he could forget all about Blunt.

A large, battered book with curling pages lay open on the chopping block. He read the title: *Old Saxon Remedies*. A handful of bluish-purple flowers was scattered beside it, and a stone pestle and mortar stained with the same vivid colour sat in the sink.

He had just picked up one of the flower heads to smell it when the kitchen door burst open.

'Wolfsbane!' shouted Nan, struggling in with a bag of shopping in one hand and a wicker basket in the other.

Jack froze as if she'd pronounced a curse.

'*Aconitum napellus* to be more precise. Put it down. At once! Now go wash your hands. That plant's poisonous. They used to paint it on arrows when they hunted wolves.'

Jack rushed to the sink, turning the tap on full blast. Meanwhile, the sound of frantic clawing came from inside the basket.

'It has medicinal uses too,' Nan continued. She undid the leather fastening on the basket and opened the lid. 'But only if you know what you're doing.'

A groggy head appeared. Odin blinked hard as if amazed to find himself home.

'What happened to him?' exclaimed Jack, still scrubbing at his fingers.

Odin mewed pathetically. A large patch of fur had been shaved from his neck and a long wound held together by several black stitches stretched round his throat.

'We had rather a hair-raising night,' said Nan. She lifted the cat from the basket and put him in front of the stove, where he turned several circles before flopping down. 'That frog rain was only the start. I've never seen such a storm! After you ran out on us I thought I'd better drive poor Charlie home. Her bike's still in the garage.'

Jack lowered his eyes. He already felt bad enough without the pointed look Nan had just given him.

'On the way back, I could hardly see where I was going,' she went on. 'Odin came out of nowhere, jumped on the car bonnet and bounced off the other side. When I got out he was lying in the road; his heart had stopped. That's why we needed this desperate remedy.' With a sniff, she scooped the leftover wolfsbane into the bin.

'But that's crazy! What on earth was he playing at?' Jack stared at Odin, who gave another mew. 'He must have landed badly. That cut looks nasty.'

'Actually, it's a bite of some kind, which is why we went to the vet. I know about herbal remedies but I'm no expert at stitches. The wound's less than an inch from his jugular. Any closer and …'

Jack gazed at his grandmother. She looked pale and somehow smaller than usual. He turned to Odin, who was feebly licking his paw. 'That's two of your nine lives then,' he said.

'How do you mean?' said Nan.

'Remember when I fell from the tree? If you hadn't been there, we'd both have broken our necks. He's a nutter.'

'He was a kitten, Jack! His experience of climbing

was limited, mainly to my best curtains as I recall. He got into trouble, you went to his rescue –'

'Odin is *always* getting into trouble.'

'He's an adventurer, that's all.'

Jack frowned. His parents had gone on an adventure and disappeared the very day Odin had taken it into his head to climb the biggest tree in the garden. 'Stupid animal.'

'Don't say that.'

'Well, he is.'

'No, he isn't! He's brave. If it hadn't been for him, I might be in hospital. Or worse. He forced me to slow down. Otherwise, I'd never have seen that …' Nan trailed off.

'What?'

'That "thing" in the middle of the road. I only just braked in time.'

'What are you talking about?'

'It looked like – I don't know – a wolf.'

'Seriously?'

'Yes! I mean, no.' Nan hadn't meant to say anything about her premonition. Jack must never know of it. 'There are no wolves in this country,' she said firmly. 'Not any more. It was a dog. Alsatian probably.'

'Could it have attacked Odin?'

'I – I s'pose so.'

They fell silent, each lost in their own thoughts.

Then Jack said, 'So you think Odin saved your life?'

Nan's face brightened. 'Yes! In my opinion, he's a hero.'

Jack squatted down, his back against the warm stove, and touched one of Odin's white paws. A loud purring like a tractor engine started up. While he watched Nan unpack the shopping, he thought back to that bleakest of days and suddenly felt glad he'd rescued the cat from the tree. Odin had just returned the favour.

★★★

Sunlight drenched the table as they sat down to a late breakfast of pancakes with maple syrup. It felt like a celebration and once more it seemed to Jack like his life had left its usual path.

By his third helping, however, he couldn't help noticing that Nan had barely eaten a thing. 'You okay?' he asked.

'Hmm …? Oh yes, fine. Absolutely fine.'

'Was the storm really bad?'

'The worst in a hundred years they're saying. It's a miracle you slept through it. There are trees down everywhere. Looks like a bomb's exploded in the town centre.'

'Wow!'

'The supermarket was a battle zone. And some villain even helped himself to a diamond ring from Amos's.'

'No!' Jack wished he'd woken earlier. He'd missed out on all the excitement.

'He reached through the broken window and just took it. Can you believe it? What kind of character does that?'

Jack could think of at least three or four but he wasn't going to mention them. Instead he asked, 'So how long will school be closed?' *Please, oh please, let it be a week.*

'Until the electricity comes back on,' said Nan, 'which could be a while.'

Jack glanced at the lamp on the sideboard. 'But it is on.'

'For us yes, but the rest of the town's cut off, including next door.'

'Really?'

'Strange, eh?'

'Maybe it's because we're the last house.'

'Shouldn't make any difference. We're all on the same supply line.' Nan stood up, pushing her breakfast away. 'Anyway, I'm not complaining. It means I can get on.'

'You should rest,' said Jack.

'Not right now. You go amuse yourself. I've got mountains to do. You know what they say: "You can sleep when you're dead".'

Jack frowned. Nan had come out with that one before. Plenty of times. Only, on this occasion, something about the way she said it sounded decidedly morbid.

★★★

He didn't know what had got into her, but that day Nan began baking like there was no tomorrow. The house filled with all kinds of delicious smells, the windows ran with condensation, and when he ventured into the kitchen he found her pink-cheeked and distracted, hardly aware he was even there. Fortunately, he was used to these eccentric moods and so left her to it, retreating upstairs to do some work of his own.

His head still buzzed with the shipwreck, memories so vivid it was hard to believe they weren't real. *You're Jack Tideswell, you are, a piece of bloomin' magic!* Bill's words and his instruction to look after Lily had taken root inside him and he felt bad he'd lost her to the sea. He needed to convince himself *The Empress* didn't exist.

He switched on his computer, wondering again why only their house should have any power. The blue-domed lighthouse appeared, followed a few seconds later by a fanfare of trumpets. He grinned. Mac the Quack was back in business. The tiny duck marched on in dark glasses and stood in his secret agent pose, tapping one webbed foot.

To Jack's relief, his internet connection worked straight away. Within minutes he found an *Empress of Canada*, an *Empress of England* and an *Empress of Japan*. But none of them had anything to do with his ship. And he was surprised to learn that ocean liners of that sort had stopped being built years ago, when air travel took over.

Next he searched the files of numerous shipping companies. *The Empress* appeared nowhere. Nor was there any record of the Pentland lighthouse ever failing. In fact, its homepage boasted that throughout its hundred-year history, the light had never gone out.

There wasn't a scrap of information to go on. 'Bad dream. Forget it,' he told himself.

Outside, a bird whistled cheerfully. Then something in the porch below went 'thump' and the doorbell rang. He waited for Nan to answer, knowing it couldn't be Charlie. She loved their old-fashioned bell so much she always hung on the cord so it clanged at least a dozen times. This person rang only once – a loud and purposeful summons.

'Nan! It's for you!'

Below him, the radio continued to play at full volume. With a sigh, he tramped down the stairs.

As the door opened, the wind lifted his hair. A carpet of swirling leaves swept into the hall and a low chuckle came from the porch. 'Afternoon. Boisterous weather we're having!'

A tall man in a battered trench coat, which fell almost to his feet, stood on the doorstep. His face was shaded by the brim of an oilskin hat and on the ground next to him lay a large leather bag. Jack thought he looked like a travelling salesman.

'Now then. Would you be so kind as to direct me to Osmaston Hall?' The voice was rich and smooth.

'Er, yes,' Jack replied. 'There are two ways. You can either go round by the road or across the fields by the wood. It's quicker across the fields but …'

'Oh, I much prefer a direct route. Far better to travel as the crow flies.' The man took off his hat and brushed away a few raindrops. His face was tanned and unshaven as though he'd been on the road for some time, and there were deep lines around his blue eyes.

'Well, in that case, you should go over the stile further

up the lane, then walk diagonally across two fields until you get to the river. If you stick to the footpath, you eventually get to a footbridge. But that takes ages. I usually go across the stepping stones. Then I scrabble up the bank by hanging on to the tree roots and …'

The man had one eyebrow raised and his blue eyes sparkled. Jack realised he was being long-winded. He couldn't help laughing and in the next breath he found himself saying, 'You know, it's probably easier if I show you.'

'Are you sure?'

'Yes, it takes longer to explain. Really, it's not very far.'

'That would be most kind.' The man held out his hand. 'My name is Jago Flyn.'

'Jack Tideswell.'

Smiling broadly, they shook hands and Jack noticed a power in the man's grip that felt like an electric current.

CHAPTER 13

It was a warm autumn afternoon. The smell of wet grass and rotting crab apples filled the air as they tramped along the hedgerow towards the river. The last of the rain clouds had disappeared and somewhere overhead an invisible songbird trilled its heart out.

An assault course of fallen branches, broken fence posts and vast muddy puddles lay along their route. It seemed to Jack as if the storm had created a huge adventure playground. He took great delight in leading the way through it, clambering and jumping and splashing.

The stranger had no problem keeping up. His stride was strong and athletic and he made light work of every obstacle. Jack eyed the wrinkled, weather-beaten face. Perhaps he wasn't as old as he looked.

'So do you live round here, Mr Flyn?'

'No.'

The squish and squelch of their boots was deafening as they ventured across a waterlogged bridleway.

'Are you going to stay at Osmaston Hall then?'

'No, I'm here on business.'

'Oh … what do you do?'

Jago Flyn extracted a foot from the quagmire with a great sticky slurp. 'You know, this sounds like twenty questions,' he said, his eyes glinting with mischief. 'Tell you what. I'll give you three guesses. And do call me Jago.'

Jack couldn't resist the challenge. He gave Jago a long head-to-toe stare and focussed on the battered trench coat. It reminded him of pictures of the first world war.

'Um, are you in the army? A soldier?'

Jago exploded with laughter. 'Ha! Insolent rascal!' He spoke in a blustering fashion, like an old army colonel. 'I'll have you court-martialled for that. I may look like I've been in the wars – and I *am* scarred by life's slings and arrows – but I have never, upon my soul, *ever* served my country.'

Jack grinned. 'All right then.' He stared at the weather-worn face. 'What about a sailor? You look like you've been at sea.'

Jago seemed to find this funnier still. Now he sounded like Long John Silver: 'A salty sea dog, eh? Nice try, but wrong again. Yer about to walk the plank, Jack me lad. Only one more guess. What's it to be? Tinker, tailor? Soldier, sailor?'

Rich man, poor man, beggar man, thief, thought Jack. But none of those seemed appropriate. He glanced down at the hefty leather bag. 'What's in there?'

'Arrr … the tools of me trade,' said Jago, still playing the pirate. 'And no, ya can't look.'

Jack frowned. He had another idea, but this one was a wild guess. 'I know,' he began uncertainly.

'Go on then. Spit it out.'

'You're an actor!'

'Ha! Now what makes ya say that, me hearty?'

'Your voice, of course. You can do different voices.'

'Very clever indeed. And close, begad!' said Jago with a wink. 'But wrong!'

★★★

The sound of rushing water was deafening as they neared the river. The storm had turned the meandering Churn into a raging torrent which spat flumes of spray against its grassy banks.

Jack scratched his head. His usual route over the stepping stones lay several feet below the water's surface. However, the storm had provided an alternative crossing point: a fallen tree which straddled the river, stretching its long limbs up the bank on the other side. It looked risky though. He eyed Jago's heavy-duty boots, hardly the best footwear for balancing on a slippery tree trunk. The bag would be a nuisance too.

But there was no time for second thoughts. Jago had already hoisted the bag on his head and was edging out across the river ahead of him. Jack had no choice but to follow.

They made good progress until they reached the middle of the river, at which point a freak gust of wind whistled out of nowhere. It blew so hard at their backs that Jack couldn't help himself. Arms flailing like a windmill, he tipped forwards.

It all happened in a split second. Hearing his scream, Jago turned, but with the bag perched precariously on his head, his movements were limited. He had to remain perfectly upright or risk losing all his possessions. He planted his feet wide apart and bent his knees so that it looked like he was sitting on an invisible chair. Then, just as Jack began to tumble, he caught him by the scruff of the neck.

When they finally collapsed on the opposite bank, Jack was giggling uncontrollably. Despite the danger, the whole scene had been absurdly funny.

'Thanks,' he spluttered. 'I thought I was going for a dip.'

'A heart-stopping moment, to be sure,' replied Jago.

'That move you did – the one like a ballet dancer – I think that's what they call a *plié*!'

'I beg your pardon! That was a classic karate manoeuvre, I'll have you know.'

'A-ha! So you're a karate expert?'

'No.'

'I didn't think so,' Jack sniggered.

'Impertinent scoundrel.' Jago threw his bag higher up the bank and scrambled after it. 'I should have let you fall in.'

Jack leapt to his feet to apologise. But the twinkling blue eyes told him he needn't have bothered. Laughing to himself, he hurried to catch up. This adult seemed to enjoy playing games, and the more he got to know him the less ancient he seemed.

★★★

Soon they were heading up the hill towards Osmaston Wood. At the top they would be able to look down on the valley and see the Hall itself.

It was a steep climb and they were both breathing heavily. Tiny beads of sweat glistened on Jago's forehead. He unbuttoned the trench coat and for a moment his coat–tails billowed out behind him, flapping in the wind like the wings of an enormous bird.

Jack gasped. The lining of the coat was extraordinary, made of a sumptuous silky material with white pinstripes. It didn't match the battered exterior at all.

Jago also wore a striking black and white waistcoat over a maroon shirt. And there, tucked in one of the waistcoat pockets, Jack spied a small brush.

He couldn't contain his excitement. 'I know what you do!' he exclaimed.

★★★

Jago made a square shape with his thumbs and forefingers and looked through it at the Hall below. It was an elegant red-brick building, once an Elizabethan hunting lodge, with tall chimneys and pinnacles and acres of well-ordered gardens.

'Now then,' he declared. 'This is as good a spot as any.'

He opened the leather bag and with a flourish worthy of a conjuror produced a small tripod seat, a folded wooden frame, a large umbrella, several glass jars and a number of paintbrushes. Jack was amazed the bag held so much.

Jago took the brush from his waistcoat pocket. 'I need this for the finer detail,' he said.

'So you're an artist!'

With a quick nod, Jago began setting up his easel.

'And you're going to paint the Hall. Can I watch?'

'If you like, but I need to concentrate. So no chattering, please. Watercolours dry quickly. I have to work fast.'

'You won't know I'm here.'

Jack found a natural seat in the hillside and settled himself down, enjoying the sun on his face and the smell of the warm earth. A slight breeze rustled the long grass, lifting the hairs on the back of his neck, and he turned towards the wood. He had a strong sensation of being watched, yet all he could see were gently swaying trees.

Jago hung his long coat on a branch, rolled up his shirt sleeves and got down to work. In addition to the paint palette, he held five brushes between the fingers of his left hand. Whenever he needed a different colour, he switched the brush he wanted to his right hand like a juggler. Jack was impressed. He knew he would have dropped the whole lot.

At first, he couldn't make out the picture at all. It

was just a haze of pale colours with no real definition. But Jago worked fast, building layer upon layer, adding more depth and detail with every stroke until finally Osmaston Hall began to emerge from the mist.

He stopped only once, when a portly woman wearing a green jacket and riding hat came out of the house. She marched across the gravel with two black retrievers at her heels and disappeared into the stables.

Jago stretched and yawned, leaning so far back on the tripod seat that the legs sank into the ground. When the woman reappeared on an enormous grey horse he consulted a pocket watch, which he placed carefully on the easel, and went back to work.

After a lot of excited waving at the house, the woman rode off with the retrievers lolloping after her. Jack's keen eyes scanned the upstairs windows. At the far end, he spotted a figure holding a small white bundle, a baby.

'Do you draw people too?' he asked.

'No, never,' said Jago, without looking up. 'Only houses and gardens.'

'Oh … you've made the driveway longer than it really is.'

'I may have played with the perspective a bit. That's what I call "artistic licence". We're showing the place at its best.'

'You mean like an estate agent?'

Jago roared with laughter. 'Exactly! An Englishman's home is his castle. That will sell this picture.'

'Who to?'

'The lady in the green jacket, of course. Though

she doesn't know it yet. And I sincerely hope she'll be as generous as her neighbour over the hill at Dellaston Manor.'

Jack longed to know how much the owner of the Manor had paid but Jago was busy again. He worked at lightning speed. A few deft strokes here and there and suddenly there was water in the fountain, a glimpse of a chandelier through the window and a watchful stone lion at the entrance.

Using the smallest brush, he added even more minute details and outlines in black. Now there was a weathervane on the greenhouse, a cascade of late roses over the brick wall and even a peacock on the lawn.

Jack looked down at the garden. 'But there *are* no peacocks!' he insisted. 'Is that artistic licence too?'

Jago held his finger to his lips. A few moments later an eerie high-pitched cry echoed up to the woods. Jack hadn't heard it before, but somewhere down in the garden there was indeed a peacock. A compelling thought gripped him. It was almost as if by painting the bird Jago had made it exist.

By the time the lady of Osmaston Hall came cantering back, her horse steaming from its exertion, Jago was applying the finishing touches. He glanced at his watch and then up at the sky. 'Time to head back. We're losing the light.' He held out the watercolour. 'What do you think?'

Jack gazed at the painting. The weathervane on the greenhouse looked as if it might actually spin in the wind. The clouds were perfectly arranged, soft and white as cotton wool, and the woods in the background appeared dark and mysterious.

'Amazing,' he said. 'You could almost step into it.'

'Another masterpiece then,' said Jago with a wink.

In less than two minutes flat, the leather bag was packed. They ambled down the hill and while they chatted a cool breeze played on Jack's cheek. It felt like an animal sniffing at him. Once again, he glanced over his shoulder at the wood. Mounds of amber leaves lay in drifts around the trees. And when the wind stirred them, the last thing Lily had said blew into his mind: *Promise not to let go* …

CHAPTER 14

The sky had turned crimson by the time they climbed the stile and retraced their footsteps down Hill Rise. Jack gazed wistfully ahead at the two shadows falling long and thin on the tarmac. The afternoon had slipped by so quickly.

He glanced at Jago, who was whistling softly at the birds. He wasn't like other adults. He didn't ask boring questions for a start, or try to force a conversation. And when no one was talking, like now, it didn't much matter. On top of that, he liked playing games. Jack wished he could think of another one to prolong the fun.

'I know! It's your turn now,' he said slyly. 'You can have three guesses about me.'

Jago smiled broadly. 'Splendid! I love to play the detective.' He delved into his coat pocket and produced a small magnifying glass which he held to his eye. His pupil was so enlarged he looked like a comic Cyclops. He tapped the side of his nose and put on a posh voice. 'Nothing escapes the eagle eye of the great Sherlock Holmes. Show me your hand, boy.'

Jack grinned and held out his left hand. It was grubby and covered in doodles.

Jago made a big show of studying it, then shook his head gravely. 'Hmm. A textbook case, I'm afraid. Unless I'm very much mistaken, this hand belongs to a schoolboy with a guilty secret. He not only has an aversion to soap but by these squiggles I see he's also nothing but a dreamer. Am I right?'

'Oh come on, that's obvious!'

'Somewhat elementary, I agree.' Jago rubbed his chin. 'Aha! Look at this. Very revealing. Dear, oh dear.'

'What?'

'You have an addiction.'

'Really?'

'There are calluses on the ends of your fingers: see the hard skin here and here. I'd say we're dealing with either a mad violinist or … how about a computer addict?'

'Most kids like computers,' said Jack, heartily disappointed. 'You've got to do better than that. And you've only got one more guess.'

Jago traced his finger over a long line in the middle of Jack's upturned palm.

'Now then. *This* is interesting. Very interesting.'

'What now?' Jack wasn't going to be caught out by another joke. Jago, however, was looking serious for a change and had dropped the phoney accent.

'It looks to me like something important has been lost,' he said. 'Or perhaps merely forgotten. Or even misplaced. It's hard to tell exactly. But don't worry – it's right under your nose.'

'Something important?'

'Very.'

'You mean like a door key or a watch?'

'Far more precious than that.'

Jack was puzzled. This sounded like a riddle. What could be so precious? He thought of his parents. They were lost but they certainly weren't forgotten, nor were they going to turn up under his nose. 'What is it then?' he asked.

Jago shrugged. 'Search me. You're the one who should know. I'm just reading your palm. But whatever it is, you have to tell me when you find it. Then I win the game. Deal?'

Jack laughed. 'Deal!' He held out his hand and they shook on it.

★★★

A pair of skinny legs in faded denim dangled from the apple tree outside Jack's house. Charlie had been perched in her favourite lookout post for almost half an hour, awaiting his return.

As they got closer, Jack saw her staring at Jago as if he'd arrived from another planet. He sensed mischief ahead as Jago reached quickly into his pocket and, once again, fixed the magnifying glass like a monocle into his eye.

'I say, Jack,' he said, squinting at the tree. 'Strange birds in your neck of the woods. Look at that big one up there. Unusual plumage, don't you think?'

'That's Charlie,' said Jack, grinning up at his friend.

'Oh! Beg your pardon. These old eyes aren't what they were. Delighted to make your acquaintance, Charles.' Jago held out his hand and shook a branch of the tree.

Charlie rolled her eyes. 'Hullo,' she said flatly.

Jack had a terrible urge to laugh. Charlie's proper name was Charlotte, which she hated. But Charles, he suspected, would please her even less.

'Now then, Jack …' Jago's right eye twitched wildly with the effort of holding the pretend monocle in place. 'You have been a most excellent guide. And I must beg your assistance in one further matter. Will you please point me in the direction of the nearest alehouse? This afternoon has been thirsty work.'

He placed his hands on Jack's shoulders, which shook with laughter, his blue eyes challenging him to keep a straight face.

'There's a pub just around the corner on the main road,' said Jack. 'It's called The Feathers. You can't miss it. There's a big sign outside with a cockerel on it.'

'Splendid! Then *that* is where I shall roost tonight.'

As Jago spoke, the magnifying glass popped out and the two of them fumbled to catch it. Jack had to suck in his cheeks to stop the giggles escaping. 'Mind how you go, Jago,' he managed to say. He felt like a bottle of fizzy drink that was about to explode. And somehow the fact that Charlie wasn't amused made matters even worse.

Jago winked and set off down the road. He hadn't

gone very far before he bumped into a lamp post. He raised his hat in apology, then promptly stepped off the pavement in front of a passing cyclist. With a scream the cyclist fell off, and a lot of shouting ensued while Jago disentangled himself from the bicycle wheels.

Jack could take no more. It was like watching a pantomime. He bent over, his hands on his knees, laughing so hard the tears rolled down his cheeks.

'Who's the joker?' said Charlie, hopping down from the tree.

'Jago Flyn. Hee, hee, he's a painter,' Jack spluttered.

'No kidding. So tell me, how does he manage to paint if he can't even see where he's going?'

A car horn hooted angrily at the bottom of the hill. Though Jago was out of sight, they both knew he was causing chaos on the main road.

'He *can* see!' chuckled Jack. 'It's just an act.'

'Uh-huh. I think I got that. I'm not stupid, you know.' Ramming a lock of ginger hair under her beanie, Charlie waited for Jack to compose himself. 'So where've you been?'

'He wanted directions to Osmaston Hall. We went over the fields, then I watched him paint a picture of the place.'

'Doesn't look like an artist. More like a tramp.'

'That's only on the outside. Underneath he wears all this arty stuff and he sells his paintings to rich people.'

'Is he any good?'

'Brilliant. He can make places look ten times better than they really are.'

'Sounds like a con to me.'

'It's called artistic licence,' said Jack. 'He uses his imagination.'

'Well, I don't like him.'

'You've only just met the guy!'

'I don't care. There's *something* about him.' Charlie hoisted her rucksack on her shoulder. 'Is my bike okay?'

'In the garage. Why? Do you have to go?'

Charlie chewed her lip as if considering it. Then she grinned. 'Nah. I didn't lug this halfway across town for nothing. I've got a surprise for you.'

'What?'

'Wait and see. Come on!'

Together they crunched across the gravel driveway with Jack trying in vain to unzip Charlie's bag. When she bolted for the house, he gave up and cast a wistful glance back down the hill. The 'something' Charlie disliked about Jago was probably just her feeling left out, he decided. After last night's quarrel he could see why she might be touchy. Even so, he hoped he'd get to meet the flamboyant Mr Flyn again.

CHAPTER 15

Nan was making vegetable soup, gallons of it by the look of all the plastic containers spread over the counters. A huge saucepan bubbled on the stove while the whirr of the liquidiser battled for supremacy over the rock music on the radio. Nan had her back to the door, jiggling her hips in time to a thumping bass line.

'At least the power's back on,' giggled Charlie.

'It never went off,' said Jack, trying to ignore the spectacle in front of him. 'We're the only ones who've got it.'

'Lucky you! I had cold baked beans for lunch.' Charlie eyed the row of cottage pies which were cooling on a big wire tray. 'Are you having a party or something?'

Nan spun round, her wooden spoon raised like a conductor's baton. A piece of potato peel hung limply from her hair and one cheek was daubed with flour.

Jack frowned. 'What *are* you up to?'

'What does it look like?' said Nan. 'Cooking!'

'I can see that. But who for? Are we expecting visitors?'

'No.'

'Starting a restaurant?'

'No!' Nan looked flustered. 'I'm making sure the freezer's well stocked, that's all – keeping the wolf from the door.' She laughed, a high awkward sort of chuckle that didn't suit her.

Jack shook his head. Sometimes Nan gave a good impression of being bonkers. He stepped forwards to remove the potato peel from her hair. 'You worry too much,' he said.

Before he could move away, Nan had her arms around his waist, hugging him like she never meant to let go. 'You *must* tell me when you're going out,' she whispered in his ear. 'I need to know where you are.'

'Stop fussing.' Pulling away, he shot an awkward glance at Charlie, his face crimson. 'I'm not a baby!'

'Got any biscuits?' said Charlie with a grin.

'Of course, dear! Take the tin,' said Nan. 'Be careful, some of them are still hot.'

Charlie motioned her head towards the door and Jack nodded gratefully. A quick retreat upstairs was definitely the best course of action.

★★★

'Sorry 'bout last night,' said Jack, flicking a stray crumb from his T-shirt. 'Dunno what came over me.' He and Charlie sat cross-legged on the bedroom floor, the tin of biscuits between them.

'Forget it,' mumbled Charlie, her mouth full. 'Blame

it on the weather. That wind was enough to drive anyone … Mmm … What flavour's this? Marshmallow and –'

'Bonfires. New recipe.'

'Cool.'

'So where's my surprise?'

'Oh yeah!' Charlie licked her fingers, then wiped them on her jeans. Hauling the rucksack towards her, she tipped it upside down. A large slab of a book dropped on the carpet, sending up a puff of dust. 'Ta-da! *The Seven Wonders of the World*,' she announced, and before Jack could interrupt, she began reading aloud.

'"Thousands of years ago, the tallest lighthouse of all time was built in Egypt on an island called Pharos. A giant skyscraper, more than a hundred and thirty metres tall, it guided sailors into the great harbour of Alexandria. The building was a miracle of science, art and human endeavour and became known as the seventh wonder of the ancient world."'

'Charlie, I know this stuff –'

'Wait, there's more. This book came from the library and look what's inside.' She unfolded a yellowing newspaper cutting.

'"Divers have found a lost world on the sea floor at Alexandria in Egypt,"' she read. '"They believe they've uncovered the ruins of the great Pharos lighthouse, which was destroyed six hundred years ago by an earthquake. No one knows exactly what it looked like. But all that is about to change."' Charlie's eyes sparkled with excitement. 'Jack, this is about your parents! Look, there's even a picture of them …'

Jack turned away. 'Charlie, please stop –'

'I can't believe you never told me! How could you keep this a secret? Jack, look at this place. It's incredible!'

Charlie turned the book to face him and Jack was confronted with a picture he hadn't seen for years. It was an artist's impression of a vast three-storey building which stood on a tiny island at the end of a long causeway. It had a base shaped like a massive box, a tall octagonal middle section and a rounded tower on top like a mosque. It was meant to be beautiful, but to Jack it looked like a crematorium.

'I can't believe you found this,' he said, touching the edge of the newspaper. 'I'm surprised it's still there.'

The brightness faded from Charlie's face. 'What do you mean?'

'I've seen this book before,' he said. 'When I was five … after Mum and Dad died.' For a split second he found himself wishing he could burn the wretched thing. 'Nan got it from the library and we looked at the drawing together. It was her way of explaining, I suppose. I didn't understand where they'd gone.

'She told me they'd found this wonderful place under the sea. She made it sound like a fairy tale – a fallen tower smashed into a thousand pieces.' Jack shook his head. 'It was her idea to put the cutting in there – to keep them safe. Daft really. But it sort of helped.'

Charlie closed the book quickly. 'Jack, I'm so sorry.'

'It's okay. You didn't know.'

'I only went to the library cos the internet was

down! If the power had been on, this would never have happened.'

'Honestly, don't worry.'

Charlie slumped into the chair in front of Jack's computer. She'd meant to make him proud, not miserable. She stared glumly at the screensaver lighthouse which bobbed gently up and down on a perfect sea of turquoise and green pixels. From the beam on top, the word *Pharos* materialised in a burst of yellow before disintegrating into the waves.

'Why's this lighthouse named after the old one?' she asked grumpily.

'Pharos is an ordinary word now,' said Jack. 'It means lighthouse in lots of languages – French, Italian, Spanish. That's just a graphic, nothing to do with the old Pharos.'

'What's it doing on your computer then?'

'It downloaded itself. Someone sent me a disc.'

'Who?'

'I dunno!'

Charlie's eyebrows disappeared upwards beneath her black beanie.

'I found the parcel at the back of the house,' said Jack. 'No message, no stamp, no postmark. Nothing to show where it came from.' He fished the brown bag out of his wastepaper bin. 'It came in this.'

'But that looks like *your* handwriting! Did you send a self-addressed envelope anywhere? To a games company or something?'

Jack shook his head.

'Maybe you did and just forgot.'

'Charlie, I didn't forget! And look, this isn't an envelope. It's more like a sandwich bag.'

'Okay, okay. Where's the disc then?'

Jack pulled open the middle drawer of the desk. 'Here.'

As the disc changed hands, the lights in the room flickered. Jack and Charlie looked at each other, half expecting the power to go off. But, if anything, the lights seemed to burn more brightly.

Charlie made a face. She could see herself reflected in the metal disc. Scruffy spikes of ginger hair stuck out from under her hat. 'Odd-looking CD,' she said. 'What's this here?' She traced her forefinger around the tiny fish shape near the centre.

'Ow!' She slammed the disc down on top of the book and rubbed her palm. 'Damn, that thing's hot!'

All at once, a flare of blue light enveloped the disc, illuminating the room like a lightning flash. It lasted barely a second, and though there were no flames, a strong smell of burning paper filled the air.

'Jack! The book – it's on fire!' shrieked Charlie. 'Take it out. Quick! Before it sets the place alight!'

Jack picked up the book with the disc on top of it. He raced for the stairs with Charlie at his back, thumping him to make him go faster. The back door bounced on its hinges as they flung themselves outside into the darkness.

Instantly, the lights in the house flickered and went off. The rock music on the radio died and a wail of despair came from the kitchen where the cooker had cut out.

Jack kept going. Halfway down the garden, the fish pond glimmered in the moonlight. He hurled the disc in, the water gurgled and a cloud of steam hissed into the night air. Dropping the book, he threw himself down, gasping for breath.

'What the heck happened there?' Charlie flopped on the damp grass beside him and nudged the book with her foot. It was still smoking. 'Look at that, what a mess! I'm in trouble now. There's bound to be a huge fine … Hey Jack? What is it?'

Jack crouched over the book. The disc had burnt a perfectly circular hole not only in the front cover but also in hundreds of pages inside. He flipped through them. The cavity was cone-shaped and the further into the book he went, the smaller the hole became. He reached the seventh and last chapter. There the burning had stopped. All that could be seen was a dark brown ring, the size of a small coin, directly above the picture of the famous lighthouse.

'Spooky,' said Charlie, peering over his shoulder. 'It looks like there's a sun in the sky now.'

Jack frowned. It reminded him of something else. 'Looks like an enormous mirror to me.'

Charlie squinted at him.

'That's what was on top of the lighthouse,' he said. 'A gigantic mirror to reflect the sun. They could see the beam fifty miles away.'

'You mean the lighthouse was solar-powered?'

'No, silly! They used the sun to reflect the light in the day and fires at night. They didn't have our technology or –'

He broke off and looked at the darkened house. He could hear Nan cursing and banging cupboard doors as she hunted for matches and candles, and suddenly his mind raced like a hot–wired car. He leapt to his feet and scrambled back to the pond.

Lying on his stomach, he dipped his arm through a layer of thick, green algae. A frog belched close to his ear and something scaly slithered over his fingers, but at last his hand brushed over a cool, metallic surface.

'Watch this,' he said. Drying the disc on his shirt, he walked towards the house, slowing as he reached the back door. He hoped the water hadn't ruined it.

Charlie clamped her hand to her mouth. As Jack stepped over the threshold, the whole house lit up. From inside, the beep and whirr of various electrical gadgets could be heard and a blast of music came from the kitchen, accompanied by a rowdy cheer from Nan.

'So that's your source of power!' she said, hurrying over.

'Yep.'

'A-mazing!'

Jack turned the disc over in his hands. 'Maybe it's a solar-powered device. Wonder how the energy's stored?'

'It's magic,' whispered Charlie.

Jack looked up quickly. Her eyes were solemn, full of wonder. She was being deadly serious.

A light breeze blew over the garden, sending a drift of dead leaves dancing across the lawn. *You're a piece of bloomin' magic,* said a ghostly voice in his head. He felt his body sway slightly, like he was teetering on the edge of a cliff. He could feel Lily's hand in his, holding on tight.

He gripped the edge of the doorframe. No. He was just an ordinary boy. There was nothing special about him. It was madness to suppose this was anything other than … than what? A clever piece of science that had found its way into the wrong hands.

'Technology, not magic,' he said firmly. 'You should have seen the equations when it downloaded …'

Charlie marched back down the garden, returning with the book. 'Are you telling me *this* is an accident? The last chapter, the seventh wonder – the place *your* parents found! Apart from one little ring, it hasn't been touched. Use your imagination, Jack. It means something.'

'Like what?' He didn't want to use his imagination. His imagination scared him. Already a dark thought had taken hold. He'd wished for the book's destruction. He'd actually wanted it to burn – and the next moment it had.

Charlie shrugged. She had no idea why the final chapter remained intact. She rubbed the red ring on her hand which tingled like a nettle sting.

'Does it hurt?' said Jack.

'Nah. S'nothing.' She gazed thoughtfully at the disc and a grin spread slowly across her face. 'You know what? We could have fun with this.'

★★★

Jack took a little persuading, but five minutes later they were out in the road and number 12 was in darkness once more. Charlie's red racing bike, her most treasured possession, stood between them while she fastened the straps of the saddle bag where they'd hidden the disc.

'Just keep clear of the houses.' Jack checked up and down the road. 'We don't want the whole town knowing about this.'

'You worry too much.' Hopping on the bike, Charlie flashed him a grin. 'Who could possibly guess what we're up to?'

She set off, pedalling furiously up the hill towards the stile. The night air was intoxicating and she seemed to fly along twice as fast as usual. As she approached the first street light, she held her breath. It lit up, casting a circle of white on the tarmac as she passed below. A banshee shriek exploded out of her: 'Woo-hooo!'

One after another, the street lights marked her progress up the road, like spotlights in a theatre. The effect was stunning: she felt like a conjurer with a wand. Each light stayed aglow just long enough for her to reach the next and then went out.

She turned around and raced back downhill, repeating the performance at breakneck speed.

'A-mazing!' She came skidding to a halt in front of Jack, spraying tiny stones over his feet. 'Go on, you try. Then it's me again.'

Jack needed no invitation. He tore off into the darkness, laughing at Charlie who tried in vain to keep up with him.

On Osmaston Hill the wolf, who had made his lair in the wood, sat watching. Tiny circles of yellow light appeared and disappeared in his amber eyes as he listened to the children's whoops of joy. He put his nose to the ground. The wind rustled through the grass as he drew their scent towards him.

CHAPTER 16

By the middle of the next day, normal power was restored to the whole of Morton Muxloe. In the bar at The Feathers, a raucous cheer broke out as the ancient jukebox droned back to life and the embers around the fake log fire began to glow. Someone drummed his fists on the counter and called for drinks all round.

The landlady eyed the stranger asleep on the long settle in the corner. He had his boots up on the armrest and his wide-brimmed hat pulled low over his face like a cowboy in a western. Why she'd let him bunk down there for the night she'd never know. Customers were never allowed to stay beyond closing time. Yet this man, with his tall stories and silly songs, had made her break all the rules. She'd let the carousing go on far too long and when the last of the punters had gone, somehow there was an unspoken agreement he could stay.

She pulled a pint, knowing he hadn't a penny in his pocket to pay for it. Gentleman or not, he'd hit hard times. Best send him on his way.

'Rise and shine! Get that down ya, mate. Hair of the dog!'

Jago Flyn looked up. To the landlady's surprise, his blue eyes were bright and alive as if he hadn't been sleeping at all. He shook his head at the glass of beer. 'No thanks, my lovely. Today I must be sober as a judge. Important business to transact. J has to go-go! It won't do to be smelling of alcohol.'

He beckoned her closer and whispered something in her ear. The landlady rolled her eyes at the ceiling. Then, after some deliberation, she produced a key from her apron pocket and pointed to a door marked 'Private'.

In less than half an hour, Jago reappeared with his face clean-shaven and his long hair wet and gleaming. He wore a fresh white shirt under the waistcoat and his boots were shining.

'Lord, look at 'im. Don't 'e scrub up well!' shouted one of his drinking companions.

The landlady nodded her approval. Jago was far more handsome than she'd realised. 'Talk about transformation. You could get a job as one of them quick-change artists. I 'ardly recognise you.'

Jago said nothing. Instead, he seized her hand and kissed it fiercely before returning the key to her apron pocket. The bar erupted with wild stomping and applause. He tipped his hat and bowed, making his exit to the sound of wolf whistles.

★★★

At first, Jack thought it was a bird calling. A loud warbling drifted through his bedroom window, echoing the song of another bird some distance away. It sounded like a funny conversation that only the birds could understand. Then he heard footsteps – heavy boots – and a smile spread across his face. That was no bird. He jumped up from his desk and pushed open the window.

'Hey, Jago! Wait up. Where are you going?'

'Osmaston Hall,' said Jago, without stopping.

'To sell the painting?'

'Yes.'

'Can I come too? Please!'

Jago stopped short and studied the pavement for a moment. Then he looked up at Jack, who hung so far over the edge of the window he was in danger of toppling out. 'Well, all right. But you'd better make yourself presentable. Comb your hair, find some decent shoes and wash those unspeakable hands. Be quick about it. I haven't got all day.'

Within minutes, Jack was at his side.

'Now then,' said Jago. 'Oh, for pity's sake, haven't you got anything better than those?'

Jack looked down at his black plimsolls. 'Only wellies,' he replied, casually sliding his hands into his trouser pockets.

Jago narrowed his eyes. 'Show me,' he ordered.

Reluctantly, Jack held out his hands for inspection. He'd run them under the tap, but the ink stains were still visible.

Jago gave a dramatic sigh. 'They'll have to do, I

suppose. And what about my prediction? Did you find anything important?'

The question caught Jack completely off guard. He'd forgotten all about the palm reading. His eyes grew wide. Of course – the disc! Jago's prediction *had* proved true.

'Yes,' he said in surprise.

'Excellent! So? Spit it out. What was it?'

Jack opened and shut his mouth. He'd hidden the disc inside a DVD case among his film collection – a gory werewolf movie he knew Nan would never watch. He didn't want anyone else to know about it, except for Charlie, who'd sworn herself to secrecy.

Jago held up his hands. 'I can see it's a private matter. That's fine. You don't have to say anything.'

Jack bit his lip. He liked Jago and didn't want to offend him. On top of that, they'd made a deal. 'It was my horse, Indigo,' he said quickly. 'A little crystal thing. He went missing a couple of days ago.'

Jago raised an eyebrow. 'Aha! And he's special?'

'Very.' That, at least, was the truth. 'My parents bought him a long time ago. They're dead now.'

Jack stared at the pavement and waited for Jago to come up with the usual sympathetic comments people made when they heard he was orphaned. But to his relief, he only asked, 'And where was he hiding, this horse of yours?'

'Um …' Jack felt instantly guilty. Lies had a habit of growing and he didn't want to continue with this one. 'Under a book.'

'Something you were reading.'

'Yes.'

'So he *was* right under your nose after all.' With a grin, Jago licked his forefinger and drew a vertical line in the air.

Jack smiled and nodded eagerly. The palm reading had been far more accurate than Jago knew. He was very happy to concede the point.

★★★

He half expected to see the black retrievers bounding to meet them as they crunched across the gravel in front of Osmaston Hall. But the dogs were nowhere in sight. Only the peacock announced their arrival, his ear-splitting cry echoing around the buildings.

Jack felt nervous as he climbed the stone steps to the ornate front door. Close at hand, the house looked formal and intimidating, not at all the kind of place where a scruffy boy in plimsolls would be welcome. But Jago was already striding ahead, three steps at a time. It was too late to back out.

The door opened and a small plump man in a dark suit stood before them. Jack started in surprise. He had no idea where he'd seen him before, but there was something familiar about him. He wore round tortoiseshell glasses and his neat hair was slicked back with oil.

'Yes, can I help?' The man spoke abruptly as if he had no time for callers.

'Now then. We've come to see Lady Harington. My name is Jago Flyn.'

'Well, I'm afraid you've missed her. She's out riding.'

'I see. Then we'll have to wait.'

'Do you have an appointment?'

'Yes, of course,' snapped Jago with such ferocity that the man took one step back.

'Strange, she said nothing to me. She must have forgotten. You'd better come in, I suppose.'

The hallway was impressive, with a sweeping staircase and a high ceiling covered in fancy plasterwork. The black and white tiled floor reminded Jack of a giant chessboard. While the man's heels tapped loudly across it, he tiptoed behind, avoiding the lines.

They entered a large, wood-panelled room that smelled of cigar smoke and leather. A vast mahogany desk stood at one end under a glittering chandelier, and paintings of old ships covered the walls.

'I'm afraid Lady Harington won't be back for half an hour at least. She usually rides at this time of day.' The man signalled for them to sit down.

Jago ignored the instruction and walked about the room, while Jack sank into a big velvet chair. He gazed awestruck at the suit of armour that stood like a sentry next to the fireplace. Instead of a sword, it held a banner depicting the family crest below the head of a roaring lion.

'What precisely *is* your business here?' said the man.

'I'm an artist. I've come to discuss a painting,' said Jago, using the same abrupt manner.

There was an awkward silence.

'Are you the butler?' asked Jack from the depths of

the chair. He was keen to establish the man's identity. He was sure he knew him.

'No, I most certainly am not! I'm an accountant, Herbert Lonsdale. I look after the Harington finances.' Lonsdale took off his glasses and polished them on his handkerchief, frowning like a toad.

Jack's heart lurched. He'd seen that expression before. Herbert Lonsdale. HL – the monogram on the pyjamas! Incredible as it seemed, this was the man from the cabin on *The Empress*. He looked younger somehow and had a lot more hair, but Jack was sure he was the same person.

He glanced at the paintings on the wall. 'Mr Lonsdale – sir – have you ever been on a ship?'

'What an odd question! No, I haven't. And I never will if I can help it. I detest the water.'

'Oh,' said Jack, crestfallen. 'So you've never heard of a boat called *The Empress*?'

Herbert Lonsdale looked startled. '*The Empress*! Why – how could you possibly know –'

'You mean she exists?' said Jack eagerly.

'No. Er, not yet anyway. She hasn't got past the design stage. Still on the drawing board, so to speak.'

'I see. Then it can't be the same ship. The one I'm talking about looks old-fashioned, like something out of a history book.' Jack pointed at one of the paintings on the wall. 'A bit like that.'

Lonsdale looked up in surprise. 'Well, yes … actually *The Empress will* look like that. She'll be built with modern technology, of course, but furnished like the ocean liners of old. An Orient Express of the sea and a cruise ship second to none,' he added proudly.

'Really!' Jack could barely contain his excitement. So he hadn't dreamt about an old ship at all, but a new one that had yet to be built. 'Can I see what she looks like? Do you have any drawings?'

Lonsdale glanced towards the desk where a bundle of rolled-up papers lay. 'Certainly not. I've said far too much already. The project is in its infancy. We don't want our competitors knowing the details and – I say, leave those alone!'

Jago had moved swiftly to the desk and picked up a bundle of plans. While he scrutinised them, his eyes flicked to Jack and back again. He dropped them with a thud.

'Thank you!' fumed Lonsdale. 'Now tell me, boy, how did you hear of this ship?'

Jack's mind reeled. What if he really *had* seen the future? A shiver ran down his back and he didn't know how to answer. As he stared at Herbert Lonsdale, all he could see was the man in the cabin calling him a thief.

'The lad lives locally. He must have overheard some gossip,' said Jago, without taking his eyes off Jack. 'Perhaps your employer has been talking with neighbours?'

'I hardly think Lady Harington would discuss such a sensitive project with the neighbours!' Lonsdale blustered. 'She has far more sense ...'

There were footsteps in the hall and a woman's voice called, 'Herb, I'm back. Earlier than I expected, I'm afraid. Chesterfield is lame. Something spooked him in the woods.'

Lady Harington strode into the room, a big woman with ruddy cheeks that looked as if they'd been blown up with bicycle pumps. Her green jacket, jodhpurs and riding boots were covered in mud and there was a long scratch on her forehead.

Lonsdale was at her side in an instant. 'Geraldine, my dear, what happened? Are you hurt?'

'Can't think what got into him. He's usually such a steady lad. He panicked. Put his foot down a rabbit hole and I went over his head. Herb, I'm fine! Please don't fuss!' Lady Harington turned to Jago and Jack. 'I didn't know we were expecting company?'

Before Lonsdale could draw breath Jago was speaking. 'I beg your pardon for this intrusion, Madam. My name is Jago Flyn and this is my nephew, Jack.'

Jack clambered out of the chair to shake hands, blinking with surprise at his new status.

'I'm an artist. I specialise in painting historic buildings. But I fear we've called at a bad moment. You've had an upsetting accident.' Jago spoke in a voice Jack hadn't heard him use before, a voice full of authority and power.

Despite her riding ordeal, Lady Harington was all ears. 'Not at all,' she replied. 'Takes more than that to rattle me. I'm strong as an ox.'

Jack tried to hide a smile. Lady Harington was just like an ox and her large flaring nostrils seemed to emphasise the resemblance.

'I happened to be in the area and your house took me by surprise,' said Jago. 'Quite the most impressive example of Elizabethan architecture I've seen in years. The place has clearly been renovated with a great deal of sensitivity.'

Lady Harington beamed and patted her dishevelled curls.

'Most of my paintings are commissioned,' continued Jago. 'Particularly since my little coup at Buckingham Palace. But yesterday the weather was perfect, I felt inspired and I took the liberty –'

'You've painted the house!' Lady Harington sat down, clapping her hands in delight. 'Show me, show me!'

Jago reached into the depths of his leather bag and produced a long tube. He made a great performance of removing the rolled-up picture inside. By the time the watercolour was revealed, Lady Harington was on the edge of her seat, gasping with pleasure.

'But how wonderful! What a likeness: you've captured the atmosphere of the place perfectly. Do look, Herb. What do you think?'

Herbert Lonsdale studied the painting and shrugged. 'Call me a philistine but the proportions don't look right. The drive is too long.'

Ignoring him, Lady Harington traced her finger over the windows. 'So much light,' she said. 'And such attention to detail. Here's the weathervane and the lion at the gate and oh! – you can even see Percy peacock. Magnificent!'

'Thank you.' Jago allowed himself a slight smile. 'I

would like to show this at my next exhibition in London. That is why I'm here. I came to ask for your permission.'

'You don't need Lady Harington's permission to show this picture,' said Lonsdale bluntly.

'True. But I came as a matter of courtesy. It seemed the polite thing to do since I did, in fact, trespass into the grounds.'

Lady Harington looked disappointed. 'Oh, don't worry about that. So you mean you don't want to sell the picture?'

'No. This is unique. I want to hold on to it.'

'Oh dear, what a shame. Surely I can persuade you? I would give you a good price.'

Lonsdale raised his eyes heavenwards.

'I'm afraid not,' said Jago. 'I've already been persuaded to let my Dellaston Manor painting go. Mrs Morgan was most insistent.'

'Della Morgan has one of your paintings? Well, I can be insistent too. Name your price!'

Jago turned to Jack, who had been hugging his knees in delight throughout the exchange. 'Now then, my boy. I'm not sure about this. What do you think?'

As far as Jack could see, this was just another of Jago's games. And he was clearly enjoying himself, winding Lady Harington up like a clockwork mouse. 'I think you should let the lady have the picture,' he said.

Jago looked directly into Lady's Harington's pleading eyes; her lashes fluttered and everyone held their breath. 'Very well,' he sighed. 'But I cannot part with the painting for any less than two thousand pounds. Cash.'

Lonsdale spluttered and began to protest, but Lady Harington held up her hand.

'And a brief tour of the house would well and truly secure the deal,' Jago continued. 'I hear Osmaston Hall has quite the most impressive collection of medieval wall paintings.'

'Done!' cried Lady Harington. She loved nothing better than to show off her house and her knowledge of its history, particularly if the audience included a handsome connoisseur of art.

'Herb, please organise the payment. There's cash in the safe. Mr Flyn, Jack, come with me.'

★★★

Herbert Lonsdale scowled, thoroughly vexed by the turn of events. He didn't like being mistaken for the butler and he'd been rattled by the questions about *The Empress*. And he wasn't at all happy about Lady Harington's fluttering eyelashes. In his opinion, Flyn was nothing more than a cheap salesman. It was preposterous that he should breeze in as though he owned the place and breeze out again with a cool two thousand pounds.

Lonsdale thumped a button on the desk. A section of the wood-panelled wall flew open to reveal a small safe. He walked over and punched in the secret code on the electronic keypad alongside it.

Outside, Percy shrieked in alarm. Lonsdale glanced over his shoulder. He could see nothing through the latticed window except a magpie sitting in the tree.

Damn peacock, he thought. He went to the window and was surprised to see several more magpies on the lawn. Percy was busy rattling his feathers and charging at them with his head down. Unimpressed, they simply hopped a few feet away and regrouped. Lonsdale counted them: one for sorrow, two for joy, three, four, five, six, plus the bird in the tree. He'd never seen so many magpies in one place before.

He returned to the safe, took out several wads of cash and slammed the door firmly shut. Then he punched in the code once more.

From its branch in the ash tree the magpie watched intently, its eyes shining like black beads.

CHAPTER 17

Jago had a spring in his step as they headed away from Osmaston Hall. 'That woman has far too much money for her own good,' he said. 'She didn't even bother to haggle over the price.' He patted his waistcoat pocket, which bulged with crisp, pink fifty pound notes.

Jack gave the artist a sideways glance and said nothing.

'What?' Jago threw his hands up in the air like a man under arrest.

Jack frowned. 'You don't really have an exhibition in London, do you?'

'No.'

'And you never painted Buckingham Palace.'

'No.'

'And Mr Lonsdale was right. You didn't have an appointment. Lady Harington wasn't expecting you at all.'

'Well, we had to get past the pompous toad somehow, didn't we? You can't conduct business like that on the doorstep,' said Jago. 'Perhaps I did embellish the story a bit – oh, all right, a lot – but she liked the picture, didn't she? Of course she did. There was genius in it, Jack. One hundred per cent pure Jago genius! You can't put a price on that. And you know what? I *could* paint the Palace if I wanted to. The Queen has only to ask!'

Now Jago sounded pompous. The beginnings of a smile flickered across Jack's face.

'Artistic licence,' Jago continued. 'We all stretch the truth sometimes, show people what we want them to see.'

'Hmmm,' said Jack. 'You're good at stretching the truth. You said I was your nephew!'

'Ah, now that *was* a blunder, I agree.' Jago's eyes twinkled. 'I mean, who in their right mind would believe that I, Jago Flyn, distinguished artist to Her Majesty no less, would have such a scruffy, snot-nosed scamp for a relation.' He elbowed Jack off the path.

'You are the biggest liar!' Jack shoved Jago back, knocking him into a bush, and soon the two of them were locked in a scrimmage of arms and legs, each trying to wrestle the other to the ground. Eventually Jago gave in, collapsing first on his knees and then flat on his face with a roar of defeat.

'Very distinguished!' shouted Jack, shaking with laughter. He didn't mind Jago claiming he was his nephew, not in the least. In his heart he wished it was true.

'By the way,' said Jago, brushing the twigs and mud from his coat, 'what was all that about the ship?'

Jack stopped laughing. 'It's nothing,' he said. 'Probably a coincidence but … I think I've met Mr Lonsdale before.'

'On a ship called *The Empress*?'

'Yes.'

'The ship that has yet to be built?'

'I know it sounds strange …'

'Very!'

'I had this dream – well, more of a nightmare really – about a shipwreck. Everything about it was so real, like I was actually there. And … well, he was in it.'

'Now that *is* a coincidence! Especially when he's got the plans on his desk. Practically psychic. Has anything like this happened before?'

'Never.'

Jago looked over at the woods, his brow creasing in thought. 'What brought it on, I wonder? Tell me more. When did this happen?'

But before Jack could answer, something hard and sharp hit him on the shoulder and he cried out in surprise. A large stone lay at his feet.

'Bull's-eye!'

The sound of boyish laughter rippled up the hill. Jack felt his cheeks burn with shame. He knew the voices at once: Blunt and his mob. They were leering and gesturing obscenely from behind a clump of bushes further down the path.

'Trouble?' said Jago.

'Morons. Ignore them,' replied Jack.

They walked on, and another larger stone landed with a thud close by. Jago picked it up and looked at Jack, who was doing his best to fight back tears.

Jago weighed the stone in his hand for a moment.

'Wait there.' He marched purposefully in the direction of the gang.

The bullies came out of hiding and, sensing a battle, grouped themselves around Blunt, who stood arms folded, feet apart, commando style. As Jago drew near, he spat on the ground.

'Whassup, Grandad?'

Jago dropped the stone with an ominous thud at his feet. 'Now then. Listen carefully, because I'm not going to repeat myself. You will *never* go near that boy again.' His words carried such force they sounded more like a prediction than an order.

'Oh yeah? And who are you, then? His bodyguard? Don't make me laugh.'

'Shall I show you what will happen if you ignore me?'

'Yeah, go on.' Blunt smirked at his friends. 'I'm sooo scared.'

Jago reached into the pocket of his trench coat and pulled out something metallic. The boys shifted uneasily, expecting some kind of weapon. But Jago merely put the metal object to his lips and blew hard. There was no sound and nothing appeared to happen.

Blunt exploded with laughter and pointed a contemptuous finger. 'Is that it? He's only blowing a whistle at us!'

'It's about time someone did,' said Jago with a smile.

The boys fell about, hooting with derision.

Further up the hill, Jack cringed. He couldn't hear what was being said but Blunt's reaction was clear

109

enough. A blaze of fury welled up inside him. What was Jago playing at? This was no time for silly games.

Then, long before anyone else, he heard it – the swish of parting grass like a hundred swords unsheathed and the heavy panting of an animal on the run. The hairs rose on his neck as he turned towards the wood. Running full tilt down the hill, its thick, dark coat rippling over its long body, was a wolf.

With a mixture of terror and fascination Jack watched it advance, his heart drumming almost as fast as its approaching feet. It was heading straight for him. At the last moment he shut his eyes. A strong breeze lifted the hair from his face and the animal whistled by so close it seemed to pass right through him, its soft fur brushing his hand.

The bullies were no longer laughing. Instead, their faces grew long with horror as they realised what was charging their way. One of them swore loudly, another screamed, and they all turned on their heels, running for their lives like a herd of stampeding cattle.

The wolf accelerated, his long legs moving with such apparent ease that his body seemed to float over the ground. He gained on his quarry with every stride, his sights set on the straggler at the back of the group.

Blunt lagged well behind the others. He'd never been a good runner and was nearly out of steam. Glancing back, he let out a scream. The creature was so close he could see its shining teeth and the saliva hanging in glossy threads from its jowls. He made a break and bolted towards the nearest tree, snapping several branches as he scrambled his way up.

For a moment the wolf slowed, then appeared to change its mind, continuing its pursuit of the other boys. Jack's heart sank. 'Don't let him get away,' he murmured.

Jago raised the whistle to his lips again, and even though the wolf was more than two hundred metres away, he stopped in his tracks and turned to listen. Jago signalled towards the tree where Blunt had taken refuge and the wolf began galloping back up the hill.

'So he's yours!' gasped Jack.

'Not exactly,' said Jago. 'No one owns Alpha. He's a wild animal. But wherever I go, he follows. So if he has a master at all, it's me.'

Alpha had reached the tree and was up on his hind legs, growling savagely. Blunt, meanwhile, scrabbled to a higher branch, but he had chosen a spindly-looking tree and the further he climbed the more it bent under his weight.

'Now then,' said Jago, offering the whistle to Jack. 'It's your call.'

'What do you mean?'

'Alpha will stop when you tell him. One short blow on this will suffice.'

There was a crunch as the slender branch on which Blunt perched began to give way. Jack watched as the thug who had terrorised him for the best part of a year attempted to edge his way to a safer spot. But his movements only prompted another ear-splitting crack. The branch crashed to the ground, leaving Blunt hanging by his fingernails to a jagged stump. His legs were dangling only a few feet above the wolf.

111

Alpha leapt in the air, catching one of his trainers in his mouth. Blunt flailed and kicked out. 'Lemme go, lemme go,' he squealed.

The trainer came off. Alpha tossed it to one side, growling, and Jack glanced down at his own feet and the black plimsolls. His fist tightened around the whistle. Blunt and his crew were nothing but worms. He hated them.

'Stop him! Please! Call him off!' Blunt screamed at Jago. He was losing his grip and blood trickled down his ankle. But Jago merely held up his hands and shrugged, as if confirming he had no say in the matter.

Alpha lunged again. This time Blunt fell to the ground, landing on his back with a heavy thud. Too winded to move his body went still, and for a second he blacked out.

When he came round, two huge paws were on his chest, pinning him to the ground. He stared up in terror. The wolf's amber eyes were locked on to his with such intensity it was impossible to look away. Alpha curled back his lips and snarled, showing his long, white incisor teeth. Blunt began to weep.

And then it was over. The weight suddenly lifted from his chest and he could breathe. He turned to see where the wolf had gone.

Standing nearby with the whistle in his mouth, Jack stared down at him. Alpha sat at his feet, waiting for the next command.

Blunt's eyes grew wide.

'That's right,' said Jago, pulling him up by the

sleeve. 'You've been given a last-minute reprieve. Count yourself lucky, because I'm not sure you deserve it. Now get out of here before he changes his mind.' He jerked his head at Jack.

Blunt backed away, tripping over the discarded trainer. Then he turned tail and fled as fast as he could down the hill towards the river where the other boys had gone.

Alpha watched until he became nothing but a speck in the distance. Then he threw back his head and howled.

The hairs stood up on Jack's arms. The noise rose high then changed pitch, ending so abruptly it sounded as if Alpha's voice and heart were both breaking at once. 'It's okay, you did enough,' he said. Without thinking, he reached out to touch the ruff of fur below the wolf's ears.

Alpha froze. The contact, though slight, seemed to confuse him and his hackles rose.

Jack looked anxiously at Jago. 'I didn't mean to –'

'Let him be,' said Jago. 'He doesn't understand. You can't befriend a wolf.' He took the whistle from Jack and pointed in the direction of the wood.

For a moment Alpha stood his ground, his eyes fixed on Jago in a long stare. His nose wrinkled with the beginnings of a snarl. Then his tail went down and he shot away.

CHAPTER 18

For the rest of their brisk walk home Jack bubbled with excitement. He wanted to know everything about Alpha. What was he doing in Morton Muxloe? What kind of wolf was he? Why was he following Jago? If he was wild, why did he respond to a whistle?

But Jago's mood had changed. He seemed distant and preoccupied, and Jack's curiosity only made him irritable.

'I've never seen a real wolf before. Does he live in that wood?' said Jack. 'You know, I think I sensed him when you were painting. Where does he come from? Obviously not here!'

'Of course not,' snapped Jago. He strode on so quickly Jack thought he was going to ignore him. Then he added over his shoulder, 'Algonquin.'

'Al – gon – where?'

'Canada,' said Jago.

Jack stopped dead in surprise. How had Alpha travelled across an ocean? He ran to catch up, but on seeing Jago's furrowed brow, he decided to save that question for later. Instead he asked, 'Is he really wild?'

'Yes.'

How, Jack wondered, was Alpha surviving in an English wood? He supposed there must be enough rabbits and deer to eat. Another question occurred to him. 'Would he attack a cat?'

'If it crossed his path. He's a hunter, remember. Why?'

Jack explained about Odin and how Nan had nearly had an accident after seeing the wolf. As Jago listened, his face grew even more serious.

'I see,' he said. 'Then Alpha is venturing closer to town than I thought. It's time for us to move on.'

'You're leaving?' exclaimed Jack.

'Yes. My business here is done.' Jago tapped his pocket containing the wad of cash.

'Where will you go?'

Jago didn't answer straight away. Instead, he gazed at the rolling hills in the distance. 'Which way does the wind blow?' he muttered. Then, glancing back at Jack, he seemed to recollect himself. 'What I mean is I'm free as a bird on a breeze. Nothing to tie me down. I shall go to the Pentland coast,' he said decisively, 'and from there by boat to Belgium.'

'Belgium!'

'Yes. Why not? They have a saying that every Belgian is born with a brick in his stomach. They love their houses. Even more than the English. They'll love my paintings too,' said Jago with a wink.

Jack smiled half-heartedly. He'd barely had time to

take in all that had happened that afternoon, but he was certain of one thing – he didn't want Jago to go.

Everything had changed in the past two days. It was uncanny. Since Jago had arrived the sky seemed bluer than usual, the birds were singing more noisily and whatever he wished for seemed to come true. He'd begun to feel lucky for a change. And meeting Jago was part of it. The way he'd stepped in and tackled the bullies had been amazing too. Beneath the funny-man exterior, he had nerves of steel.

'You were great this afternoon. Thanks for helping me out,' he said. 'I owe you.'

'Don't mention it. I've no time for thugs. Good thing you were in charge. Not sure I'd have been so merciful.'

There was an awkward pause.

'So when will you go?' asked Jack.

'Tomorrow morning. Bright and early. The sooner the better, I think – under the circumstances.' Jago held out his hand. 'Well, it's been a pleasure, Jack Tideswell.'

Jack nodded. There was nothing more to say. He gave Jago a grin and when they shook hands, it seemed as if a surge of electricity passed between them, just as when they'd met.

★★★

The front door closed with a gentle click. Jack leant against it and stared at his black plimsolls in a kind of daze. Despite his triumph over Blunt, he suddenly felt flat and empty. Jago had gone and that was that. He'd probably never see him again. If only he'd kept quiet about Nan's meeting with Alpha. Maybe he'd have been in less of a hurry to leave.

He crossed the hallway and climbed the stairs, recalling his last glimpse of Alpha as he'd bolted for the woods. What a shame he'd been so frightened. His fingers curled softly over the banister, remembering the feel of the wolf's coat. It had been so dense and luxurious; he'd longed to lay his cheek against it. He gave a shrug. Odd that a creature who seemed so nervous of humans should have ventured into town at all. What had possessed him?

A hissing sound erupted under his feet.

'Oops. Sorry, puss. Did I make you jump?'

Odin, who'd been curled up on the landing, lifted his nose and sniffed Jack's outstretched hand. A low growl rumbled in the back of his throat.

'Hey, silly! It's only me.' Jack bent down to stroke the cat's head. Odin's claws flashed at him and a bright bead of blood appeared on the back of his hand. 'Ow! What was that for?'

Odin was on his feet, his back arched, the ugly black stitches on his neck bulging. He spat savagely and for a moment it looked as if he was about to attack again.

'Oh no you don't.' Jack shooed the hissing cat with his foot, forcing him down the stairs. 'Get out of here!'

'Jack? Is that you?' called Nan from the kitchen.

Odin fled, colliding with Nan's legs as she appeared in the hallway.

'What's going on?' she said.

'Stupid animal scratched me,' replied Jack, sucking at the blood.

'What! Here, let me see.'

'It's nothing.'

Nan frowned in the direction of the study where the cat flap was banging to and fro like a machine gun going off. 'Where've you been?'

'Out.' Jack started back up the stairs. He was in no mood for one of Nan's inquisitions.

'What do you mean "out"? I thought we had an understanding. You're supposed to tell me when –'

'You weren't here.'

'I was at the garage. I told you, I wanted to get the car checked. Jack, wait. *Don't* turn your back on me!'

Jack stood still. He hated the way she worried all the time. It didn't do either of them any good.

'Don't ignore me,' said Nan. 'I'm your grandmother. I'm *supposed* to take care of you.' Her voice was fretful. 'If anything happened to you, I'd never forgive myself.'

Jack swivelled to face her, his eyes burning. 'And nothing ever *will* happen to me if you have your way,' he said. 'Nothing at all! Stop going on. Let me live!'

Nan stared at him in astonishment. 'What's got into you? How dare you talk to me like that?'

Jack didn't reply and a silence followed which seemed to go on for ever. He knew she wanted an apology but he didn't see why he should give one.

'Right then,' said Nan eventually. 'Have it your way. Get on with your life. I assume that still includes school. For your information, you start back tomorrow.'

Jack's heart sank. He'd hoped the unscheduled holiday would go on much longer. And after the excitement of the last two days, school was the last thing he wanted. He glared at Nan. She couldn't have dreamt up a worse punishment if she'd tried.

'Dinner'll be on the table in ten minutes,' she snapped.

Jack watched her walk towards the kitchen, her bony shoulders hunched and stiff. There was only one way to retaliate. 'I'm not hungry,' he snarled, and marching up to his room, he slammed the door.

CHAPTER 19

He flung himself on the bed, punched the pillow, then lay face down, waiting for the anger to subside. When it didn't, he grabbed a tennis ball from the windowsill. Thok. The ball belted the wall opposite, leaving a small, satisfying indent in the plaster.

The computer screensaver flickered.

Distracted, he watched the blue-domed lighthouse shuttle across the screen, its slender spire glinting like a needle. At least he still had the disc. He slid off the bed, fished out the DVD case from the bookshelf and stood for a moment, tapping it against his side. Maybe he should call Charlie. Nope. On second thoughts, bad idea. She'd only try to cheer him up. He was in no mood for company.

Music blared from the radio downstairs and his eyes closed in frustration. Nan was singing along with some cheesy boy band – out of tune. It drove him nuts the way she pretended to be happy when she was cross. If only he could switch her off.

He slumped down at the desk, remembering the previous evening's fun. What a laugh! How she'd screamed when the appliances had cut out. He removed the disc from the DVD case. What kind of crazy technology could power a house like that anyway?

His fingers brushed the keyboard and his homepage appeared. He punched in a question.

'Which metal conducts electricity best?'

236,000 results in 0.3 seconds.

"At ordinary temperatures silver is the best conductor, followed by copper, gold and aluminium," read the first entry. "However, when supercooled, some pure metals become 'superconductors' with nearly zero electrical resistance."

Jack sat back and flipped the disc over to examine it. No electrical resistance? That made sense, sort of. His index finger tapped the keyboard as he thought about it.

Outside, the street lights glowed and the dusky fields fell into darkness.

He clicked on 'superconductors'.

A rectangular chart full of squares and numbers and symbols popped up. With a groan, he recognised the periodic table. It showed all the chemical elements known to man – his science teacher was mad about it. For some reason, the fifth column and fifth row were illuminated in blue. And where they met, the symbol 'Nb' was raised on a tiny 3D platform.

'Niobium,' he read. 'Never heard of it.'

He put the disc down and immediately the blue highlight disappeared and the platform sank back into a square. His nose wrinkled at the screen. 'Random,' he muttered.

There was a fanfare of trumpets and Mac marched on, throwing an orange ball in the air. A message from Charlie had arrived. Jack clicked on the tiny duck to remove him. Mac blinked and hung his head. Then he lifted one webbed foot, booted the message ball away and trudged after it with a melodramatic sigh.

Jack drummed the desk. The disc had an antique quality which was why he'd thought it might be bronze. But its bluish tinge made him wonder. His fingers returned to the keyboard.

He spelt the letters out loud: 'N-i-o-b-i-u-m.'

Click went the mouse.

92,906,308 results in 0.41 seconds

"Niobium is a rare earth metal with many special properties. It is highly resistant to heat, anti-corrosive and very strong."

Impatiently, Jack clicked on. Physicists used the metal in particle accelerators. Click. Special jewellery was made with it. Click. It was mixed with steel in bridges, car bodies, pipelines, railway tracks, ships. Click. Camera lenses, television screens, even people's glasses were coated with it …

How can it be rare if it's everywhere? he thought.

He picked up the disc again and a memory flashed into his head: Herbert Lonsdale angrily snatching his broken glasses and calling him a thief. Why was every detail of that dream still so vivid? He thought about meeting Lonsdale that afternoon. It had felt weird, especially when he'd started going on about *The Empress*. What if –

The screensaver flicked back on and Jack chewed

his lip. What if he'd glimpsed a real event, something bad that was going to happen? Not a dream or any kind of premonition. Supposing he'd actually been there – in the future?

A sensation like pins and needles shot up his arm. The disc had begun to glow bluish white in his hand. He stood up quickly and it suddenly flared so brightly he couldn't even see his own feet.

It was happening again. Only this time he realised that the machine-like thrum wasn't caused by the computer: it came from the disc itself. He could feel the vibration going right through his skin into his bones and an overwhelming tidal tug drawing him forwards. He reached out to steady himself, but the desk, his bed, the entire room had fallen away.

He couldn't fight it and he realised he didn't want to. He was wide awake, and whatever the disc was made of, it was about to superconduct. *You asked for an adventure*, he told himself. *Well, now you've got one.*

★★★

'Gotcha!'

Jack groaned. He was lying face down, his mouth full of grit and his lungs squashed flat. Gulls cried overhead and a sharp rock pressed under his chin. He wriggled desperately, trying to free his arm which was being held behind his back.

'Oh no yer don't! Yer on my beach. Why yer spyin' on me?'

'I wasn't!'

'Liar!'

As Jack gulped for air, his captor yanked him up by the scruff of his neck and spun him round. An older boy in cut-off jeans and a pale blue shirt stood, hands on hips, glaring at him.

'I saw yer,' he said, his black hair whipping across his face in the wind. 'You was watching me.' He stepped forwards and pushed Jack in the chest, his thick eyebrows daring him to disagree.

Jack spat the sand from his mouth.

'Why don't yer fight?' said the boy.

'I don't want to.'

'What d'yer mean, yer don't want to?'

'You're bigger than me.'

'So? I know plenty of little fellas wot fight.'

'Well, I'm – not – one of them,' snapped Jack. He wasn't little; he was tall for his age.

'What's wrong with yer then?'

'Nothing!'

'There is.' The boy jabbed him in the chest again. 'Where's yer self-respect. What are yer? A man or a muppet?'

Jack glared back. 'Numpty,' he muttered.

'And what's one of them when it's at home? You bin reading them ickle baby books? Humpty Dumpty sat on the –'

And that was what finally did it. Jack was way beyond nursery rhymes, and he'd had enough of the jabbing finger. 'It's "man" or "mouse", you moron!' he shouted.

'Oh yeah?' The boy raised his fists with a grin. 'Reckon 'umpty's got the 'ump! Come on then, li'l mouse …'

Motivated by some deep instinct which told him to make his whole body like a battering ram, Jack charged forwards. At the last moment, he twisted sideways, dropping his shoulder low. He didn't see the boy's astonished expression, but as his head thundered into his midriff, there was a moment of intense satisfaction: he knocked the loudmouth clean off his feet.

'Ooof!'

What happened next, however, took them both by surprise. Beyond the mound of sand where the boy had been standing was a precipice. The two of them crashed over it.

There were rocks on the way down and they hurt like hell. Jack's knee crashed into the boy's head and something sharp gouged his ankle. Above them the gulls screeched in alarm, but their own yells, mixed with the clatter of tumbling stones, were decibels louder.

Eventually, they came to a sprawling halt on a stretch of soft sand, Jack on his front and the boy spread-eagled on his back.

'Bloomin' maniac! Thought yer said yer didn't fight!'

'I LIED!' roared Jack. A trickle of blood ran down his ankle. He bit his lip against the pain.

Groaning, the boy sat up and put his head between his knees. Drops of blood from his forehead stained the sand.

'Here!' barked Jack. He pulled a filthy tissue from his pocket. 'Take it.'

125

With a grimace – either of disgust or pain, Jack couldn't tell which – the boy mopped his face. Then he put his fingers in his mouth to remove what looked like a piece of tooth. Throwing it aside, he heaved himself up.

'Bill Armitage,' he said, extending a hand. 'It *is* my beach. No one comes in autumn, leastways not after the 'olidays. That's my *Princess* over there … What's the matter? Cat got yer tongue?'

Jack peered into the boy's big, open face. 'Bill?'

The bushy eyebrows should have given it away; the voice too. It *was* him, the engineer from the ship. Only he was younger, much younger. Jack's heart gave a thud. This time the disc had sent him backwards rather than forwards.

He glanced along the beach. A small boat, Bill's *Princess*, was pulled up on the sand nearby, a fishing rod sticking out the back with its line trailing in the water. And beyond, on a craggy island in the sea, stood a familiar sight: the Pentland lighthouse.

'Do I know yer?' asked Bill, hoisting him up.

'Yes! I – I mean no.' Jack grinned awkwardly. 'Well, not yet anyway … I think we're going to be friends!'

'We're bleedin' blood brothers already. Look at us! What's yer name?'

'Jack Tideswell.'

'And yer climbed down 'ere in them shoes?'

Jack looked down at his plimsolls, then up to the cliffs which rose behind them. Hundreds of thousands of gulls thronged every ledge and crevice. He nodded.

'Blimey. Can you swim an' all?'

'Course I can!'

A grin stole across Bill's face. 'Hmmm. A mouse wot swims.' His eyes flicked towards the sea.

Without a word of warning, he set off down the beach, chunks of wet sand flying around his heels. As he ran, he peeled off his shirt and, with a quick backwards glance, whirled it about his head and whooped like an Indian warrior.

Two black gym shoes lay discarded among the rocks. Jack was close behind. When his feet hit the water's edge, he yelled too. The surf was ice cold and made his ankle sting like an animal had chewed it.

'Last one in's a bloomin' –'

The wind stole Bill's final words but Jack had a shrewd idea what they might be. He ran even faster. All the king's horses and all the king's men couldn't have stopped him. Bill was asking for it.

A wave rolled in and he plunged towards it, disappearing through the wall of water which poured down like a white mane. The shock of immersion was wonderful. Within seconds he forgot the cold, forgot his stinging ankle, forgot everything in his life that felt unfair and lost himself in his own private battle against the breakers.

It took several dives to get beyond them and by the time he surfaced, Bill was nowhere to be seen. He paddled about, listening for a tell-tale splash or shout. But apart from the gulls with their endless creeling, he was alone.

A small boat toiled across the choppy waves towards the lighthouse. In the prow, he could make out three figures, standing shoulder to shoulder, too far away to notice his tiny bobbing head. His courage began to fade. Where had Bill got to? Surely he could handle the current?

All at once the water erupted below him and before he knew what was happening, a pair of broad shoulders lifted him clean out of it. 'Let go!' he screamed. Two hands had fastened around his ankles, tipping him backwards.

For a split second, while his arms flailed, he could see the lighthouse quite clearly. A man with binoculars watched his plight from the walkway on top. Just before he slammed down, gulping a horrible salty mouthful, he saw him wave.

'Ha ha ha!' Through the haze of bubbles came muffled howls of laughter. 'No one can hold their breath as long as me!' roared Bill as he reappeared.

'Wanna bet?' spluttered Jack, furious at being caught out.

'Yeah, bring it on!'

'How much?'

'Pound note says yer won't last two minutes.'

'Easy!' Jack flicked back his wet hair, spraying Bill in the face.

'You ent got the lungs, Mouse.'

'Watch me.'

Jack dived again, so wrapped up in the moment he completely forgot he was in another 'here and now'. Being with Bill was fun. Despite his rough edges, Jack liked him and wanted nothing more than to win his admiration.

The money didn't much matter, which was lucky, because in his enthusiasm Jack had overlooked one important detail. There was no such thing as a *pound note*, at least not in his 'here and now'. They'd stopped printing them more than thirty years before.

★ ★ ★

Later on, Jack couldn't help laughing. As things turned out, Bill didn't have a penny on him. He was so embarrassed he wouldn't let the subject drop. Jack had won fair and square; he'd pay him back 'one day', he said. To prove it, he wrote 'I.O.U.' in the sand with a big stick he was using to prod the fire they'd made.

The wind had picked up and no amount of driftwood seemed sufficient to make a good blaze. So, belatedly, they'd begun building a firewall of rocks, each trying to outdo the other over who could lift the biggest.

While they worked Jack's eyes kept returning to the letters in the sand. As far as he was concerned, Bill had already settled his debt on *The Empress*. He wanted to tell him everything, about the ship, Lily, the light … but he stopped himself short. *It'll freak him out*, he thought.

Instead, he asked about the visitors he'd seen.

'Oh, them.' Bill dropped a huge rock into position and stood back to survey his handiwork. 'Them's the Brethren.'

'Are they monks or something?'

'No, you clod! Don't you know nuffin? They're from Trinity House – officials. It's them what runs the lighthouses. My dad's the keeper.'

Jack nodded. 'I think I saw him earlier. The man with binoculars?'

'That's 'im. Always bloomin' spyin'.'

'Can we go and see him?' It occurred to Jack he could warn the adults about the light.

'Nope.'

'Why not? You live there, don't you?'

'Sometimes.' Bill gave the fire a prod. 'I'm mainly with mam on the mainland.'

'Oh.'

'It's easier fer school,' explained Bill. 'I help when I can. He doesn't want me today.'

'Why?'

'They're talkin' – 'bout improvements.'

'There's a problem with the light?'

'No! Works perfick.'

'How do you know? What if there's a fault? What if some day it breaks down? Suddenly the power could fail and the next thing you know –'

'Ent never gonna break down!' Bill cut in. 'Not while my dad's keeper. Anyways, if the main light goes, we've got a backup. Plus two sets of batteries in case the electric fails. 'Ere we go – look!'

The light had come on. As it swept across the bay, Bill grew animated. 'It's got its own signature flash, see, every five seconds. That's how you know it's the Pentland,' he said proudly.

'There's three lenses wot revolve round the lamp, bleedin' massive things. We has to dust 'em every day, and polish 'em with vinegar. Then once a year we –'

He broke off. Jack's hand was on his shoulder. 'Wot?'

'I have to go.'

Bill looked disappointed. 'You cold or summat? I can fix that.' He marched over to his boat.

Jack pulled on his plimsolls. He wasn't cold and he didn't want to leave. The Pentland light had triggered the tugging sensation and it was getting stronger by the second. The disc was pulling him back.

'Bill, listen. Have you ever seen magic happen? Right in front of your eyes?'

'Once or twice,' said Bill over his shoulder. 'Watched a bloke cut a woman in 'alf once. Bit boring really. Ah, 'ere it is!' He held up a jerry can and an oily rag.

'That's just a stupid trick! I mean the real thing.'

'Wot, like witches and broomsticks?'

'No! The kind where you go backwards and forwards. In time.'

'Teleporting and stuff?'

'Sort of.'

'Load of rubbish.'

'That's what I thought. Then –'

Bill wasn't paying any attention. He doused the rag with liquid from the can. 'I'll show yer a piece of bloomin' magic. Stand back.'

He picked up a stone the size of a tennis ball and tied the rag around it. Then, after weighing the bundle in his hand, he lobbed it high into the air. It landed dead centre

131

in the pile of smouldering wood. A crackle, a hiss and a great deal of spitting followed before an explosion of flames reached into the sky.

'HowZAT!'

Bill spun round, arms raised in triumph.

Above him, the gulls circled and screeched.

'Mouse?' The bushy eyebrows met in the middle. There was no cheer of approval, no friend to join him in a war dance around the flames. The beach was empty. Jack's magic had beaten him to it.

★★★

The screensaver lighthouse glowed luminous in the dusk of the room. Six letters slid down its yellow beam into the sea: P – h – a – r – o – s.

Despite what had happened, Jack felt surprisingly calm. He'd made up his mind. There was something he had to do – for Lily, Bill, even toad-face Lonsdale.

A small amount of money lay on his desk, with a shiny silver pen that had belonged to his father and his crystal horse, Indigo. He put the items in his rucksack, taking care to wrap Indigo in a nest of tissues inside his favourite old, red hoodie.

Then he folded up the train timetable he'd printed out. His plan was simple. Tomorrow he'd skip school, take the Great Eastern line to Dunton and walk across The Spike peninsula to Wakeham. From there it was only a fifteen-minute boat ride to the lighthouse.

Bill's reassurances about the backup system hadn't

convinced him. He had to find the keeper and warn him about the light. He'd seen with his own eyes what was going to happen. And the only one who could stop it was him.

Brimming with excitement, he picked up the mysterious disc. *What kind of crazy device is this?* he thought. First it had catapulted him into the future, to an event which had very nearly killed him. Then it had blasted him to the past, landing him in his first-ever fist fight!

One thing, at least, was clear. He understood now how Bill had come to recognise him on the ship. And Lonsdale too, for that matter … though there'd been no reason to call him a thief. He'd been on his best behaviour at Osmaston Hall.

Downstairs, the DJ on the radio announced another song. To his relief, Nan had given up singing. He tucked the disc in the hoodie along with Indigo and zipped up the rucksack. He'd have to wear his uniform and act normally in the morning. She'd go nuts if she knew what he was up to.

Exhausted, he collapsed on the bed. Lily had haunted his dreams for two nights running and he had a feeling tonight would be no different. Perhaps when he'd seen the keeper she would leave him in peace.

He pulled off the plimsolls and a sprinkling of dry, white sand fell to the floor, sparkling on the thick pile of the carpet. He studied it for a moment. 'Humpty Dumpty sat on the wall …' At least Bill couldn't accuse him of doing that.

CHAPTER 20

It was long past midnight at Osmaston Hall and several fallow deer had crept into the walled garden to nibble at the shrubbery. A tawny owl hooted overhead and in the distance, a dog fox called to his mate. The marauding deer munched on, stooping low among the holly bushes to reach the tender bark.

A strangled cry filled the air. The deer stood to attention, watchful as sentries, their ears twitching. A long, rasping choke came from somewhere nearby: some creature was breathing its last. The deer had heard enough. With one collective leap, they bounded away in fright.

The house itself was in darkness, except for the soft blue glow of a laptop computer in the ground-floor office. Two big moths dive-bombed the screen, kamikaze-style, and Herbert Lonsdale swatted them aside. He couldn't be bothered to close the window.

He scratched his head, tapped in some calculations and groaned. *The Empress* project was going to cost the Harington business a small fortune. At this rate it would take at least five years and the profits from every shop, office and hotel they owned to get the hare-brained scheme afloat. Geraldine might just as well play Monopoly with her properties.

But Lady Harington could not be dissuaded. 'You can say what you like, Herb, it's what Victor wanted.'

Romantic stuff and nonsense, thought Lonsdale moodily. There was nothing legal to bind her to a dead man's whim. Lord Harington had been dead and buried for a year. It was time she realised that this ocean liner was nothing but a fantasy.

A scratching sound behind him interrupted his thoughts. The latch which held the window ajar had come undone and the room filled with a cool breeze. Lonsdale got up, shut the window and stood with his hands in his pockets looking out at the garden.

In the darkness, the enormous topiary bushes that lined the lawn resembled sleeping giants. Everything was perfectly still and quiet … except … Lonsdale leant forwards, squinting. There appeared to be something hanging from the silver birch tree.

Overhead, the clouds parted and for a moment the garden was bathed in moonlight. Lonsdale gasped in horror, realising what he'd been looking at. It was one of the grisliest sights he had ever seen.

Before he could do anything about it, a gloved hand covered his mouth. There was no time to struggle. He felt a sharp pain on the side of his neck and collapsed unconscious on the floor.

A small, wiry figure in a dark tracksuit gave the

accountant's sprawling body a shove. No response. Beneath his black balaclava, two impish eyes beamed with pleasure. Holding the high-powered stun gun to his lips, the intruder kissed it lightly before replacing it in his belt.

Moving swiftly, he went to the safe and entered the code, removing several large wads of cash which he put in his backpack. Moments later he padded across the hallway and up the sweeping staircase, his black trainers squeaking on the marble steps.

Loud, manly snores came from a room at the end of a long gallery. A broad, mischievous grin spread across the thief's face. Apparently, *Lady* Harington was not such a *lady*like sleeper. She sounded like a giant balloon deflating.

Stealing into the room, he made straight for the wooden jewellery box on the dressing table and started examining the contents with his torch. Tiny flecks of coloured light danced across the ceiling and he sighed as if he'd never seen anything so beautiful. Into the backpack went a large sapphire ring, a gold heart-shaped locket, a diamond tiara and a bright turquoise bead necklace which Lady Harington had been given as a child. The necklace had not fitted around her broad neck for years.

She stirred in her sleep. 'Whoa there, boy! Hold your horses …'

The thief froze, his hand hovering over the stun gun.

Lady Harington opened her eyes and clutched at her sheets. 'Steady, Chesterfield,' she murmured, 'steady, boy … only a fox.' Then, with a great creaking of bedsprings, she rolled over and the snoring resumed.

The thief let out a low whistle of relief. This mountain of a woman would not be easy to silence, especially for someone his size.

He hurried back along the gallery, passing beneath the portraits of Lady Harington's ancestors. They looked fearsome in the torchlight but he barely gave them a glance. Something far more exciting had caught his attention, through an open door at the other end.

In a high-ceilinged room painted with fleecy clouds, two pinpricks of light winked at him. Padding across a circular cream rug, he paused to look around. The Harington family nursery, where generations of children had played and grown up, still seemed to echo with their voices.

His torch flashed to and fro, resting briefly on a white cot. Through the bars, beside a pile of neatly folded bedding, a small army of soft toys gazed up at him. He put a finger to his lips as if to hush them. Then, with astonishing speed, he bounded forwards and climbed the bookcase to the top.

The winking lights turned out to be nothing but a pair of yellow glass marbles which had spilled out of a board game. Yet he scooped them up in delight, polishing them on his sleeve before adding them to his haul.

Then he did something even more remarkable. Instead of walking down the stairs, he swung one leg over the oak banister and slid to the bottom, flying off the end and landing silently on the chequered floor with his arms raised. Two cartwheels, a backflip and several deep bows to an imaginary audience concluded the performance before he hurried back to the office.

With a great deal of effort, he dragged the prostrate body of Herbert Lonsdale towards the desk. From his tracksuit pocket, he produced a small electronic device and connected it to the laptop. It was a portable palm reader. This would give him top-level access to the Harington bank accounts. He put the unconscious accountant's hand on top of the device and dialled into the bank.

Within seconds Lonsdale's fingerprints were verified and the thief gained entry into *The Empress Trust Fund*. He keyed in a figure – £2,000,000. In the next moment, the money disappeared from the account.

★★★

Less than ten minutes later, Herbert Lonsdale began to stir. He hauled himself into his leather chair and slouched over his desk, his head throbbing. For a moment he couldn't think what had happened. Then, with a shudder, he remembered the grotesque sight in the garden. He pulled himself up, clutching his back in pain, and staggered to the window.

Yes, it was still there. Percy the peacock hung from the silver birch, his long turquoise neck bent at an awkward angle. Most of his beautiful tail feathers lay scattered on the lawn amidst a pool of blood, their round blue-green tips like staring eyes. Percy had paid the price for being a much better guard dog than Lady Harington's two retrievers who were, even now, still slumbering in the kitchen.

Lonsdale rubbed his aching temples and turned back into the room. He noticed the safe door was open and finally it dawned on him: there had been a burglary. He looked around nervously. The safe was bound to be empty but he went to check anyway.

All at once there was an explosion of screeching and chattering and Lonsdale almost leapt out of his skin. Some sort of creature was inside the safe. He backed away as a blur of black and white flew up into his face and clawed his cheek. Shrieking in pain, he put his hands up to bat the thing away.

Now, at long last, the dogs began barking in the kitchen and footsteps thumped on the stairs. Lonsdale wheeled around frantically but he couldn't see his attacker anywhere.

The door creaked open and, very slowly, the barrel of a shotgun appeared. Lady Harington stood at the other end of it, wearing a fearsome expression, her long white nightdress billowing out like a galleon in full sail.

When she saw Lonsdale, she lowered the gun. 'What the devil's going on? Herb, are you all right?'

Herbert Lonsdale sat on the floor, gibbering. 'W-w-w-one for s-s-sorrow,' he stuttered, pointing a finger heavenwards.

Lady Harington crouched down and put a comforting arm around him, appalled to find her old friend in such a state. He was trembling with fear and blood trickled like a teardrop from a cut near his eye. She looked up

139

and saw something white flash near the ceiling where he kept pointing.

'I say, there's a magpie on the curtain rail. How on earth did he get in?' She bustled over to the window and undid the latch.

The bird let out a jarring rattle of a cry as she approached. 'Tsche, tsche, tsche …'

'It's no good scolding me. It's not my fault you're stuck inside,' she said. 'Out you go.'

The bird swooped down. As he flew off shrieking into the night, the deer which had regrouped in a huddle by the woods dived for the ink-black shadows.

CHAPTER 21

Nan was slicing a loaf of bread with such vigour the table shook as if an avalanche was approaching. Jack's cornflakes slopped from side to side in his bowl, but he pretended not to notice and carried on reading the back of a cereal packet. Odin sat on the windowsill, perfectly still, his green eyes flicking from one human face to the other.

Last night's angry words hung between them. Nan wanted an apology; Jack remained tight-lipped. Apart from anything else, saying sorry seemed two-faced when he was about to embark on a trip that would make Nan's hair stand on end. She couldn't cope with him straying one mile from home, let alone a hundred or more.

Odin gave a querulous mew – and was ignored. He set about licking his wound as if he hadn't wanted any attention in the first place.

Nan handed Jack his packed lunch. The sandwiches were like doorstops and she hadn't bothered to cut off the crusts. But he couldn't help noticing she'd included a generous helping of her special biscuits. He felt a pang of guilt and looked down.

In the hall, she tapped the barometer as usual. The needle moved to high pressure. 'Fair and warm,' she said, breaking the silence at last. 'No need for a coat then.'

'I'll take it anyway.'

'Really?'

'You never know, I might need it.'

Nan stared at him, shaking her head. The disappointment on her face was unbearable. He wanted to tell her he wasn't being deliberately awkward. There were reasons – good reasons – for what he was going to do. He wanted her to be proud, not sad. Yet if he told her the truth, would she let him go?

He grabbed his coat and walked out. At the end of the drive he turned to look back, wishing he'd hugged her. Nan stood at the kitchen window, watching him, her shoulders slumped. He waved and saw her hand go up. But her expression didn't change.

★★★

Hurrying along the main road, he glanced at his watch. He had twenty minutes to get to the station, buy his ticket and find the right platform. He couldn't afford to hang around.

As he reached The Feathers pub, however, his pace slowed. Three police cars straddled the pavement outside, one of them with its blue light flashing. A woman in a pink dressing gown stood in the doorway, surrounded by uniformed officers.

'No. You listen to me,' she shouted, jabbing the

nearest man. 'This is *my* pub, you got no right to barge in. I told you, he ent here!'

A rumble of angry male voices followed and one of the men tried to push past. The landlady erupted. 'Why would he be hiding?' she shrieked. 'Are you calling me a liar? He's gone, I tell ya!'

'All right, all right.' A slim man in a long, grey overcoat pushed his way through the uniforms. 'There's no need for all this. Look love, I know you've had a rude awakening.' He looked sternly at the officers around him. 'But we need to find this man. Did he tell you where he was going?'

'No. As it happens, he didn't!' she spat. 'What's it to you?'

'There was a burglary last night,' said the detective. 'Up at Osmaston Hall.'

Jack ducked behind a row of wheelie bins that filled one corner of the pub garden.

'So?' the landlady said. 'What's that got to do with 'im?'

'He was there yesterday, selling a painting. Her ladyship gave him a tour of the place herself. We just want to ask the gentleman a few questions, eliminate him from our enquiries.'

'Oh yeah? You reckon he was casing the joint. Is that it? Always thinking the worst, you lot. Well, you're wrong. He was here with me last night. All night. I can swear to that!'

'I see,' said the detective calmly. 'And was there a boy with him, his nephew, by any chance?'

'No. Didn't even know he had a nephew. Why?'

'He had a boy with him yesterday, bit of a rough sort by all accounts. Poor man who let them in got assaulted last night: knocked unconscious. He reckons the thief was no bigger than a child of twelve or thirteen. Could be the same boy.'

The detective paused and in the silence that followed, a bird screeched overhead. A magpie strutted along the ridge of the pub roof, its bright eyes fixed on the scene below.

The detective glanced up, then continued, 'So if you don't mind, we'd really appreciate your co-operation. We need you to tell us everything you know about this Mr Flyn.'

Through the gap between the bins, Jack saw the landlady shrug, then jerk a thumb over her shoulder. 'Go on then. But it won't take long. Ent much to tell.'

Jack slid slowly to the ground, his heart pumping. *A burglary at Osmaston Hall? Lonsdale assaulted!* He clutched at the long grass around him. How could they think he was responsible? Part of him wanted to laugh out loud. It was mad. *He* was the prime suspect! The stench of the bins made him gag and he realised he was about to throw up. He crawled on all fours to the hedgerow.

Afterwards, he sat in a crumpled heap, hugging his knees. So now he knew why Lonsdale had called him a thief. He was tempted to rush in, find the man in the grey overcoat and tell them they'd got it all wrong. But the more he thought about it, the more it seemed like a bad idea. He'd watched enough crime programmes to know he'd wind up in the police station making a statement. And that could take hours.

He scrambled to his feet. Nothing was more important than getting to the lighthouse. Whatever happened, he had to stick to his plan.

★★★

Morton Muxloe railway station was a grand red-brick building with a high, vaulted roof. As Jack arrived through a side entrance, the chimes of the clock tower sounded. The station announcer was giving details of a departing train, but with all the noise he couldn't tell if it was his.

He pushed his way through the tide of commuters pouring out of the building on their way to work. He hadn't realised how much his school uniform would stand out. Deciding to avoid the booking office where someone might remember him, he made for the automatic ticket machine in the main hall.

Luckily, the queue was short, but while he waited in line he got another shock. The police were here at the station, too. Three officers patrolled the platforms and another two were engrossed in conversation with a station official under the departure board.

He scanned the list of trains. The Eastern Express was due to leave platform one in three minutes! He fumbled in his wallet for the right money. Several coins spilled to the floor, bouncing and rolling in all directions, and he dived after them.

'Need any help?' said a deep voice. A giant black

boot came down, trapping one of the coins.

Startled, Jack looked up. It was the man in the grey coat from The Feathers.

The detective bent down and picked up the runaway coin. 'Coppers can be useful,' he said, pressing a two pence piece into Jack's hand and chuckling with pleasure at his own joke. When Jack didn't join in, he asked, 'You from Muxloe High?'

Jack nodded.

'Where you off to then?'

'I'm, um ...'

'It's okay, I don't bite, you know.' The detective grinned. His teeth were big and yellow and there seemed to be far too many of them.

'I'm – er – going to the dentist,' Jack blurted.

'Oh, bad luck.' The detective paused for what seemed a lifetime. 'Checkup or fillings?'

'Checkup.'

The detective turned away to survey the rest of the station. Jack thought he'd been dismissed, but as he stooped to pick up his rucksack, the policeman fired another question: 'So where is this dentist of yours?'

Jack glanced up at the stations listed on the Eastern line and picked one of them. 'Fenstreet,' he lied. He could see the station clock over the detective's shoulder. As the second hand pulsed its way around the dial, he was conscious of his heart knocking against his chest. His train was leaving in two minutes. At this rate he wasn't going to make it.

He looked up hopelessly at the roof where several

pigeons fluttered around the metal rafters in a state of agitation. *Trapped, like me*, he thought. *Please make this man go away*. Aloud he said, 'I've got to go. I'm going to miss my train.'

The detective's eyes rested firmly on Jack. 'Fenstreet, eh? Bit out of the way for a dentist. I don't think it's even got a station, lad.' He looked at the display board and frowned.

Jack searched the list again. To his dismay, the station had mysteriously disappeared.

'How old are you, son?'

'Fourteen.'

'And what's your name?'

Jack fought the panic rising inside him. The policeman was tenacious as a terrier after a rat. He struggled to think of a name other than his own. But his mind had gone blank. *Jack Tideswell* – that was the truth and those were the only words in his head.

He opened his mouth to speak and was about to give himself away when a bloodcurdling scream came from the far end of the station. A woman's cry echoed to the rafters, sending the pigeons into an even greater frenzy.

A surge of people spilled out from platform seven, running and shouting for help. The newspaper vendor called out, 'What is it? A bomb scare?' and when no one replied, he hurriedly pulled down the shutters on his shop with a crash.

The detective was already halfway across the concourse, heading towards the commotion. Jack wasted no time. He pumped the coins into the machine, grabbed his ticket and tore off in the direction of platform one.

The guard stood poised with the whistle in his mouth. He seemed hesitant about letting the train go. There was clearly a security problem, yet no one had told him to hold the train. He waved Jack on board and looked down the platform at the driver, who had his head out of the window.

'Well? Are we going, or what?' the driver bellowed.

The guard took a deep breath and made up his mind. He blew the whistle, the brakes hissed and the Eastern Express bound for the Pentland coast lurched forwards.

★★★

Everyone in the carriage had crowded on one side, jostling each other for a better position at the window.

'Good lord,' said a businessman. 'Is that a wolf?'

'Nah, can't be. Alsatian more likely,' said another man. But he sounded unsure.

Jack's heart leapt. He hurried forwards, wriggling through the crush of bodies. It was Alpha! He was running flat out along platform seven, parallel to the departing train. Behind him, a huddle of frightened people gaped and pointed. And in their midst a woman sat on the ground being comforted by a station official. She looked white as a ghost.

Suddenly, the detective in the grey overcoat appeared. He stepped clear of the crowd and pulled out a gun.

A gasp ran round the carriage.

'Noooo!' yelled Jack, thumping his fist against the window.

The other passengers turned to look at him and a woman holding a toddler on her hip said, 'It's not a pet, love. It's savage. Gave that poor lady the fright of her life.'

'Bang, bang,' said the toddler excitedly.

It was like watching a silent movie. The policeman went down on one knee and took aim. Jack didn't hear the shot but he saw the pistol recoil just as Alpha took an almighty leap off the end of the platform.

The passengers craned their necks to see what had become of him, but the train had picked up speed and an incoming engine pulling a long line of freight wagons cut across their view. There was a general groan of disappointment.

'Bad dog all gone?' There was a tremor in the toddler's voice.

'Yes, all gone,' said his mother, hugging him close.

Jack screwed up his eyes, trying to make out the distant figure in grey. The detective was up and running, his long coat fanning out behind him. He reached the spot where the wolf had jumped, but it was impossible to see his expression.

Jack prayed there wasn't a body lying on the asphalt beside the track. 'Run, Alpha,' he whispered under his breath. 'Run!' Why couldn't these people understand? The wolf hadn't come to the station to terrorise them. He was simply looking for his master. Perhaps Jago was on board at this very moment. He glanced around the people in the carriage.

Everyone was talking, their faces animated by the drama. 'I blame the owner,' the businessman said. 'Completely irresponsible. A dog that dangerous should be muzzled. Imagine if it attacked a child.'

The mother with the toddler nodded in agreement. 'If you ask me, only a thug would own such a brute in the first place.'

Jack pushed past them, angry tears pricking the corners of his eyes. Alpha wasn't a brute. He was wild … beautiful. Only yesterday he'd transformed his life by seeing off Blunt and his gang. And today he'd come to the rescue again. It was Alpha's timely diversion that had enabled him to catch the train. So that was twice the wolf had saved him.

He moved down the rocking train from one carriage to another, looking for the one familiar face that would share his point of view. But Jago was nowhere to be seen. Doubling back, he found an empty carriage and threw himself into a seat by the window.

By now, the Eastern Express had left the outskirts of Morton Muxloe and was hurtling through open countryside. Ploughed fields spread out on either side and the Rollright Hills stretched into the distance like sleeping dinosaurs.

Jack pressed his nose against the window and watched his home town grow smaller and smaller. With a pang of loneliness, he opened his rucksack to inspect the nest of tissues inside his red hoodie. Indigo felt warm in his cocoon and the smiling J on the horse's back gave him a burst of courage. It was just a train ride. And a longish walk. He'd be home before dark.

He sat back, closing his eyes, and tried to picture what Charlie might be doing. He wished she was with him. He knew she would have something sensible to say.

CHAPTER 22

Stamping her feet against the chilly air, Charlie waited outside the school gates. For the millionth time in her life, she wished Nan would give in and let Jack have a mobile. But no, apparently they not only fried people's brains, they scrambled dreams too. Nan had made her promise she wouldn't sleep with hers by the bed, not even under the pillow.

She plunged her hands in her pockets and stared down the road. 'Oh no, that's all I need,' she moaned. Limping round the corner, swearing loudly at his friends, Blunt was headed her way.

His face darkened when he saw her. 'It's all-out war now. Your mate's gone too far,' he shouted.

Charlie looked at him blankly.

'Set his dog on us, didn't he? Look at this!'

As he came closer, Blunt yanked up his trouser leg, revealing four scratch marks which ran lengthways down his calf to his ankle. Charlie wrinkled her nose. The skin around them was inflamed and raised into wheals that resembled long worms.

'He's gonna be so sorry he messed with me,' said Blunt.

'What *are* you talking about?' Charlie replied. 'Jack hasn't got a dog.'

'Belongs to that old geezer he hangs out with. They were up at the Hall yesterday. We watched 'em. Reckon they went back and did that burglary last night.'

'What? Jack wouldn't –'

'Oh yes he would. He's got a strange choice of friends, if you ask me.' Blunt looked her up and down. 'He's gonna pay for what he did.'

'Is that right?' Charlie couldn't keep the sarcasm out of her voice. 'And what are you going to do?'

Blunt grabbed her by the collar, pulling her towards him. 'It's not what we're gonna do, it's what we've already done,' he hissed.

'If you've hurt Jack –'

'I ent laid a finger on him,' said Blunt, coolly. 'Didn't need to.' Then before she could back away, he leant forwards and planted a disgusting kiss on her lips. 'Hope for your sake I ent got rabies,' he said, enjoying her horrified expression.

Charlie lifted her hand to slap him, but he anticipated the movement and caught her wrist. Incensed, she spat at him, 'Rabies? You're barking mad already! When you start foaming at the mouth, no one's going to notice the difference!'

Gormley snorted loudly.

Blunt glared at him and shoved Charlie backwards so hard she crashed into the railings.

When they were gone, she struggled to her feet. She could feel the impression of the wrought iron in her back. *Idiots!* What did Blunt mean: 'It's what we've already done …'? And what was all that about a burglary? She rubbed her sore wrist with a growing sense of unease. Jack was no thief but he'd definitely gone to Osmaston Hall with Flyn.

Charlie pulled a face. She didn't like the painter one little bit. Even though he played the fool, she knew he was smart – sharper than a razor. She felt a twinge of jealousy. Jack hadn't replied to her message the previous evening. Being with Flyn was probably more fun, especially if he'd given Blunt a good scare.

The school bell rang and she glanced back along the road one last time. Maybe Jack was fed up with having a girl for a friend. Shoulders hunched, she headed into class alone.

CHAPTER 23

Jack woke with a start, roused by the sound of someone shuffling a newspaper. A businessman in a pinstriped suit lounged in the seat opposite, his shaved head just visible above his tabloid. 'Big Blow: storm costs millions,' read the headline.

Jack rubbed his eyes. The train was pulling out of a small station which appeared to be in the middle of nowhere. There were no houses, no shops, no cars, and apart from an old lady napping on a bench, no people. He stared at the sleeping woman. She had a voluminous purple coat bundled around her like a blanket. Two starlings perched on the wicker basket next to her and a white plastic bag danced along the platform at her feet.

As the train picked up speed, he just caught the place name: Fenstreet. No wonder the policeman had been suspicious. This place wouldn't have a dentist. It was odd there was even a station.

'Now then. Where exactly are you running to?' said the businessman, as if resuming a conversation they'd already begun.

Jack almost leapt out of his skin. The man tossed the paper aside and looked directly at him, his brilliant blue eyes accentuated by the shaved head.

Jack's heart thumped. 'Jago! I didn't recognise you.'

'Thought I'd smarten up my act.' Jago made an extravagant gesture at the suit. 'Finest Savile Row cloth. What do you reckon?'

'Great,' said Jack uncertainly. He hadn't thought Jago was the kind of person to wear a suit. 'Are you in disguise?'

'Certainly not! Why, should I be?'

'It would make sense. They're looking for us, Jago. There's been a burglary at Osmaston Hall.'

Jago sighed. 'I know. There were blue lights all round The Feathers this morning. I had to fly the coop early. Most inconvenient.'

'Shouldn't we tell them we had nothing to do with it?'

'Oh, I don't think that's necessary. They'll catch the culprit soon enough. We were simply in the wrong place at the wrong time.'

'But they've got a description. They think the thief's a child.'

'Indeed?' Jago raised his eyebrows.

'It wasn't me, if that's what you're thinking!'

'Of course not. I don't doubt your honesty for a minute. I was merely wondering at the audacity of a child who would dare to break into a stately home. It's ambitious, to say the least. Don't you agree?'

'I s'pose so.' Now Jack found himself half-wishing he *was* the thief.

'No. I'm afraid there's no going back. I have business elsewhere. And Alpha needs to move on. He was getting restless, as you know.'

'That's the other thing,' said Jack, his voice catching. 'I think Alpha may be … hurt. He frightened some people at the station. The police tried to shoot him!'

Jago seemed unperturbed. 'Alpha can look after himself.'

'But he could be wounded, lying half-dead somewhere. You can't just leave him. How will he find you?'

Jago merely smiled, then nodded towards the window.

Outside, the violet-blue sky seemed bigger than usual. Giant shafts of sunlight speared the clouds, hitting the rolling hills like laser beams. In the middle of them, an animal moved along a distant ridge, travelling so fast that its streamlined body appeared to float over the ground.

'Alpha!' Jack's heart hammered as if a bird had been released in his chest. 'I don't understand … How did he catch up with us?'

'Wolves have tremendous stamina. They can travel great distances.'

'But …?' Jack glanced at his watch. The train had been travelling for a good hour at high speed. How had the wolf managed to come so far?

'Alpha is as old as the hills themselves,' said Jago. 'He isn't governed by time. Neither am I. Let me show you.' He clapped his hands.

Immediately, there was blackness outside as if the train had entered a long tunnel. The rocking motion of the carriage stopped and a deathly silence hung over it.

Jack stared at the seat opposite, the blood pounding in his ears. It was empty. Jago had disappeared into thin air. Before he had time to wonder how or why, the daylight returned and he found himself looking out at the hills once more.

The train slowed, pulling into a station. He recognised the place straight away. There was the old lady in the purple coat dozing on the bench, a couple of starlings swooping down towards her basket. A white plastic bag lifted by the breeze of the incoming train flew up from the railway track and cavorted towards her.

The signs dotted at intervals along the platform confirmed that this was Fenstreet. It had all happened in the blink of an eye, like déjà vu. Except Jack knew for certain it wasn't a trick of the mind.

With a long hissing sigh, the doors of the train opened and he heard footsteps approaching at a run. A bag landed inside the carriage with a thump – a large leather bag – and just as the doors began to close, a familiar figure in a trench coat and oilskin hat swept in.

'I ditched the suit. Not really my style, was it?' said Jago, breathing heavily. He took off the hat and a shock of dark hair fell across his brow. Brushing it from his eyes, he slammed into the seat opposite.

'Magic,' whispered Jack, half in appreciation, half as a statement of truth. He turned to the window. Alpha had disappeared, though he knew he wasn't far away. He could sense him still running, as surely as he could feel the blood pumping through his veins. In a moment he would see him … Yes! A column of sunlight fell across the folds of a hill, revealing a speck of brownish grey racing down the edge of a long gully.

Tingling with excitement, Jack turned back to Jago. 'Well? Come on! Explain!'

'We just replayed time,' said Jago matter-of-factly. 'Only for a minute or so, but enough to create a slightly different version of the present. One in which my hair was never cut. It was a bad decision anyway. I could tell you didn't like it.'

'But how … who are you?' said Jack slowly.

'Exactly the same person I was five minutes ago. Despite the change of appearance.'

'No, that's not what I meant and you know it. Jago, you said you were an artist.'

'I am. And a very good one too.'

'Yes, but that's not the whole truth, is it?'

'The whole truth is a slippery customer, Jack.' Jago leant forwards and reached behind Jack's right ear, producing a pack of cards out of nowhere. After shuffling them thoroughly, he arranged them face down on the table between them, like the pleats of a fan. 'Pick one,' he said.

Jack chose a card near the centre and turned it over. It wasn't from a normal deck. Instead, it showed a character in a broad-brimmed hat and breeches, standing in front of a stall covered in cups and balls and knives. He was holding up a short stick like a baton.

'There are two kinds of magician,' said Jago. 'One is a common conjuror like this.' He tapped the card and the character on it began to move, juggling three cups in the air above him. 'He's a showman – a fast-talking, two-bit hustler who cons people out of their money with cheap tricks and smooth patter. A fraud, in other words. Exactly what Mr Lonsdale thinks I am. Couldn't see any magic in my art, could he? No. Now, turn the card over.'

Jack could hardly take his eyes off the juggler but he did as he was told. On the reverse side of the card, which should have been plain green like the others, he saw a second image. A youthful figure in a white robe and a long, red cloak held a wand above his head. A sword, a golden chalice and a pentacle star revolved around him, catching the light as they turned.

'Here, on the other hand, is the genuine article. The true magician,' continued Jago. 'A Magus. He has nothing to do with illusion or deception. The magic he creates is real. He's a master of metaphysical secrets who can bend reality according to his will.'

'Like you!' cut in Jack. 'You're a Magus!'

Jago shook his head. 'I wish I was, but that *would* be stretching the truth,' he said with a smile. 'I have an ancestor, a very distant one, by the name of Hermes Trismegistus. Now, he *was* a Magus. But he lived centuries ago and the gifts I've inherited are limited, to say the least. That little time slip just now was a drop in the ocean compared to his power. The truth is neither black nor white, Jack. I'm more than a common conjuror, but I'm a long way from a true Magus.' He

160

turned the card on its side and spun it round so that the two images became a blur.

'A drop in the ocean?' exclaimed Jack. 'Is that what you call it? What you did was amazing.' He leant across the table and touched Jago's sleeve, his eyes alight. 'You're probably closer to a Magus than you think.'

Jago stared at Jack. He was so startled he took his eye off the spinning card and it tumbled to the floor. Jack wriggled under the table after it. As he picked it up he noticed something about the Magus he hadn't seen before. The belt around the magician's waist was, in fact, a bright red snake.

'Ugh! What's this? It looks as if it's trying to swallow its own tail.'

Jago laughed. 'These are Tarot cards,' he said. 'Used by fortune tellers to predict the future. They love their symbols. Snakes can shed their skin and be reborn. It's a sign of immortality.'

'A moment ago, before you disappeared, you said you weren't governed by time. Are you –?'

'What? Immortal? Look at these wrinkles. What do you think?'

'What about Alpha?'

'Ah, now he's a different matter. Alpha is a piece of pure magic, as mysterious as the elements themselves. He'll live beyond you and me – to the end of time, I shouldn't wonder.'

'But – you said you met in Canada. Al – gon ...'

'Algonquin. So I did. He lived among the Indians there for a while.'

161

'Why didn't you tell me this before?'

'Would you have believed me? The boy who ignores magic under his own nose?'

Jack's jaw fell open.

'When I read your palm I knew there was magic in it. I predicted you would find it too. Was I wrong?'

Jack hung his head. It occurred to him he hadn't told Jago the whole truth either. 'No. All the while it was staring me in the face,' he said. 'I'm sorry. I lied about finding Indigo.'

'Doesn't matter.' Jago waved his hand as if batting away a fly. 'Listen. It's said that a Magus arrives in a person's life when a change is about to happen. He's the guide we encounter just when we need him most, the one who leads us into a new realm. I'm convinced you and I have crossed paths for a reason, Jack, though I'm not sure yet what it is. As I said, I don't have all the answers, but perhaps I have some. Tell me, why are you here on this train?'

Jack was already rummaging in his rucksack. He held out the disc. 'It's because of this,' he said.

He smiled into Jago's twinkling eyes. Here, at last, was someone who might be able to explain things, someone who would reassure him he wasn't going crazy, someone he could trust. Jago would be able to shed some light on the mysterious object.

CHAPTER 24

'Where did you get this?' Jago spoke in a tone of hushed reverence.

'Someone sent it to me. I don't know who,' said Jack. 'It was posted through the back door, the one we don't use.'

'A door that isn't used? How odd.'

'It was wedged in the cat flap.'

'Ah, I see. Then the door *is* used.'

'Yes, I s'pose so … but only by Odin.'

'Hmmm,' said Jago. 'That makes sense. A lot of sense. I wouldn't be surprised if there's an animus involved here.'

'A what?'

'Think about it. It's only your cat that uses the door. So it isn't likely the postman, or any other ordinary person, would make such an important delivery there. But to an animus, it's the obvious place. A point of entry used by a real animal.'

'Jago, I don't get it! What's an animus?'

'Oh! An animus is a human spirit that takes the shape

of an animal. The word comes from ancient Greek – *anemos* – meaning wind. Alpha is probably the oldest animus there is. They say Hermes himself breathed some of his soul into him.'

'Alpha is the spirit of a Magus?'

'Yes.'

Jack gazed down at the disc in Jago's hands. 'So what kind of animus brought this to me?'

'I've no idea. I told you, I don't have all the answers.'

Jago turned the disc over. As the train sped along, the metal caught the light from the window and made him squint. He reached into his pocket and produced the magnifying glass which had caused such hilarity on the day they'd met.

Jack smiled, remembering how Jago had pretended to be short-sighted and crashed into a lamp post. It was hard to believe that the man sitting before him now, with his face so still and serious, was the same person.

The silence seemed never-ending while Jago examined the disc.

'It's got niobium in it,' said Jack.

'Hmm?'

'A rare metal.'

'A super alloy. Yes, that's hardly surprising.'

'So what is it?' asked Jack, unable to contain his curiosity a moment longer.

Jago placed the disc on the table between them and pointed at the tiny fish engraved near its centre.

'This is a clue. It's a letter, the first one in the Greek alphabet. They call it –'

'Alpha!' exclaimed Jack. 'Why didn't I see that before? Did Alpha deliver this to me then?'

'No. I'd have known. It's far more likely he'd have tried to stop it reaching you. This thing's dangerous.'

'Dangerous? How? What *is* it? Come on, Jago, you've got to tell me!'

'I'm trying! So many questions! Give me a chance.'

Jack mouthed the word 'sorry' and made a zipping motion across his lips. But under the table, his knees jiggled with impatience.

'That's better. Now, where was I? Ah, yes … Alpha isn't just the letter A, it's also the Greek number one. The man who made this loved numbers. He was always first when it came to solving mathematical puzzles.'

Jack stared at the symbol. The letter A and the number one. What did that mean? He tried to sit still so he could think straight. He remembered Charlie tracing her finger over the little fish just before the disc caught alight. Jago was right, it *was* dangerous.

'Now look. What do you see here?' Jago handed him the magnifying glass and pointed at a dark line engraved round the edge of the disc. It was barely thicker than a human hair and looked like a simple circle. But as Jack focussed the glass, he could see it was another clue.

'It's a kind of zigzag. No, wait. These are letters too … they're all the same!' His eyes gleamed. 'It's the letter M. Dozens of them.'

'We'll make a detective of you yet,' said Jago. 'M for myriad. It's the largest number the Greeks had a name for. The man who made this invented his own system of

165

numbers using myriads. Then he calculated how many grains of sand it would take to fill the universe. He was obsessed with the idea of infinity.'

Jack was on the edge of his seat. 'So? Who is he?'

'Who do you think? A and M. Can't you guess?'

'No!'

A storm cloud seemed to pass over Jago's features and he appeared reluctant to say the name.

'Jago, please!'

'Very well. This was made by Archimedes, the greatest mathematician that ever was.'

Jack gaped at him. 'But he lived centuries ago.'

'Before the current era, yes.'

'That's impossible … I mean … it made my computer work. And the street lights!'

'I dare say it did.' Jago's eyes narrowed. 'Nevertheless, it isn't modern magic. This tarnished piece of metal is an ancient mirror, or at least part of one. It's also an instrument of death.'

★ ★ ★

A bluebottle fly buzzed noisily between them and landed on the carriage window. It crawled up the thick glass pane, pausing every so often to rub its legs together like a miser expecting money. Jago sat lost in thought, his face like thunder.

'What do you mean?' Jack was asking.

Jago looked at him blankly, as though he'd forgotten he was there. 'Hmm?'

'What kind of mirror? How can it be an instrument of death?'

Jago roused himself. 'Archimedes wasn't just a mathematician. He was a skilled engineer,' he said. 'He invented all kinds of weapons to fight the Romans – giant catapults to fire rocks, huge claws to lift ships from the water. But most famous of all were his burning mirrors. They were death rays, so powerful he could set a whole navy alight without even stirring from the battlements. And this is the centrepiece of one of them.'

As he spoke, Jago held the mirror at an angle, focussing the sun's rays directly on the bluebottle. In less than a second there was a fizz and a crackle and the fly fell to the floor, its small roasted carcass reduced to cinders.

A strong smell of burning filled the carriage and an instant later there was an almighty bang, like a gun going off. They both leapt in astonishment. The train window had cracked. Long, jagged lines radiated outwards from the point where the fly had perished, creating a crazy paving effect that stretched past several rows of seats.

Jack clapped a hand to his mouth. Burning the library book had been bad enough, but this was vandalism on an altogether different scale. Jago had his palms upturned as if to say, 'What happened there?', and suddenly Jack couldn't help it: his shoulders began to shake. Apparently, even a real, live magician, descended from a Magus no less, was capable of serious mistakes. Jack threw himself across the seat, hooting with laughter.

Jago ran his index finger over the place where the fly had been and pursed his lips. 'This isn't funny, you know.'

'I know-ho-ho ...' Jack laughed even harder.

'I *meant* to do that.'

'You didn't!'

'I did.'

More peals of laughter erupted from Jack.

A reluctant smile twitched at the corner of Jago's mouth and the thunderous mood that had settled over him seemed to lift. 'All right, I admit it. That did take me by surprise. But you have to agree, it proves my point. This is deadly.'

Jack sat up at last, wiping his eyes on his sleeve. The laughter had cleared his head. 'Yes, but that's not the whole story. It isn't just a – what did you call it? – a death ray. It can't be. I stepped right inside the light and I wasn't burned at all.'

Now it was Jago's turn to look astonished.

'It took me to the shipwreck,' said Jack.

'You saw the future?'

'I didn't just see it. I *went* there,' said Jack. 'And to the past. I met the ship's engineer when he was a boy.'

'How?' Jago's eyes shone with the same craving for knowledge as Jack's had earlier.

'I don't know,' said Jack honestly. 'It just happens. It's a bit like reading a book. One minute you see the words, the next you're in it. Only this is real.'

A silence fell over them, then Jack spoke. 'Archimedes was interested in infinity, you say. He must have made a light so fast and powerful it could cross the boundaries of time.'

'The man was a genius, I'll give him that. But I didn't say he was a god,' said Jago gruffly.

'You never know. Maybe he was halfway Magus like you. Or … or …' Jack trailed off. Alpha suddenly felt very close; he could sense him. He glanced out of the window and an idea flew into his head. What if the spirit of a Magus had been nearby when the mirror was created? Jago had said Alpha was as old as the hills. Maybe he'd been with Archimedes when he made the mirror?

'Or what?' said Jago.

'Nothing.' The idea seemed too fabulous for words. Yet he could feel a breeze tickling his neck, just like he had at the woods.

The train rattled over a set of points in the track and its rhythm changed. Disturbed by the vibration, a cascade of tiny glass pieces fell from the cracked window to the floor.

In the distance, an approaching train sounded its horn. Jago looked at the glass on the floor and stood up quickly, his face darkening again. 'Get up,' he barked. 'Move!'

They hurried towards the interconnecting doors that led to the next carriage. The first door hissed shut behind them just as the oncoming train rocketed past. A muffled boom reverberated through the train and they staggered sideways. As Jago caught Jack, he wrapped his great coat about him. The door blasted open and a shower of glass rained over them.

From beneath the coat, Jack could hear the wind howling. He pulled back the folds of material to peek into the carriage. It looked as if a monster had been set loose. There was glass everywhere, the seats were ripped, a section of ceiling hung down and a gale roared in through the open window. He could smell the sea, almost taste its salty tang, and despite being scared, he felt elated.

Shouts of alarm came from the next carriage. The train lurched and its brakes screamed. Someone had pulled the emergency cord, bringing them to a halt alongside a school playground. Children stopped their lunchtime games to gaze at the blasted carriage, pointing and shouting in excitement.

'Dunton!' exclaimed Jack. Over the rooftops, he could just see the Ferris wheel turning. 'We made it.'

'Not quite.' Jago raised an eyebrow. 'The station's a good mile down the line. Time to make ourselves scarce, I think.' He handed Jack the mirror. 'Now then. Be careful with that. Damn thing doesn't just wreck trains. It destroys people too.'

Jack nodded. With a shiver, he watched Jago climb down to the track. What if the mirror was *only* capable of destruction? Suppose it had shown him a future he could do nothing about? What if …

He shut his eyes tight. *Stop it*, he thought. Believing he was on a wild goose chase to doom and disaster would only make that outcome more likely to happen.

He hastily packed the mirror away. Then he jumped down, crunching on the gravel next to the rails. One or two of the children who were clinging to the wire fence around the playground raised their hands to wave.

Jack waved back. He knew he had to press on, but for those few moments, as he scrambled up the embankment after Jago, he would have given anything to be on the other side of the fence with them.

CHAPTER 25

The doorbell of number 12 jangled furiously. When no one answered, there was a scuffling in the porch and the letterbox clanked open.

A pair of hazel eyes scoured the hall. Apart from the gentle ticking of a clock, the house was silent. The only sign of life was a small frog sitting at the bottom of the stairs. He puffed out his chest and chirruped hopefully.

The hazel eyes narrowed into a frown and the letterbox crashed down.

On the other side of the door, Charlie threw her schoolbag on the ground and kicked it in frustration. Jack was either out or, worse still, ignoring her. She scooped up a handful of gravel and hurled it at his window. 'Oi! Are you up there?'

The blank pane of glass stared down at her like an unblinking eye.

'Where are you then?' she growled under her breath. She *had* to see him, to warn him about what had happened today. First there'd been Blunt and his creepy threats, then in afternoon registration their teacher had mentioned the burglary. The police were coming tomorrow to talk to everyone in assembly. Convinced the thief was a child, they were looking for witnesses. What if Blunt tried to pin the blame on Jack? When it came out he'd been to Osmaston Hall, it wouldn't look good.

Charlie hoisted her bag on her shoulder and was about to head away when she heard a screeching sound in the back garden, followed by Nan's angry voice, 'Serves you right, you hooligan! What gives you the right to come in here and do that! There's no use denying it – I saw you with my own eyes!'

There was no reply. Charlie assumed the trespasser must be lost for words. She crept around the side of the house and made her way across the lawn.

Nan's voice came from behind a row of laurel bushes. 'I wondered why they kept disappearing. I found one lot halfway down the road, completely mangled. You must have dropped them from a great height. That's theft *and* vandalism, you know.'

Charlie brushed past a long border of catmint. In places the plants were flattened, where Odin had rolled in delirious enjoyment of their scent. The cat, however, was nowhere to be seen.

'Well, it can't go on. Those wind chimes are important. But then, you already know that. Don't you?'

Again, no reply. But there was a strange clattering sound, like a stick being rubbed back and forth along iron railings.

'It's no good. You can't get out. Not alive anyway.'

Charlie's step quickened and as she rounded the laurel bushes, a long rasping cry filled the air, 'Tsche, tsche, tsche.'

Unaware of Charlie's presence, Nan crouched over a large wire box, a curious contraption consisting of three compartments. Perched in one of them, its wings spread wide in defiance, was an enormous magpie. When it saw Charlie, it lowered its head, rattling its beak along the bars of the cage, first one way, then the other. Another grating cry exploded from it, 'Tsche, tsche, tsche.'

Nan turned her head. 'Oh Charlie! You made me jump. No need to look so alarmed, dear. It's only a trap.'

The magpie flew upwards, battering its wings against the wire roof.

Nan ignored it. 'You see that perch on the top? It works like a trap door. When the bird settles there, it gives way under his weight.'

Charlie shook her head in bewilderment. 'What are you going to do with him?'

'I'm going to wring his neck,' said Nan calmly.

'But that's horrible! Why?'

'He keeps attacking my wind chimes.'

'Magpies can't help liking shiny things. Are they that special?'

'*Yes*, they are!' said Nan firmly, though she looked a little flustered. 'And what's more, he'll kill off all the song thrushes next spring. Magpies are terrible thieves. They take the eggs and chicks from other birds' nests. I'm not the only one who thinks they're a pest. This is quite legal, you know.'

Charlie stared at the imprisoned bird. She hadn't realised it was such a predator. Even so, it seemed to her that Nan wasn't bothered so much about the fate of the song thrushes as the loss of her precious wind chimes.

The bird fluttered to the ground again, its black and white plumage stunning as a harlequin's costume. Charlie was dazzled. Its long tail shimmered with emerald green and its bright eyes looked so intelligent she wondered how it had let itself be lured in.

Watching her closely, the magpie seemed to read her mind and stooped to peck at something. A string of glass beads lay in the grass at the bottom of the cage. They looked so cheap Charlie thought Nan must have found them in a Christmas cracker. But she could see why the magpie had been tempted. They sparkled with rainbow colours.

Nan had hastily pulled on some old gardening gloves. 'Charlie dear, why don't you go in and put the kettle on?'

Charlie didn't move.

'Right then. I suggest you look the other way.' Nan unfastened a door at the side of the cage and reached in.

Charlie couldn't take her eyes off the bird, which was beating its wings in desperation. Without thinking, she leant forwards and tugged at Nan's sleeve. 'Don't, please. Stop!'

It all happened in a split second. Charlie hung so fiercely onto Nan's arm she couldn't move. The magpie saw its chance and bounded forwards, its white wing tips reaching like fingers for the sky.

'No!' screamed Nan, grabbing hopelessly at the air.

The magpie screeched back, climbing higher and higher until it was nothing but a black dot. And even then its cries could still be heard, like angry laughter. 'Tsche, tsche, tsche ...'

Just before it vanished, Charlie saw something glint like a distant star and her breath caught in her throat. She glanced down at the trap. The glass beads had gone.

★ ★ ★

Nan slumped against the garden wall, her fists clenched, her face grey. There was nothing she could do about it. The bird had given her the slip.

'I'm so sorry,' Charlie was saying over and over. 'Really, really sorry.'

'You shouldn't have interfered.' Nan wanted to curse out loud, but she bit her tongue. There was no point in making Charlie feel worse. She couldn't expect her to know why the magpie's invasion had been so serious.

The wind chimes had been much more than musical ornaments. Nan had fortified her house and garden with a collection of powerful charms. Dangling from the roof gables and various carefully chosen trees, they provided a ring of protection that kept her small corner of the world safe from any source of malevolence – or so she hoped.

Since the day the seagull had arrived the metal pipes hadn't stopped jangling. Then she'd noticed that, one by one, they kept disappearing. The magpie had been dismantling them, breaking down her defences until she felt sick with worry.

'Where's Jack?' she asked.

'That's what I want to know,' said Charlie. 'He hasn't been in school all day. I thought maybe he was home ...'

Nan gazed at Charlie's bewildered face. She was grateful she was propped against the wall. Her legs had just turned to jelly.

★★★

The boot of the Beetle, unlike other cars, was at the front instead of the back. It bulged with belongings: jumpers, boots, sleeping bags, even a kettle and an old camping stove. Nan hadn't known what to pack, so she was packing everything.

'Please let me come with you,' Charlie pleaded.

'Out of the question,' snapped Nan, heaping things on the back seat. 'Here, put the torch in the glove box, will you?'

To Charlie's surprise, Odin already lay stretched out on the parcel shelf. Nan never went away without him. She gave the cat a frown. 'Wouldn't it be nice to have some company? I know you've got Odin but ... it's such a long way.'

'I'll be fine.'

'I'm good at map reading.'

'I know how to get there.'

'But it'll be dark –'

'I've got headlights! Charlie, I'm familiar with the route. I've been to Wakeham before.'

At Charlie's suggestion, they had checked the web

history on Jack's computer. After finding the Eastern Express timetable and his research on the lighthouse, it didn't take a detective to guess where he'd gone. 'You've been more than helpful,' said Nan. 'Jack doesn't give much away. I'd no idea he was in such trouble.'

Charlie had told Nan all about Blunt and the bullying, Jack's friendship with Jago Flyn and the burglary at Osmaston Hall. She'd held back only one piece of information, keeping her promise to Jack not to mention the mysterious disc to anyone.

'He's my friend! You have to let me go. You have to!'

'Charlie Day, be sensible!' Nan lobbed a tin of cat food into the car, narrowly missing Odin's head. The cat yowled.

'You're angry because of the magpie,' wailed Charlie.

'It isn't that at all! Look, I don't know how long I'll be gone. I certainly won't be back tonight and you've got school tomorrow. Even if I agreed, your mum wouldn't.'

'But –'

'I really haven't got time to argue.'

And that was that. Ten minutes later Nan set off, the Beetle belching black smoke as it lurched down the drive.

Charlie stood amidst the exhaust fumes, grinding her foot in the gravel. It wasn't fair. Jack was on an adventure, a dangerous one. What if he needed her? She couldn't bear to be left out.

A trail of oily wet spots glistened on the drive. She kicked the gravel, spraying stones in all directions. Stupid wreck of a car. About time Nan traded it in.

CHAPTER 26

The boats in the little harbour lay sideways in the mud, ropes and rigging clattering against masts in the wind. The sound, usually so cheerful in summer, had a hollow ring to it, making the tiny seaside village seem even more deserted than it really was.

Jack sat glumly on the quayside dangling his legs over the wall. *Plaice to Eat*, Wakeham's fish and chip shop, had a closed sign on the door and the pavement outside the grocer's was empty. Gone were the fishing nets and crab-baiting lines, the water pistols and brightly coloured windmills that spun in the breeze. Apart from a woman pushing a pram and a man painting the upside-down hull of a boat in his garden, no one was about.

He stared at the mudflats in the harbour and watched a crab scuttle out from beneath a pile of seaweed. He and Jago had hiked nearly seven miles across The Spike peninsula, dropping down the coastal path just as the sun had begun to fade. He'd rushed ahead, so excited to see the red and white tower of the Pentland lighthouse

179

standing on its throne of rock beyond the headland. All they had to do was hop on a boat and they'd be there.

Or so he thought.

The crab disappeared under a yellow buoy, one claw raised as if in a mock salute. Jack threw a stone after it. He hadn't expected the tide to be out, or the harbour master's office to be shut. And he certainly hadn't thought all the hire boats would be gone, vanished like the windmills with the summer crowds.

'Leave it to me,' Jago had said. 'Can't do much about the tide, I'm afraid. But I'm sure I can find us a boat.' And with that he'd disappeared inside the Lock and Quay Inn, from which he hadn't returned.

Jack's stomach rumbled. He pulled up his red hood against the chilly air and burrowed in his rucksack for one of Nan's biscuits. Mmm. Lemon and crunchy sugar with a hint of … A pang of longing went through him. The mystery ingredient tasted of pancakes.

Overhead, the gulls circled closer and one cheeky individual landed on the stone bollard right next to him. Barely looking up, he threw it some crumbs, and instantly regretted it. Half a dozen birds descended, flapping and fighting and screeching madly.

'Get lost! Shoo!' he yelled, drumming his feet against the harbour wall. But the gulls wouldn't leave him alone. The large pushy one came so close he could feel its wings fanning his face. He got up, retreating to a nearby bus shelter. Even then, the bird followed, settling on the roof above him with two others.

A burst of raucous laughter spilled out of the pub

and his shoulders sagged. If Jago didn't hurry up, there'd be no daylight left. He watched the woman with the pram finish her tour of the harbour and stop outside the grocery store. Glancing around, she parked the pram in front of the window and darted in, setting the doorbell jingling.

With a huff, Jack got the mirror out of the rucksack. His fingers traced a pattern over the tiny fish symbol and he thought about Lily. Soon he'd see the keeper and everything would be sorted: she and *The Empress* would be safe. It all seemed straightforward … So why did he keep getting this nagging feeling they'd met for some other reason?

A breeze lifted his hair and suddenly the gulls above him cried out in alarm. With a whoosh, the wind circled the shelter and sent them spinning into the sky.

Jack leant forwards, staring up after them. Despite their best efforts to escape, they were being dragged like toy kites from one side of the harbour to the other.

It would have been funny if it hadn't been so violent. He looked around him. The trees were perfectly still and even the rattling of the boat rigging had died down. All the wind's energy seemed to be directed at the gulls alone.

Was it something he'd done? He quickly hid the mirror in the pocket of his hoodie. The birds had been a nuisance and he'd got annoyed, but he hadn't meant to punish them.

And then he saw him. Beyond the harbour master's hut, there at the very end of the jetty, stood Alpha, his eyes locked like lasers on the cavorting gulls.

'So it's you,' he muttered. It took a moment for what he was seeing to sink in. Then Jack was on his feet, running flat out in sheer delight.

At the sound of his footsteps, Alpha lowered his head and immediately the birds scattered, blown away like scraps of paper, their misery at an end.

It was as if the wolf had conjured the wind just to get his attention. Although now he had it, he'd grown visibly nervous. As Jack reached the jetty, Alpha's tail dropped and he started to back away. Desperate not to frighten him, Jack slowed down, glad for once of the black gym shoes which allowed him to tiptoe softly across the wooden duckboards. Without meaning to, he had Alpha cornered.

Nothing moved, the wind barely sighed, and Jack became conscious of a great hush all around. It felt as if he'd stepped through an invisible curtain into another realm. 'You can't befriend a wolf,' Jago had said. But Jack couldn't help himself. This was no ordinary wolf and he was going to try.

He'd advanced almost halfway along the jetty when Alpha gave a low growl. It wasn't loud, more of a warning rumble at the back of his throat, but Jack dropped instantly to his knees, making himself small. 'It's okay, I won't hurt you.'

Ears twitching, Alpha put his nose to the ground, drawing Jack's scent towards him. He lifted one paw tentatively.

Jack's eyes closed. *Come on, you can do it,* he urged. *I won't move a muscle.*

A second later he heard the click of claws on wood. A wet nose touched his palm, his chin and then his cheek. It was all he could do to stop himself laughing out loud. And when he finally opened his eyes, Alpha's broad face was so close he could see himself reflected in his pupils.

'You made it!' he whispered.

Alpha bowed his head. Without thinking, Jack reached out to touch the patch of dark fur between his eyes. The wolf flinched but didn't pull away, and very gently Jack let his hand fall over the great ruff framing his face. Alpha's coat was remarkable, soft and luxurious underneath, with a layer of tough guard hairs on top: some jet black, some pure white, others grey and tan, and a few of burnt gold.

'Those people at the station said you were bad. But you're not, are you? You were only trying to help.'

Alpha stood quietly, his ears flicking forwards to listen.

'Look at this.' Jack reached into his hoodie for the mirror. 'See the symbol here? Alpha – that's you!'

The amber eyes gleamed. At the mention of his name, Alpha's tail moved from side to side, and he nudged the mirror with his nose.

'You were there when he made it, weren't you? It's like a puzzle. A and M, one and infinity, Alpha and the Magus. Did you blow your magic into it?'

Every hair on Alpha's body seemed to bristle proudly, making him look enormous.

'I wish you could tell me. Because if I'm wrong and this is destructive, I can't change anything.'

The wolf whined.

'What is it?'

Alpha's front paws twitched. He was having to control every nerve and muscle just to keep still.

'There is a way you can tell me, isn't there?' said Jack. 'You control the wind. You can speak with that! Go on, then. If there's any good in this mirror of yours, why don't you show me?'

Alpha lifted his muzzle, sniffing at the air as if to catch the scent and meaning of Jack's words. Then his eyes flicked to the quayside. Instantly, a breeze stirred, gathering force around the two of them and gusting across the harbour so fast that Jack had to lean back to stop himself falling over.

A trickle of water appeared, the first hint of an incoming tide, and the boats shifted restlessly on the mud. Their rigging rattled, the sign at the Lock and Quay clanged and a dustbin in the high street fell over, tipping its contents into the gutter.

Outside the store, the pram rocked backwards and forwards on its springs and a pair of pink arms stretched upwards for attention. Then, as the wind moaned louder, the rocking grew fiercer until, with a noisy ping, the brake on the back wheel gave way and the pram began to roll down the hill.

'Alpha, no!' yelled Jack. 'What are you doing?'

The wolf laid his ears against his head and snarled. For a moment it looked as if he might attack, then he backed away. With three or four big strides, he raced back along the jetty and launched himself into the rushing tide.

Jack didn't have time to see what had become of him because he was running too, running faster than he'd ever done in his life before. The pram rattled and bounced across the uneven stones and above the noise he heard the baby wail.

He didn't know if he would make it in time. Then, just as the pram reached the harbour wall and the first wheel left the ground, he was there, snatching at the silver handle, his lungs fit to explode. Below him, the water bubbled and swirled, pouring into every nook and cranny on the harbour floor. He tugged the pram back and hung on to it, fighting for breath.

'Sshh, sshh, you're okay,' he panted.

But the screaming baby refused to be comforted. Two little fists grasped hopelessly at the air and with every yell its whole body shuddered.

In desperation, Jack pulled the mirror from his pocket, holding it to the light so that it sparkled and winked. Almost immediately, the cries subsided and ten tiny fingers grabbed at the edge of it. With surprising strength, they pulled the mirror close.

A pair of sky-blue eyes shone up at him, reflecting the fish symbol from the disc. With a tingle of recognition, he stared at the white blonde lashes.

'Lily?' he whispered.

The lashes blinked. Beads of tears slid down one rosy cheek onto the cotton pillow beneath and where they fell, something familiar caught his attention. Hand-sewn in black and gold thread, a lion's head roared above a family crest.

Stunned, he glanced around the harbour. Had Alpha intended this? His memory rewound to his first trip to Osmaston Hall. While Jago had been busy painting, he'd spotted a figure at an upstairs window ... someone cradling a white bundle ...

Lily chuckled and all of a sudden the mirror flashed, glowing brighter than ever before. For a second she looked startled. But instead of crying, she grasped the disc tighter and laughed again, completely unafraid.

Jack took a deep breath. When the tugging began, he let his mind go quiet. This time he was more than ready. This time he would trust the magic, because he was finally beginning to see that Alpha was behind everything.

CHAPTER 27

He found himself standing on exactly the same spot on the quayside. But the pram had disappeared and the place felt decidedly different. It was morning for a start; the sun was high in the sky and the air smelled clean and sweet like it had just rained. The roofs glistened and water ran down the street gutters, spilling into the sea which lapped against the harbour wall.

A white delivery van drew up outside the Lock and Quay, splashing through a puddle. Its brakes squealed and a pop tune Jack didn't recognise blared from the cab.

'Easter holidays, is it?' called the driver as he hopped out. 'All right for some!'

Jack smiled and waited for him to disappear. Then slowly – very slowly – he turned round, scanning every window, every doorway. Lily was here somewhere, she had to be. She'd known who he was on the ship. She'd even mentioned seeing him on the quay.

If she really *was* a Harington, there'd been no sign of her when he'd toured Osmaston Hall with Jago. So for some reason, their paths were meant to cross here. Alpha had made sure of it.

The doorbell of the grocery store jingled. A middle-aged man emerged, a newspaper tucked under his arm and a white terrier yapping at his feet.

Jack glanced past him, along the high street and back to the quay where his eyes settled on the bus shelter. A girl in a long jumper and purple leggings sat cross-legged on the bench inside. She was scribbling at something with such energy her blonde hair swung about her face like a curtain.

She looked up briefly and stared straight at him. It was obvious she didn't recognise him. But there could be no mistaking her. Perched like an elf on a toadstool, she seemed younger than on the ship, her features slightly rounder, her hair a fraction shorter: Lily.

He hurried towards her, suddenly hopeful. What if he could do something, here and now, to alter her future? There must be a way. He thought of Jago's time trick on the train. If only he could send events down another track.

'Hullo!' he blurted. 'What're you doing? Can I see?'

Several sheets of paper cascaded to the ground.

Startled, Lily dived after them, her face turning crimson. 'Um, I dunno. They're not very good. I don't think you'll –'

'Here, let me help. I'm Jack, by the way. Jack Tideswell.'

As he spoke his name, the wind gusted and three brightly coloured drawings sailed over his head, narrowly escaping his clutches as he leapt to catch them.

'Oh nooo,' groaned Lily.

'Hang on!' he shouted.

He had to run fast. Two of the pictures had already flipped and cavorted out to sea, while the third landed near the jetty, its corners curling in the breeze. Once, twice, three times he pounced as it skipped along the duckboards and settled just out of reach.

'Stop it, wolf!' he muttered. He trapped the drawing with his foot and frowned at the distant hills. 'I know you're there. I don't need ...'

He looked down.

'... proof.' Beneath his gym shoe lay a crayoned sketch of the Pentland lighthouse. In the bottom right-hand corner, Lily had signed it: 'L Harington, age 6½.'

'Thanks,' she said shyly when he returned.

'I like the fish in the sea,' he replied. Every single one looked like the symbol on the mirror.

'Oh, them. They're just for fun. It's the lighthouse that's important. I can't get the spective right.'

Jack gave a knowing nod, despite having no idea what she meant. Then it dawned on him. 'Ah! Per-spective.' It seemed a long word for a small child.

'Uh-huh. See how close it is to the quay? I made it too big.' Lily put her head on one side. '*And* it's leaning over.'

'Looks fine to me.' He decided to show off too. 'I'd say that's artistic licence.'

She squinted at him.

'It's where you bend the rules. You know, stretch the truth a bit.' He put his fists together, then prized them

189

apart like a body builder with a chest expander. 'I've got a friend who's a painter. He does it all the time.'

'No way. That's terrible!'

'Why?'

'Because … what if a building fell down?'

Now it was Jack's turn to look confused.

'I can't do wobbly drawings,' said Lily.

'I don't understand.'

'When I'm an architect!'

'Oh, I see!'

'What's so funny?'

'Nothing.'

A hurt look filled Lily's face. She screwed up the picture and threw it on the ground.

'Hey, I wasn't laughing at *you*.'

Her eyes flashed at him.

'Honest! It's just the idea you could make a building fall over by …'

Her lower lip trembled.

'You're right. An architect has to be accurate,' he said swiftly.

'Ex-actly.' She folded her arms. 'And I'm rubbish!'

It wasn't a promising start. Jack wisely decided to hold his tongue. He retrieved the crumpled picture and flattened it on the bench between them, while Lily swung her legs furiously. The lighthouse *was* tilting, as she'd pointed out, but it looked solid and reassuring on its rock of grey. And somehow the way it leant over the sea gave it a friendly feel, like a stooping giant. The fish rushed up towards it as if they were about to leap into the sky … And now he looked more closely, he could see another creature: a mermaid.

A tingle ran through him. 'This is brilliant! You've got imagination. If you ask me, that's much more important than being precise. You have to let your mind soar. How else will you get a big idea?'

The legs stopped swinging.

'Imagination is *the* most powerful muscle in your body,' he said grandly. It was one of the few things he could remember his father saying. 'It gets you from A to B. Everyone has to picture the future to make things happen, right?'

There was no answer so he ploughed on. 'I can see you now, sitting in your office in one of those big leather chairs. You know, the sort that swivels? And –'

He broke off. Lily was scribbling with a blue crayon. She had already covered half a sheet of paper with an image he vaguely recognised.

'I draw this one a lot,' she said. 'But it's hard to get right.' Her hand flicked across the page as if by working fast she could capture something elusive. 'In the morning when I wake up, I keep my eyes shut. Then I see it. The dome floats in the sea like a bubble. It's so blue you don't notice it at first.'

Stunned, Jack gazed from the sketch to Lily. She'd produced a rough version of his screensaver, from a bird's eye view. Until now, he'd never noticed that the twelve supporting feet resembled the hours on a clock face.

'It's like a watch,' he murmured.

'I know ... but it's something else. Can you guess?' Around the dome, Lily drew a thick blue circle like a dial. 'This is a glass tunnel. For people to look out.'

Jack didn't need to be told. The details were imprinted in his memory. What made his mind spin was the knowledge that the image on his computer hadn't been some random graphic after all. The mirror and Lily were somehow connected. It had shown him a preview of the building that was unfolding in front of him.

'It's a lighthouse. Obviously,' he managed to say.

'Yes! What do you think? Like it?'

'I love it. You're a genius. When did you have this brainwave?'

'I dunno.' Lily blew out her cheeks, popping first one, then the other. She tapped her head. 'It's been in here – like – for ever. I'm a doodler, Mum says. It started ages ago.'

Goosebumps crept down Jack's spine. He thought of the ten tiny fingers gripping the mirror in the pram. Before their leap, the disc had flashed so brightly ... Something told him it hadn't only downloaded the graphic to his computer. It had transferred the idea to Lily, too.

His eyes flicked to the hillside. Was this why Alpha had brought them together? Something about this fantastic, crazy design was important.

He grabbed the crayon and screwed up his eyes to picture the screensaver. 'Make the spire taller. And how about it doesn't just float? You could make the whole thing move.' He added some waves. 'What's it called? Have you got a name?'

'Not yet.'

He scribbled some more.

Lily squinted at his untidy writing. 'Far-os.'

'Not "far", but "fair". Fair-os. It's named after an ancient lighthouse in Egypt which actually did fall down.'

Lily snatched the crayon back. 'Then how about …' Her tongue stuck out while she drew some fish shapes under the sketch. '… we build it where the old one used to be?'

'A new lighthouse floating over the old one? Lily, that's amazing. Then people can see the ruins!' His parents would definitely have approved. He grabbed another crayon and coloured in a fish. So would Alpha.

Glancing up, he caught Lily watching him closely.

'How do you know my name?'

'Um …' His mouth opened and closed. 'Didn't anyone ever tell you? When you were little, your pram almost ran off the quay. I caught it.'

'Wow, thanks! Were Mum and Dad there?'

He shook his head.

'Busy working, I 'spect.'

'Are they here now?'

'Nope. Paris. They're always off somewhere.' Lily stared glumly at the sea. Then her face brightened. 'Anyway, it's my turn now. We're going on a cruise. Gran promised and it's her boat so everyone has to do what she says.'

A knot tightened in Jack's stomach.

'She's organising a party and everything,' Lily continued. 'I'm going to be seven!'

He swallowed hard. 'And your grandmother is Lady Harington?'

'You know her?'

'Sort of. I went to her house once.'

'Osmaston Hall! Isn't it great? You know the suit of armour? At Christmas, Tux made the head fall off. Stupid dog! He scared himself so bad, he had to sleep with me.' She leant in close, lowering her voice as if confiding a secret. 'I'm in a bunk bed now. Gran says I'm old enough. Plus I need to practise for *The Empress*!'

Jack forced a smile. It was hard to look impressed when all he wanted to say was 'don't go'. But it was the adults in charge he had to warn. Telling Lily would only terrify her.

The sun glinted on top of the lighthouse and for a moment the red and white stripes seemed to go blurry. He suddenly felt lightheaded, as if standing on the edge of a cliff.

'So you live in Wakeham?' he said, blinking hard.

'Yep.'

'Ever been inside that place?'

Lily eyed the lighthouse and shook her head furiously.

'Why not?'

'It has ghosts.'

'Says who?'

'Mrs Mortimer in the chip shop.'

'That's ridiculous!'

'She tells everyone. When the wind blows, you can hear a wolf howling. *And* a child crying.'

Jack got unsteadily to his feet. The sunlight on the

tower was almost blinding and he could feel the familiar tug of the mirror. 'She's after more customers. People like ghost stories.'

'Well, I don't! Sometimes at night I hear it.'

His head swam. The bus shelter, the quayside, the harbour itself were beginning to slip away. He grabbed Lily's hand.

'Listen to me. Forget Red Riding Hood, okay? Wolves aren't big and bad. They're amazing.' He wanted to tell her about Alpha, how it was because of him they'd met. 'Only the luckiest people hear them. Next time it happens, I want you to try something.'

Lily looked at him wide-eyed.

'Make a wish. A big one.' He glanced at the hills. 'It'll work, you'll see.'

She nodded solemnly. 'Do you have to go?'

''Fraid so.'

Jack let go of her hand and tried not to think of the last time he'd left her. He'd hardly rewritten events. He wondered if he'd made much difference at all.

Then, as he walked away, hurrying out of sight along a lane behind the shelter, he heard her talking to herself. Her voice sounded stern and unafraid. 'I know a wish. That wolf better get ready. One day I'm going to build –'

★★★

'Pharos,' he said, leaning into the pram. 'Not far, but fair!' A smile crinkled the corners of his eyes and he thought of his parents. Lily's sketch had made him feel

195

closer to them. *Not far, but fair.* Strange how that distant place connected them all.

He gently prized the mirror from the tiny clenched fist and Lily's bottom lip trembled. Quick as a flash, he covered his face with his hands. When he pulled them away, her eyes danced.

A moment later the shop door jingled and footsteps thundered towards them. He wrinkled his nose in disappointment and to his surprise Lily copied him, pulling a silly, lopsided face that made him want to laugh and cry all at once.

'Oh my God, Lily, no! What happened?' The woman he'd seen earlier raced towards them, clutching a magazine.

'The brake came off,' he called. 'It's okay, I stopped it in time.'

'But I was only gone a minute!' Arriving breathless, the woman swept Lily into her arms. 'My poor darling. There, there, hush. I'm here now. I should never have left you. Think what would have happened if … oh God, I'm done for. What if they find out?'

Jack looked at her blankly.

'It's my job!' she wailed. 'I'm supposed to look after her.'

'I won't tell, don't worry. It wasn't your fault anyway. The wind blew and then …'

He decided to say no more. And when, eventually, the woman stopped wringing his hand, he smiled politely, did his best to ignore Lily's outstretched arms and turned away, relieved to escape without an inquisition.

If she only knew, he thought as he hurried off to find Jago. With a sniff, he peered back through the dusky gloom along the jetty.

The tide continued to rush in. Above the distant bawling from the pram, the boats clanked, rising on their moorings as if lifting from graves. The lighthouse had come on, casting its long beam across the harbour. But Alpha, the cause of the drama, was nowhere to be seen.

CHAPTER 28

The fire crackled in the Lock and Quay and shadows from the crowded bar leapt across the ceiling. The warmth was overpowering. Despite the raised voices and raucous laughter, Jack's eyes began to droop.

As promised, Jago had found them a boat. But the owner, a scrawny man called Tattoo, was in no state to take them out. He leant heavily on Jack's shoulder and burped like a foghorn. 'Yous'll have to wait fer mornin',' he said. 'I's three sheets to the wind.'

Jack's eyes batted sleepily. Tattoo's words made him think of Lily's drawings floating across the quay.

Jago steered him away from the bar and settled him in an old leather armchair, using his rucksack as a pillow. 'You hungry?' he asked.

Jack shook his head. All he wanted was to sleep.

'I'll have them fix us some eggs in the morning.'

Jack felt so tired it was an effort to speak. 'Jago,' he murmured.

'Hmmm.'

'Alpha's here. He made it!'

'I know. Now get some rest.'

'You do? How?'

'You don't have to see him to know where he is. You sense him. I thought you worked that out on the train.'

'Yeah, but … I really *saw* him. We were on the jetty. He came close enough to let me stroke him and –'

'Yes?'

'I got this feeling … he wants to help me.'

Jago's brow furrowed and he opened his mouth to reply. But it was pointless. Jack was already fast asleep, oblivious to the world.

★★★

Much later, as the bar began to clear, an old man struggled to his feet from a seat in the corner. On his way to the door, he paused in front of the armchair where Jack lay curled up. He wagged a finger at Jago: 'You take care of 'im, you hear. Precious, he is.'

'Of course,' replied Jago, curtly.

The man swayed on his feet a little. 'Don't know how lucky you are. You got yer boy with you.'

'Yes, indeed.'

'Mine's gone,' the man blurted.

'I'm sorry to hear it. Keep your voice down, you'll wake him.'

But the man paid no attention. 'Went to sea, you know, on them damn cruise ships.' His voice grew louder. 'What could he do, eh? Didn't need no keeper no more, did they? Run the light by computers now …'

'Enough!' Jago rose quickly to his feet. 'You've had a skinful, old man. Go home, sleep it off.'

The man stared at Jack without moving. 'Can't sleep,' he muttered. 'Broke my 'eart when he went away. My job, my boy, my life – all gone! 'Ere, stop it. What yer doin'?'

Jago had caught him by the sleeve, spinning him round so their faces were only inches apart. 'What *is* your problem?' he hissed. 'This boy of yours – dead, is he?'

'Why no! Leastways, I 'ope not.'

'Then don't talk as if he is. Your child's alive. Stop whining and be thankful. Now then. Get out of here!'

Jago's eyes glinted and the old man backed away. 'You – you ent got no heart,' he stammered. 'Yer son's 'ere, safe by the fire! Mine's gone!'

Jago shook his head. 'No, old man, you're mistaken.' His voice dropped to a growling whisper. 'My son died, many lifetimes ago. And if that has made me heartless, so be it.'

He opened the door.

An icy draught swept into the pub and with it there came a harsh cry: 'Tsche, tsche, tsche.'

Something sharp brushed across the old man's face and his hand went up to his cheek. A paper-thin scratch had appeared, a tiny drop of blood weeping from it like a tear.

'Whassat?' he gasped, staring into the rafters.

Jago didn't reply but took his arm again, propelling him into the night. 'Goodnight, sir,' he said through clenched teeth.

'All right, I'm goin'! Get yer 'ands off me.'

The door closed with a thud and Jack stirred in his sleep. Jago threw himself angrily into the chair next to him.

Outside, the old man rubbed his cheek with his coat sleeve. It was cold and the sound of the sea hitting the harbour wall made him dizzy. He steadied himself against a dustbin and as he waited for his strength to return, a flash of black and white caught his attention.

He ducked his head to get a better view through the pub window. Two black eyes appeared to be watching him from one of the beams near the ceiling. He blinked, trying to focus more clearly, but when he looked again, they were gone.

Frowning, his gaze fell on Jack once more. Something about that lad made him think of his own son. What in the bloomin' world was it?

The fresh air nipped his ears and a memory stirred: two boys playing on a beach, his own dear Bill and a smaller, dark-haired child. He'd watched them run into the sea. Of course, how could he forget? It was the day the Brethren had come to tell him the lighthouse would be automated.

Frank Armitage, former keeper of the Pentland lighthouse, scratched his head. It was like seeing a ghost. The boy in the armchair was the spitting image of the lad on the beach. But no way could he be the same child. Years had passed and he'd be a grown man by now, same as Bill.

The old keeper gave a shrug. The beer must be rotting his brain. Pulling up his collar, he shuffled away.

★ ★ ★

Jago scribbled furiously, irritated beyond all reason. The piece of charcoal in his hand flew across the paper as if it had a life of its own. Dark, smudgy lines radiated outwards, and rather than forcing their direction he let them flow.

There was a flutter of wings overhead.

'Come here, Pi,' he snapped, without looking up.

A dark shape shifted from one beam to another and a cascade of dust fell to the floor.

'Don't be stupid. Why are you hiding?'

A boy in a black tracksuit and trainers emerged from the shadows. 'That man, he saw me. And I –' his voice trembled '– I don't like it when you're angry.'

'Well, he's gone, interfering fool. And I'm not angry now.' Jago placed the charcoal on the table and rubbed his blackened fingers. 'Come.'

'What'ya doing?' said Pi, creeping forwards. He leant over the broad arm of Jago's chair, his white blond hair flopping over his pale face. 'You've drawn *him*!' he gasped, pointing at Jack.

'Yes.'

'But … you never draw people! Only houses.' Pi took the sketch in his hands. 'It's good … different. No straight lines, just a jumble of swirls.' He looked at Jago out of the corner of his eye. 'You like him, don't you?'

A muscle twitched in Jago's jaw.

'He makes you think of your own son. That's it, isn't it? You were thinking of him!'

202

'Quiet! Or I shall be angry again.' Jago snatched the drawing back and tossed it on the fire. The edges turned brown and flames danced briefly in the grate.

'Now then,' he growled. 'Tell me what you've been up to. I hope you've brought me good news?'

'Better than that.' Pi's face lit up. 'I've brought you treasure!'

He crouched down behind the armchair, unzipped a backpack and reappeared with a small black box. His fingers traced the swirling gold letters on the top. 'Amos, Jeweller,' he whispered, opening the lid with a flourish. 'Look at that. Sweet, innit?'

A glittering diamond ring winked in the firelight. Pi took it out of the box and tried it on various fingers, all of which were far too skinny.

'You shoulda seen us,' he laughed. 'Easiest night's work I ever 'ad. Alpha was really on form. A whole bunch of coffins came crashing into the street – shazam! – straight through the window. All I had to do was reach in and take it.'

Jago raised an eyebrow, unimpressed.

A shadow of disappointment passed over Pi's face. 'Anyways, that's just for starters,' he said. He rummaged in the bag again and produced a sapphire bracelet, a gold heart-shaped locket and a diamond tiara, which he arranged on the arm of Jago's chair. Then came a pair of emerald earrings, an amber brooch and a child's turquoise necklace.

'Osmaston Hall, I assume?' said Jago.

'Hit the jackpot! What a place, eh? Did you see

them stairs? The longest banister in the world. Bleedin' brilliant!'

Jago massaged his temples. 'Please don't tell me you slid down it.'

'Course I did! Wheeee-Jeronimo!' Pi mimed the acrobatic landing he'd performed. 'Don't look like that. Nobody noticed.' He clicked his fingers and dug into the bag. 'Wait. I nearly forgot. Saved the best till last, didn't I? How 'bout these?' He held out the two yellow marbles. 'See how they shine? Like cats' eyes!'

At last, Jago's face softened. He pulled Pi towards him and ruffled his hair so that it stood on end. 'You're worse than a real magpie. These worthless bits of glass mean more to you than that diamond ring, don't they?'

Pi pouted. 'Well, they *are* bootiful,' he insisted. 'And I can't help it if I'm like that. You're the one who decided what sort of animus I should be.'

'True. But there really was no need for you to help yourself to all these trinkets. Those were *not* my instructions.'

Pi hurriedly scooped the jewels back into the bag. Then he reached inside his pocket and held out a crumpled peacock feather. 'I did what you wanted too. I gave that mean man such a fright. In fact, I don't think he's ever been so *stunned* in all his life!' He held an imaginary gun to his own neck, fired it and slumped dramatically into a chair, his tongue lolling grotesquely out of his mouth.

'Good. He deserved it,' said Jago. 'And what about his precious ship?'

Pi handed him a bunch of rolled-up papers.

'What's this?'

'Plans. You said you wanted to see what it looks like.'

'Aah yes … And the money?'

'Gone!'

'To a good home, I trust? I'm tired of scrimping.'

'Your account, naturally. Via a hundred others. Lots of toffs will be in trouble before they trace it to you. And by then, we'll be gone … won't we?'

Jago clapped him on the back. 'Yes, my little scavenger. At long last we've got a way out.'

'So …?' Pi got up and circled Jack's chair. 'Where is it, this escape route of ours? Can I see?'

'Be my guest.' Jago nodded at the rucksack under Jack's head.

Pi spat on his palms and rubbed them together. With the dexterity of a pickpocket, he slid his hand inside the bag. 'Oo, what's this?' Indigo, Jack's horse, glittered in his hand. 'Pretty! Can I have it?'

'Absolutely not.'

'But I like it!' Pi made the horse prance around Jago's chair. 'Finders keepers!'

'No arguments. And you can put the pen back too.'

Pi grinned sheepishly. He returned Indigo to the rucksack along with Jack's silver pen which he'd hidden up his sleeve. Then he rummaged again, his tongue poking out the corner of his mouth and his eyes rolling in mock concentration.

When the mirror finally lay in front of him, his face fell. 'Is that it? The legendary mirror of Pharos? It's a piece of old junk! I thought it would be shiny.'

Jago laughed. 'It's been at the bottom of the sea for centuries. It'll shine brighter than anything you've ever seen when the time is right.'

'Come on then. Let's take it. We've waited long enough.'

'We can't … Not yet.'

'Why?'

'I need to know how it works.'

'But you're a Magus.'

'Not any more. How many times have I told you?'

'But you still have *some* power. And now you've got this, the rest will come back.'

'It isn't that easy.'

'Then … what are we gonna do?'

'Watch and wait. He'll show us.'

'Him! What can *he* possibly show *us*?'

'He's made two leaps already, remember? Future *and* past. He's learning.'

'Yeah, yeah.' Pi gave Jack a jealous look. 'Beginner's luck.'

'Be sensible. This was delivered by an animus. What does that tell you?'

'Er …' Pi tapped his bottom lip theatrically. 'Someone meant him to have it?'

'Precisely.'

'Who then? His parents?'

'Unlikely. They died in the ruins. However, I have no doubt they uncovered it. Oh yes.' Jago nodded his head purposefully. 'Afterwards, there were reports of a blue light in the sea. The locals said it moved too fast for a fish. My guess is someone picked it up.'

'But that was seven years ago! Why would anyone wait so long?'

'*Think* about it,' said Jago excitedly. 'He's twelve now.'

'So?'

'The age a Magus must be tested.'

'Hang on!' blustered Pi. 'He's not a Magus!'

Jack stirred in his sleep and the two of them fell silent. Then Jago said, 'Alpha is keeping unusually close. He likes the boy ... And there's something about that house ... I swear he was guarding it. That's why I painted it – to get a look inside.'

'You're paranoid! Alpha follows you.'

Jago shrugged and stared into the fire.

'Oh come on. Alpha's the one who led us to him. We'd never have found the mirror otherwise. And what about the storm? He brought the town to a standstill. *Your* orders.'

'What if Jack wanted the same thing?'

'That's daft! Why bring chaos to your own town?'

'A fledgling Magus at the end of his tether ...' Jago took the mirror from Pi and studied it closely, as if hunting for a clue he might have missed. 'He doesn't know his own strength.'

'Don't make me laugh. He can't even throw straight! And what about them boys? They walked all over him. Why would Alpha listen to him?'

Jago smiled. 'I didn't mean that kind of strength. But

you're right, Alpha won't disobey me. He wouldn't dare. Hermes assigned him to serve his descendants. And we both know what happens to an animus who defies his maker.'

Pi nodded vigorously. 'Exactly. Alpha may not be your animus but he won't let you down.' His face looked pale and anxious again. 'And me? What do you want me to do next?'

'Go after that old fool who was here earlier. Fetch the keys to the lighthouse. He'll have them somewhere. He still cleans the place.'

'Consider it done.' Pi began to back away, happy to return to the shadows.

'Wait,' snapped Jago. He unfurled the plans of *The Empress* and pored over them, muttering to himself. 'What is it about this ship that's so damned important? The seventh wonder shows up seven years after his parents die and sends him here ... That wolf's up to something, I'll stake my life on it.'

Pi laughed nervously. 'Forget the ship. Ent never gonna sail anyway. Their loot's gone!'

'Stealing a bit of money won't stop a project like this. I hardly think you've bankrupted them.' Jago's fingers drummed on the arm of the chair. 'We must keep a close watch, make a plan of our own. Yes, that's it ... something to short-circuit the connection between them ... I suggest we copy these to our London friends.'

'And say what?'

Jago's mouth formed a thin line. He studied Jack thoughtfully. Then, like a father tucking a child into bed, he gently pulled the red hoodie around him and returned the mirror to his bag.

'Dear boy,' he whispered, brushing a lock of hair from Jack's eyes. 'I know how much this ship means to you. But something's going on and I need to make sure Alpha behaves.'

His fingers, black with charcoal, made a beckoning motion. From the shadows, the magpie swooped down and hovered in silent allegiance beside him.

'Tell them I'll be in touch. For technical advice. It can't take much to disrupt a ship's navigation system and throw it off course. We need a trick up our sleeve. A little backdoor program … Set the ball rolling. Go.'

Though fast asleep, Jack was aware of a faint breeze on his face and the sound of wings. In his dream Lily swam up to him and turned from a mermaid into a beautiful white gull. A throng of other gulls lifted her off the sea and away they flew towards the lighthouse, calling his name. They sounded insistent, desperate even, as if screaming at the ocean itself to hurry: 'Tide … swell, Tide … swell.'

CHAPTER 29

The approaching lorry flashed its lights and beeped its horn three times, the final blast changing tone like a siren as it thundered past. Nan gripped the steering wheel. 'What was that for?' she bellowed over her shoulder. 'Road hog!'

A yowl of agreement came from the back seat. Two yellow eyes blinked wearily from the folds of an old jumper. Odin didn't appreciate being woken up.

It was long past midnight and they were miles from the nearest town on a flat, straight road that ran through open marshland. A low mist clung to the land on either side but high above the stars shone brightly.

Without warning, the car in front swerved wildly, crossing onto the wrong side of the road. Its tyres screamed and the exhaust belched out black smoke as the driver struggled to regain control.

Nan leant forwards, peering into the darkness. The zigzag pattern made by the car's tail lights danced in her eyes like a bolt of red lightning. 'What's the matter with everyone round here?'

A figure appeared in the headlights, hurrying along the dotted white line that ran down the middle of the road. A voluminous purple coat swept the ground and before Nan knew it, the wearer had stepped directly in front of her.

'What the –?' She stamped on the brakes, sending the contents of the parcel shelf – boots, maps, blankets, bags – raining down on Odin's head. The cat gave a yowl as the blue Beetle screeched to a halt barely inches from where the figure stood.

A woman's face, brown as a walnut and lined with age, stared through the windscreen. She had one hand resting on the bonnet, the other raised.

'What are you doing?' yelled Nan, winding down the window. The smell of burning rubber filled her nostrils. 'Get out of the road! You'll get yourself killed.'

The woman's lips moved soundlessly as she fought for breath. She straightened up and pushed the matted grey hair from her face, revealing a red gash over her right eye.

'What on earth's going on?' said Nan.

'Hocus-pocus, jiggery-pokery, foul play!' Finding her voice at last, the woman came hurrying to the driver's window, gesturing wildly across the marsh. 'At the station. This morning. The same train twice!'

Nan gazed in bewilderment where the woman had indicated. In the distance lay the twinkling lights of Fenstreet.

'The station?'

'My station!'

Nan looked again across the marshes. There weren't any stations nearby. The East Coast line ran directly through Fenstreet but the place was too small to have its own stop.

'There!' cried the woman. 'You just choose not to see it! Look!'

A shiver ran down Nan's spine. The woman's eyes were crystal bright and seemed to be looking right inside her. She turned back towards Fenstreet full of expectation, though she wasn't certain what she was meant to see.

'Oh!' Her hand touched her upper lip. To one side of the village, a row of blue lights had appeared. She had to squint hard because they kept fading in and out of view, as though she was using badly focussed binoculars. Finally, they seemed to fix themselves and the outline of a building materialised below them. In the middle, a tower pointed up at the night sky. Without being told, Nan knew there would be a clock at the top of it. A special kind of clock that ran backwards as well as forwards. It *was* indeed a station, though not the sort used by ordinary passengers.

She stared with newfound respect at the ancient face. The old woman was the custodian of a 'time junction'. Beneath that purple coat caked in marshland mud was a Seer who supervised the comings and goings of a special kind of traveller: Time Trippers.

The woman nodded at her as if she had spoken out loud. 'That's right. I'm Sybil Ayres,' she said. 'I know who you are.' Before Nan could reply she slammed her hand down on the car roof. 'He tried to slip through without me noticing. But I won't be hoodwinked by tricks and disguises. I know the business of everyone who passes through my station. That's my job!'

'He? Who are you talking about?'

'A fraud, a thief, a hellhound …' Sybil's voice became shrill. She pulled a white plastic bag from one of her enormous pockets and held it open. A slimy, red smear ran down the inside. At the bottom, staring glassily up at the night sky, lay two dead starlings, their necks broken and wings smashed.

Nan looked from the contents of the bag to the gash on Sybil's face in horror.

'Came at me like harpies they did, just as the train pulled out. But he can't stop these old eyes from seeing. Oh no. I reached into his mind, read his thoughts. I know who he is!' Sybil pulled a dirty rag from one of her pockets and dabbed at the wound. She laughed bitterly. 'He's lived many lives, used many names, but our Mr Flyn isn't as elusive as he thinks.'

'Flyn?'

'Jago Flyn!' Sybil spat the name out like it was a curse.

'Are you sure?' Nan's stomach tightened as she recalled what Charlie had said about Blunt's wounded leg. 'Did he have a dog with him?'

'A wolf,' corrected Sybil. 'Nothing has ever moved through my station at such speed.'

The colour drained from Nan's face. She shut her eyes tight. She had wanted the wolf to be an illusion, something she'd dreamt up. 'It's real then?'

213

'As real as you and me.'

Nan swallowed hard, forcing herself to ask the next question. 'Was anyone with them?'

'A boy with his head full of the sea …'

'No. Not Jack!'

'He has a treasure of some kind. I saw it in his thoughts, shining like a great light. Hard to tell what it is exactly – I'm not sure he knows himself – but it made me think he's a traveller. One of us.'

A traveller, my Jack! Oh God. Nan felt numb. 'And Flyn wants this treasure, I suppose.'

'Of course. To escape his worthless life. He thinks it'll restore his old power.'

'Power? What is he?' whispered Nan.

'He *was* a Magus,' said Sybil. 'Fallen, cursed and banished!'

Nan had heard enough. She unbuckled her seat belt as quickly as her shaking hands would allow and got out of the car. 'You've got to help me! I need to find Jack. Fast!' She glanced towards Fenstreet. Under normal circumstances, it would be impossible for her to use a time junction. She had neither the skill nor the status. But here was the custodian standing right in front of her. Surely she'd allow it, just this once.

'No, I'm sorry,' said Sybil, seeing straight away what was in Nan's mind. Her tone became officious. 'It's against the rules. In any case, I've shut the station down. Flyn must have no bolt-hole. We're closing every junction from here to Timbuktu. He won't be using our network again.'

'But that puts Jack in even more danger. There must be something you can do?'

Sybil shook her head. 'I came here to tell you to turn back.'

'What!' Nan looked appalled. 'He's a child. We can't leave him to his own devices.'

'He's not defenceless, far from it. When the wolf slipped past, I caught a thought so powerful I could almost smell it. Like the promise of rain … Listen to me! Your grandson has the blood of a Magus in him and the wolf knows it. Jack has the means to defeat Flyn, to stop him causing chaos in our world.'

Nan's eyes widened in terror.

'Magical intervention is out of the question,' said Sybil. 'If we go barging in, he'll never discover his true potential.'

'The blood of a Magus?' gasped Nan.

'Don't tell me you're surprised. It runs through your family from Hermes himself. Why deny it? For heaven's sake, you've always feared your own gifts, forever doubting and –'

'Let me get this straight,' Nan cut in. 'You know this from the wolf?'

'Yes.'

'The passing thought of a creature who keeps the company of a villain. What if it's a lie? A distraction? Another trick?'

'Not possible.' Sybil drew herself up haughtily. 'I see only thoughts which are true.'

'Uh-huh. So the great Sybil Ayres is never wrong,

is that it? No one ever slipped under her radar? No one ever caught her napping?'

Sybil's face fell. 'Well, I –'

'My magic isn't one hundred per cent perfect,' snapped Nan, 'but at least I don't mind admitting it. Jack is my life. There's no way I'm going home without him. So you can stick your precious rules up … I'll manage on my own, thanks very much.'

'Now wait a minute,' blustered Sybil.

But Nan was already getting in the car, shooing Odin from the driver's seat where he'd crept to escape the clutter which had fallen on top of him. She slammed the door, turned the ignition key and revved the engine. Midway through closing the window, she paused.

'One more question,' she said grimly. 'You said Flyn was banished. So tell me, what exactly did he do?'

Sybil looked uncomfortably at the ground.

'Something unforgivable, I assume,' hissed Nan.

'He killed a man. Revenge for the death of his son.'

Nan shook her head and glared at the old witch. Then she pressed the accelerator to the floor. Four wheels churned into the marshland mud and Sybil had to jump clear to avoid the splatter.

★ ★ ★

Alpha watched the blue car snake its way along the narrow coast road that led to The Spike peninsula. From his vantage point high on the hill, it seemed to move slowly, trundling between the hedgerows like a tiny clockwork toy.

His ears twitched as he strained to catch the sound of its engine. He knew what lay ahead. Nan had already shown him on the night of the storm. He'd seen the fear in her face and watched spellbound as her vision had unfolded.

His amber eyes flicked to the place where the accident would happen. A badger had just ambled across the road and was rooting for grubs in the velvety soil of the verge. In a moment it would pass over the very spot where the front offside wheel would leave the ground and climb into the sky.

Lifting his head, Alpha summoned the wind. The long grass stirred, the fur on his broad shoulders parted and a light breeze delivered the mechanical rumble he'd been waiting for. He breathed in. The hot, metallic scent which hit the back of his throat tasted bad. Something was wrong.

His eyes narrowed, focussing on the wet tarmac of the road. Though several hundred metres away, he could see with forensic precision the drops of liquid that glistened like beads of poison on the black stones. The trail led all the way back to Morton Muxloe, where Blunt had crept into the garage to loosen the oil filter and fuel line.

Alpha growled. He didn't understand the anger and unkindness of human beings. All he knew was that it existed. Like a sponge, he let it soak into him, digesting it as he had the pile of worms in the playground. Then he blew it all out, turning it into storm winds that filled the universe with dark energy.

As the car drew closer, another low growl rattled in his throat. Nan didn't like him, he knew that. Her cat had fought him tooth and claw and would have scratched his eyes out if he'd let it. But he couldn't help straying into her territory. He'd had no choice. The mirror – his mirror – had drawn him there. So had the new Magus who knew how to make its light work.

The car no longer looked like a toy. It was moving fast now, its wheels squealing as it tore round the corners. Alpha inhaled and the grass rippled towards him, whispering with messages only he could decipher. He could sense Nan's fury as keenly as he could smell the burning metal. It seeped into his bones, making his legs quiver.

The desire to run became all-consuming. He couldn't keep still a moment longer. Every muscle in his body tightened, then flexed like elastic. With a snarl, he sprang forwards, pouring down the hill towards the sea. He had to reach the place in the road where Nan's journey was about to end. There was something he had to do.

★ ★ ★

Nan ignored the red lights on the dashboard and threw the Beetle around another bend. She prayed the engine would make the last few miles to Wakeham. If it was ruined, then too bad. All that mattered was finding Jack – before anything terrible happened.

Cursing, she gave the two furry dice a swipe. It was useless trying to wrap them round the rearview mirror. As soon as she hooked them out of the way they came loose again and swung in her face. She wished she'd never bought them.

A low-throated growl came from the back seat.

'I can't help it!' she yelled at Odin. 'We're in for a rough ride. So keep your hair on.' Gears screaming, she accelerated along a straight stretch of road, creating a tunnel of light between the dark hedgerows.

Odin's grumbling turned into a hissing fit. And when that failed to reclaim her attention, he let out a high-pitched wail. The noise went on and on, like an untuned violin searching for the right note, until her ears were ringing.

'For pity's sake,' she moaned. But something about the desperate cry made her glance up the hillside. 'What the – oh please, dear lord – No, not now!'

In spite of the darkness, she recognised the black outline straight away. It was the same grim shadow that had been preying on her mind since the night of the storm. Only now it wasn't just in her head. The wolf had found her. Tearing down the slope with his feet barely touching the ground, he looked like a demon.

'Oh no you don't!' she muttered. Alpha had altered his course slightly, heading for a section of road just beyond the next bend. Nan ducked her head down like a rally driver. 'You won't stop me this time!'

Teeth clenched, she took the corner fast, crunching the rear of the Beetle against a grassy bank. The steering

219

wheel spun in her hands and the engine screamed in protest, but she managed to keep going, pulling out of the turn with the car rocking on its axles.

For one jubilant moment, she thought she'd made it. The wolf seemed to have vanished; the way ahead was clear! She rammed the gear lever into fourth and put her foot down.

But as the needle of the rev counter climbed, her throat grew horribly dry. Suddenly her eyes were stinging as if she'd rubbed them with soap and she couldn't stop coughing. Dense black smoke was billowing from the engine, filling the car interior, making it impossible to see where she was going.

It was too late to brake. Too late to scream. The Beetle swerved from one side of the road to the other, then hit the verge with such force it cleared the ditch, crashed through the hedge and surged upwards, turning a giant somersault in the air.

As its headlights searched the sky, a ghastly screeching broke out. Nan knew it must be Odin, yet the noise sounded strangely far off. Her head felt heavy, she couldn't catch her breath and the world seemed out of focus, spinning and fading to an endless grey.

With a deafening crunch, the car fell to earth. Barely ten metres from where the cliffs met the sea it ploughed forwards on two wheels, then crashed down on all four before creaking to a standstill.

A bright circle of blood bloomed on the windscreen. For a few seconds the only sound was the incessant blaring of the horn. Then the petrol tank ignited. The explosion ripped open the front bonnet and a wall of flames poured out, crackling and licking at the night sky.

As Nan came round, a desperate sob escaped her. Her head rested awkwardly against the steering wheel and she couldn't move or feel her legs. Her magic had been right; her life was over. 'Jack,' she moaned weakly. 'Oh Jack, I'm sorry.'

She closed her eyes, accepting the inevitable. And it was then she felt it: a sharp breeze blowing in through the smashed windows, sweeping the hair from her face and dispersing the smoke in an instant. Though it hurt to lift her head, she made herself look out.

The flames had changed direction, bending up and away from the car in a great curving arch which looked almost like a rainbow. The Beetle jolted forwards and she groaned. Its front wheels had jammed against a rock. Whatever was drawing the fire away was strong enough to move the entire car.

The fiery arch lit up the surrounding hills as brightly as if it was day. Stunned, Nan's eyes ran along it to the place where it touched the ground. Standing on a boulder, near the cliff edge, was Alpha. His head was tipped back and fire came from his mouth, like a dragon. Except he wasn't creating the flames, he was consuming them, sucking them in and making them disappear.

She could hardly bear to watch. The grass streamed towards him on all sides, a whirlwind of debris spun over his head and his whole body shook as the column of fire drilled into him.

'Stop, please!' she muttered. 'What are you doing?'

221

By removing her pain, the wolf was inflicting a terrible torture on himself.

She slumped back in her seat, her spirit fading again. As the blackness invaded her mind, she prayed Alpha wouldn't destroy himself. She needed him to stay alive – for Jack's sake.

CHAPTER 30

The first fingers of dawn smeared the sky with an ugly bruised purple as Jack and Jago set out to meet Tattoo. Jack pulled his red hood over his head, shivering, and scanned the coastal path. There was no sign of Alpha but he was hardly surprised. He'd woken with a hollow ache in his chest and known the wolf was nowhere nearby.

A small motor boat bobbed up and down by the jetty, and at the sound of their footsteps, Tattoo rose out of it like the Incredible Hulk. The boat had seen better days. Blue and white paint flaked from its battered hull, and on the prow where the name should have been, a bare rectangular patch was visible.

'What's she called?' asked Jack, clambering aboard.

'Ent got no name,' grunted Tattoo. 'Bought her off a marine salvage bloke. Couple of months back.'

'She's definitely seen better days,' grumbled Jago. He cast a disparaging glance over the boat. 'She's watertight, I assume?'

'Course!' Tattoo tugged violently at the starter cord on the outboard motor. The engine spluttered into life and he sat down heavily, clutching the tiller in silence.

The stink of diesel fumes gradually wore off as the boat bumped over the waves out of the harbour. Behind them, the Lock and Quay pub grew smaller and smaller until very soon Wakeham had disappeared in a misty haze.

Ahead, the Pentland lighthouse rose out of the sea, tall as a church spire. Sitting in the prow, Jack's spirits lifted. At last he was going to meet the keeper and he might even be Bill's father. Hugging the thought to himself, he wondered what sort of man he'd be. Patient and kind, he hoped. A good listener too. He wouldn't bat an eyelid when he heard the incredible story of *The Empress*. 'Forewarned is forearmed,' he'd say, or something like that. Then he'd promise to warn the authorities and everyone would be safe.

White caps of foam danced on the waves and a fish jumped alongside the boat. Jack smiled to himself, remembering Lily's drawing. He turned to see if Jago had seen the fish too. But Jago sat hunched over, looking so grim-faced Jack wondered if he was seasick.

'Hey, you okay?' he called.

The corners of Jago's mouth twisted in a strange smile. 'Never better,' he replied, before resuming his vacant study of the boat's hull.

Jack frowned. Maybe he was wishing he was elsewhere. For the first time it occurred to him that he'd taken his friend's help for granted. Without this detour, Jago could be halfway to Belgium by now – on business of his own.

Feeling guilty, Jack delved into his rucksack and edged towards the stern. He nudged Jago with his elbow and held out a clasped hand.

'Now then. What's all this about?'

Jack's fingers slowly unfurled to reveal Indigo, his blue horse. 'I want you to have him.'

'Whatever for?'

'As a thank you. I'd never have got this far without you.'

'I couldn't possibly –'

'Why not?'

'It's from your parents.'

'That's the point; he's special. Look, he's even got a J on his back!'

Jago shook his head.

'Remember you predicted I'd find something important – right under my nose,' Jack persisted.

'It doesn't matter.'

'It does! You've been right all along about everything. I didn't believe in magic then. And I wasn't sure I could trust you. I didn't even want to tell you about …' he glanced sideways at Tattoo and whispered, 'the mirror.'

'You didn't know me. You still don't,' muttered Jago.

'I do! You're my friend. Take him, please, to remember me.'

The boat bounced hard over a choppy wave and a gull screeched wildly overhead.

'No, it's yours. And if you're not careful, it'll get smashed. What made you bring such a fragile thing anyway?' Red-faced, Jago turned away, glaring at the sea.

Jack's fingers tightened around the horse until its tiny hooves dug into him. Why was Jago being so pig-headed? It was a gift; he should be happy! He looked at Tattoo, who'd been listening to the exchange. The hard man turned away too, a smirk of amusement creasing his cheeks.

The boat bumped over another wave. Jack felt like flinging Indigo in the ocean and for several moments he could think of nothing else. He stared at Jago's fiercely jutting jaw. What was eating him that he looked so miserable? He copied the expression, making a face like a gargoyle. Somehow it helped and feeling slightly better, he slipped Indigo in his pocket.

By now, the lighthouse loomed over them, a stern-looking building with vertical arrow-slit windows. Close up, its thick red and white stripes looked hard and uncompromising, nothing like the candy-cane tower Jack had seen from the Ferris wheel.

'Where are we going to land?' he asked.

A jagged reef of rocks sprang up like teeth and huge waves crashed over them. Tattoo raised his eyebrows and said nothing. With difficulty, he steered them around the other side of the island where a landing stage revealed itself below two flights of steps. While Tattoo and Jago struggled to secure the boat, Jack wriggled past them. Unable to wait a second longer, he scrambled up on the prow and leapt off, slithering on the wet stones.

'Oi, watch it! What the 'ell you playing at?' bellowed Tattoo.

Jack paid no attention. He was already racing up

the steps, the roar of the ocean in his ears. Perhaps it was his own excitement, but even the shrieking gulls seemed to will him on. Finally, he was here: the Pentland lighthouse. With a whoop of joy, he tore across the patch of grass in front of him, climbed two more steps and flung himself, breathless, against the painted white door.

To his surprise, it fell slightly ajar and a bunch of keys clanged to the ground inside. He glanced back at Jago and Tattoo. They were still busy tying up the boat, cursing and shouting at each other.

'Hello?' he called through the gap. 'Anyone home?'

No reply.

The heavy hinges creaked as he opened the door wider. Hoping the keeper would hear him, he cleared his throat loudly and took a step or two inside.

The air was chilly and his footsteps sounded hollow on the stone floor. Half expecting a hand to grab the scruff of his neck, he turned slowly. The circular room was nothing like the cosy interior he'd imagined. On one side, there was a small kitchen with a kettle on the cooker and a single mug by the sink. But apart from that and a faded red sofa, most of the space was occupied by equipment.

Orange wiring ran down the walls to a row of sealed grey units, the largest of which had a display of tiny red, green and yellow lights. Frowning, he went over to it. The living quarters must be on another floor. This was obviously a control room. His fingers brushed across the lights, pausing at the last one. 'Power Fail' read the label below it.

A fluttering sound came from overhead.

His eyes travelled up the spiral staircase, which curled like a serpent to the floors above. A sprinkling of dust cascaded down, and someone giggled.

'Hello?' he called. 'Who's there?'

He started up the stairs, half wondering if the ghost story Lily had told him might be true. On the first floor, he passed a room containing two curved bunks. There were no mattresses on them, just a pile of old crates. *It's empty, that's all,* he told himself.

A scuffling sound came from higher up.

'Hey!' he yelled.

He could have sworn he'd seen a trace of a boyish grin and a flash of white blond hair. He raced up two more flights of stairs and arrived, panting for breath, on the landing at the top. Ahead of him, a door stood partly open. *Lantern Room,* he read. So this was where Bill's famous lamp must be … along with the joker who wanted to play hide-and-seek. He gave the door a wary shove with his foot.

Daylight flooded in on all sides through shiny latticed windows. The room appeared to be empty apart from the light itself, which stood on a platform in the centre like an exhibit in a gallery. Puzzled, Jack advanced slowly towards it. 'I know you're in here,' he said.

Three circular lenses enclosed the lamp like giant shields. They were covered in rings of polished glass in which he could see his own image, repeated dozens of times. He frowned. Not even a toddler could have squeezed behind them and yet … that was where the watching eyes seemed to be.

He went over to the window. No one in their right mind would have hidden on the walkway outside; it was far too exposed. He checked anyway and, as he'd expected, found it windswept and empty.

Below, the door clicked gently shut.

'Jack!' thundered Jago.

'Up here! I saw someone – a skinny kid with blond hair.' Jack ran from the room and hung over the banister. 'The keeper's not here.'

Jago's upturned face showed no surprise. 'I know. Come downstairs and I'll explain. Bring your bag.' His voice was cold and imperious.

Jack stepped out of view.

'Hurry up. I want to talk to you.'

Jack stood rigid, his back pressed against the wall. How did Jago know about the keeper? Why hadn't he said anything? The whole trip was pointless if … He hugged the rucksack to him, a splinter of suspicion driving deep into his heart. If Jago hadn't meant to help, then what did he want? Jack bit his lip as the strange comment Jago had made on the boat came back to him: 'You didn't know me. You still don't.'

'What are you playing at? Jack? Don't mess me around.'

Footsteps like pistol shots sounded on the stairs.

Hands trembling, Jack reached into his bag. If ever he needed the mirror to work, it was now. Whoever had sent it to him must have meant him to use it. If only that someone could have taught him how!

Beads of sweat pricked his forehead. As his fingers

closed on the disc, he noticed the metal had grown warm too. Had his own panicky feelings somehow triggered the magic? He could hear the ocean pounding and seagulls calling as they had in his dream. 'Tide … swell, Tide … swell.'

Calm down! he told himself. What if the mirror responded to him as much as the other way round? Wasn't that what mirrors were meant to do: reflect you back at yourself?

The metal thrummed but he resisted the familiar tugging. He would go when *he* wanted, not because he was scared. If there was any element of control in all of this, he needed to discover it. Right now.

Forget the keeper, forget Jago. It's up to you to find out what's wrong with the light. You have to focus!

He bowed his head and the advice he'd given Lily – his own father's words – came to him. *Use the strongest muscle in your body. It gets you from A to B. Imagination. Picture where you want to be!*

The mirror glowed and, without warning, the forefinger of his right hand stung as if he'd touched a red-hot iron. Instantly, before he could even wince, the tugging ceased. Then, for one extraordinary moment, he seemed to stand outside himself, like a spectator, quiet and detached. He let go of the mirror and it spun in the air in front of him like a tiny blazing sun.

His whole being grew calm and centred. It felt amazing, as if he'd just learned to walk a tightrope. As his surroundings turned blue-white, he held on a fraction longer, testing himself, astonished that through his own self-control he could keep the mirror so perfectly balanced.

Nothing could have broken his concentration or diminished his sense of mastery. Not even the advancing figure of Jago – or the wiry blond boy who stole ahead of him, waiting for permission to pounce. The mirror spun faster and faster. When he was ready, Jack closed his eyes and heard the gulls cry out once more as he let his mind go into freefall.

CHAPTER 31

The strange detachment he'd achieved must have had something to do with it, because this leap was unlike any other.

As he came to, the whole world seemed to be swaying. His head felt strangely light and his feet throbbed and tingled as if he was about to float away. He reached out to steady himself.

An iron rail met his hand, ice cold but reassuringly solid. While his vision settled, he clung on, watching the waves rise in and out of focus through the darkness below. 'You did it,' he muttered. 'You bloomin' did it!' He was ninety feet up on the exterior walkway of the Pentland lighthouse – exactly as he'd intended.

Behind him, a whirring noise started up and the metal floor rumbled. With a great mechanical 'clunk' the lamp came on. For a second or so, he stood blinking, bathed from head to toe in a luminous haze. Then, very slowly, the three golden lenses began to turn, directing the beam into the night like a giant searching eye.

In the distance, a curtain of sludge-green rain hung

from the clouds. Where it touched the sea, a dark shape moved up and down. Jack drew in his breath. Any moment now the beam would sweep over it and … there! Pitched on her side, with one end submerged, lay the sorry hulk of *The Empress*.

The sight of it sent a shudder down his spine. He hoped he'd done the right thing. During those few precious moments, before Jago could get to him, it had seemed the only way. He had arrived precisely at the point in time when his first leap had ended.

Stay calm, he told himself. *The knowledge you need to avoid this is right here. The light went out, then came on again. There has to be a reason …*

★ ★ ★

In the semi-darkness of the control room, a red light blinked. With a frown, Jack stood in front of it, wheeling his right arm over his head and rubbing his aching shoulder. The door to the lantern room had proved obstinate but not impossible; he'd made it to the ground floor in minutes.

On a desk nearby, numbers and letters spilled across a small screen while above him the lenses continued to rotate. Not a soul was about – he'd checked every room – and the lighthouse appeared to be functioning normally. So why was the power-fail light flashing red?

His eye rested on the telephone mounted on the wall by the main control unit. He let his arm drop and went over to it. Without hesitation, he lifted the receiver.

There was a click and a man answered.

'Trinity House Operations Centre.' The voice was gruff, half shouting above a clamour of noisy people. 'Who is this?'

'I – my name's Jack. Jack Tideswell.'

'A kid?' The man paused uncertainly.

'Beachy Head and Anvil Point. Both down, sir!' a woman cried.

'This is a direct line, son. What the hell are you doing in the Pentland? Is anyone with you?'

'No. I'm … something terrible's happened. A ship hit a sandbank and –'

'What? For heaven's sake, have you got the name of the vessel? Where is she? Speak up.'

'*The Empress*. She went down very close, maybe half a mile away.'

'Dear God –' The man broke off and the hubbub around him died. 'It's the cruise ship; she's miles off course. You there, get on to the coastguard. They must have received a distress signal.'

'The light went out,' said Jack. 'Where's the keeper?'

'What?' The man sounded stunned. 'Son, the Pentland hasn't been manned for more than twenty years. It's remotely controlled from our centre here in Harwich. Look, we've got a crisis on our hands. Ten lighthouses down and a virus overwriting every hard drive as we speak –'

'A virus! Someone did this deliberately?'

'I'm afraid so.'

'Who?'

'Hackers, terrorists, a cyber psychopath … take your pick. They've jammed the GPS and land-based radio frequencies too, effectively hijacked the entire navigation system. It's a disaster.' The man stopped. He'd lost his cool, saying more than he should. He took a deep breath. 'We're doing everything we can to restore the Pentland. Tell me how you got there.'

'But it's working,' said Jack, ignoring his question.

'What is?'

'The light. It's back on. It did go out, but now it's fine.' He stared at the monitor on the desk.

'That's not possible. Have you touched the manual override? What are you doing there?'

'I – I didn't touch anything!'

'All right. Calm down. Describe what you can see.'

'Lots of code … downloading fast …'

Letters and numbers continued to spill across the screen. They were incomprehensible to Jack, but in their midst a repeated symbol seemed to wink at him. Shaped like a fish, it was impossible to miss: the first letter of the Greek alphabet, Alpha.

'The Pentland's running independently,' the man told his team. 'Some kind of bogus program. Anyone get this? Because I'm damned if I do.'

Jack's heart thumped. The last time he'd seen equations like these was when he'd first found the mirror. It had brought his PC to life. But it couldn't be powering the lamp. He hadn't got the disc with him; it always stayed behind, pulling him back whenever a leap ended.

His gaze travelled up the spiral stairs. The giant lenses had begun turning the instant he'd arrived. What could possibly be the source of energy? Had he missed something up there?

The voices from his dream filled his head, willing him to hurry. 'Tide – swell … Tide – swell.'

He gripped the telephone tightly. 'I'm sorry. I have to go.'

'Oh no you don't. Stay right where you are. Listen, lad, we've got people on the way. I need to know what's going on.'

Jack looked at the winking symbol.

So did he. He hung up.

★★★

He'd left the door to the walkway open. It banged on its hinges and the rain drove in sideways, drenching the lantern room floor and producing a thick mist which hung about the golden lenses like a luminous curtain.

Meaning to shut it, he groped his way forwards. But he'd barely gone two steps when a starburst of flashes from the revolving glass burnt on his retinas. He stood perfectly still. His senses told him he wasn't alone.

'Jack?'

Silhouetted against the glare of the lamp, a figure came towards him, two bare feet emerging through the damp haze. 'You came back for me … Oh Jack, I knew you would!'

Tiny dots leapt across his field of vision. His mouth

236

opened to speak, but nothing came out. There in front of him, clutching the remains of a life vest, stood Lily, her nightdress ballooning around her like a white bell.

'I'm cold,' she whispered, 'ever so cold.'

Jack tore off his hoodie, his mind turning somersaults. When they'd jumped ship, he'd been holding her hand. Had he somehow drawn her with him as the light came on?

'Here, take this,' he blurted. 'I can't believe it … You're safe!'

But before he could wrap the hoodie around her, Lily backed away in fright. 'Don't – please!'

'What's the matter?'

'It's no good. I tried counting like you said, but I – I –' Her breath caught sharply and her whole body trembled. 'I can't remember anything.'

'Don't be silly. Of course you can. Put this on, you'll freeze!'

'You don't understand.' Distraught, Lily spread her arms wide. 'Look at me, Jack. I can't last much longer. You have to do something … Don't leave me here.'

For a second he couldn't work out what she meant. Then a knife seemed to twist inside him. There was no colour in her eyes, not the slightest hint of blue, and her down-turned lips were paler than the moon. It wasn't the harsh light as he'd thought. Whenever the wind gusted, her long hair merely billowed in the same curious way as her clothes. Lily was exactly where he'd left her – in the ice-cold sea. And the apparition in front of him was no more substantial than the wind itself.

Hot tears gathered behind his eyes. She was dying, frozen by treacherous waves. And the lamp itself seemed to be playing a cruel trick, projecting her soul like an eerie hologram through a million droplets of vapour.

He pressed his lips together in a red line which didn't quiver. 'I made a promise,' he said fiercely, 'and I'm going to keep it. I'm learning how the mirror works. I've found out why the light failed. I can stop this –'

He broke off. Lily wasn't listening. 'There's something coming for you,' she said faintly. 'Look.'

Her hand reached out as if trying to pluck a star from the air between them.

Bewildered, he stared at her. Her words made no sense. And slowly but surely her spirit seemed to be fading, returning to the ocean and her poor spent body.

'Wait. They're sending help; you can't give up!' Desperate to keep her conscious, he snatched at the one bright memory that connected them. 'Remember the drawing you did? Talk to me!'

Lily's face remained expressionless.

Far below a wave crashed on the rocks and a sheet of icy spray blew in. The salt water stung Jack's eyes to tears, but he refused to blink. 'You can't forget. I won't let you … Lily!'

Her stare was so glassy he thought she would never speak. Then, at last, her lips moved.

'Pharos.'

Barely audible, the word hung in the air like a sigh.

The revolving light flashed over them. As it swept

out to sea it took Lily with it, erasing her ghostly form in an instant.

'No –' Jack raced to the walkway, scouring the darkness for *The Empress*. But the waves had engulfed her too, rising like mountains that stretched as far as he could see to the rim of the world.

'Alphaaa-a-a!' he screamed. 'Where are you?'

A cold wind tugged the roots of his hair.

He bowed his head and the tears he'd held back fell angrily. First his parents, now Lily – all lost. He raked desperately through his pockets for Indigo. But the smiling J on the horse's back seemed only to mock him. And the tiny hooves raised in the air looked as if they might run away too. With a yell of utter fury, he hurled the keepsake into the sea.

A blue-white flash lit the darkness.

Soaked and exhausted, Jack flung himself down, certain it was only lightning. He pulled the hood of his fleece over his face. The magic was beyond him: he'd failed. He buried his head in his arms and wept. His world was no bigger than himself and everything in it felt hopeless.

Sobs came thick and fast and in the midst of them, a dull ache gnawed at his chest. Thinking it must be his own sadness, he drew up his knees and hugged them tight. He'd never felt so alone.

Why, when he needed Alpha most, had the wolf disappeared? A big tear slid off the end of his nose. He shouldn't have shouted when the pram had started rolling; he'd driven him away.

The ache sharpened, spreading down his back. With a sniff he tried to ignore it, but the more he thought about Alpha the worse it got, wrapping itself like a python around his ribs until his lungs grew tight and he began to cough.

A peculiar taste coated his tongue. Metal, petrol … and something else which made the hairs rise on his neck. The knowledge slammed into him. Alpha hadn't deserted him; he was in trouble. Something bad was burning his insides, consuming him faster than if he'd swallowed poison. Fire.

'What have you done?' he muttered. He struggled to his feet, his eyes raking the coastline. Alpha *had* followed him. He could sense him, just as surely as he had from the train. He was alone on the cliffs, fighting an injury which seemed to be eating him alive.

Jack filled his lungs and belly with fresh, clean air. Then, not knowing how else to help, he exhaled sharply, pressing on his abdomen. *Breathe, damn it,* he told the wolf. *Just breathe!*

He took another gulp. And another. If he could have blown out a piece of his own soul and sent it to Alpha, he'd have done it. *Use the wind, if you have to*, he pleaded. *For your own sake, let it go!*

A deafening crack sounded overhead and the walkway under his feet trembled. Out of nowhere, an explosion of flames ripped across the darkness, setting the sky alight as if daytime had arrived. Jack stumbled back, staring with wide, stunned eyes. A fiery arch, like an orange rainbow, had formed over the place where the ship had been.

Behind him, the giant lenses continued to whirr and turn, directing the lighthouse beam slowly towards the spot. Then something even more extraordinary happened. As the beam passed through the centre of the arch, a doorway of light appeared to open in the sky. Goosebumps rose on his skin. Close to the water's surface, a flurry of movement had begun. Even at a distance, he could see hundreds of glimmering shapes dipping and diving and skimming over the sea.

Almost immediately some of them took off and came streaming towards him, moving at such speed that when they drew close the rush of air nearly lifted him off his feet. He ducked down, shielding his face with his arms. He could only snatch glances, they were so bright, but amidst the glow he saw faces, silvery and shining: a white-capped steward, a teenage girl, the old man who'd tried to make him turn round …

A shiver ran through him. The whirr of machinery seemed to blot out every sound, yet he could have sworn the old man had spoken. He strained his ears to listen. More souls blazed over him and he caught it again, a faint murmur that seemed to carry a demand. 'Tide … swell, Tide … swell.'

Gentle but insistent, like the birds from his dream, the whispering grew. What did they want?

One strong spirit appeared to be travelling faster than the rest, climbing higher and higher until, moments before reaching the lighthouse, he dropped like a stone out of view. Jack rushed forwards, leaning out as far as he dared to see what had become of him.

Directly below, on a rocky ledge overhanging the sea, the glowing outline of a large man was visible. Hunched over on his knees, he had one arm plunged into the water, like an enormous bear trying to grab a fish.

Jack's heart danced. He would have recognised those broad shoulders anywhere. 'Bill!'

The big man straightened up, the light expanding around him. His eyes met Jack's. 'Ent never seen nuffin so blue!' he bellowed. 'Reckon you'll be needin' this.'

Jack's mouth hung open. A round piece of metal glinted in Bill's hand: the mirror.

'Let me 'elp, Mouse. I owe yer. Tell me what I can do.'

'But how –?'

'It were in the sea. The minute you arrived we all saw it. Ent no accident. You and that little 'orse of yours drew it 'ere somehow.'

'Indigo?'

'Aye. It took off like a bloomin' missile when you threw him in.'

A spark of joy ignited inside Jack. How or why a tiny gift from his parents should produce such a momentous effect was beyond him. But he had a pretty good idea of what he needed to do now. His eyes roamed the web of starry trails above before returning to Bill. He thought of his promise to Lily. If he could just keep his friends alive, buy himself more time …

'Bring it here,' he yelled.

'Right-oh.'

Bill set off, and in the few seconds it took him to

climb the full height of the tower, Jack filled his lungs. He could sense Alpha watching and it gave him courage. Human spirits could be transformed; Jago had said so on the train. That was what the whispering souls had demanded.

'Animus!' he cried.

The mirror responded with a blue-white flash.

Ripples of light flowed outwards along Bill's limbs, extending beyond him in a wide circle which grew and grew until it reached the souls as they swept inland, making them flicker. One by one, they tumbled towards the sea like falling leaves. Then, with a dramatic flip, they seemed to fold in on themselves and change direction. When they climbed back up, each one had transformed into a bold, bright seagull.

There was a loud clang. The largest bird of all landed beside him, dropping the mirror awkwardly from his beak.

'Careful!' Jack pounced on the disc to stop it rolling.

The seagull screeched furiously, batting his wings.

'Okay, okay. You're new to this … Me too!'

Smiling sheepishly, Jack rummaged in his rucksack for the paper bag which had contained Nan's sandwiches. A sprinkling of crumbs blew away into the night like snowflakes and the seagull squawked again.

'We're going to need this,' he said, smoothing the creases out of the bag. 'And this …' He produced his father's pen. 'I've got a job for you.'

The seagull cocked his head on one side, watching keenly as four lines of untidy letters spilled from the pen onto the brown paper. When he'd finished, Jack put the mirror inside the bag and rolled the end down. He held out the package. On it he'd written:

Jack Tideswell
12 Hill Rise
Morton Muxloe
Somershire

'I want you to deliver this. It's a long way. Think you can make it?'

The seagull hopped forwards, spreading his broad wings.

'It isn't just the distance. I'm sending you to the past. The mirror will take you back seven years. Understand? To the day of a big storm.'

He looked anxiously at the gull. The storm, no doubt, was Alpha's and he'd be waiting. Not that he blamed the wolf for the chaos. *Something had to shake me up,* he thought.

He put the parcel in the seagull's beak. 'Don't get blown away. I *need* this to arrive.'

Without wasting a moment, the gull lifted his long, white wings. Then before Jack could even scramble to his feet, he took off, banking sharply around the tower towards the coast.

Jack followed the white dot until, very soon, it was no bigger than the flecks of surf thrown up by the waves. At last he understood what Lily had been trying to tell him.

When he'd arrived, so had the mirror – that's what she'd seen in the sea. It had made the lamp work, powering the beam so she was visible too.

The hum of an approaching helicopter broke in on his thoughts. If only Harwich could have responded faster. The GPS failure must have sabotaged the rescue services too.

He shut his eyes, focussing on Bill. At least he'd won Lily and the others a reprieve of sorts.

Traces of the fiery rainbow faded to an orange mist and a strong breeze bore the seagull over the breakers towards the twinkling lights of Wakeham. In his beak the package began to glow …

Then, once more, the Pentland lighthouse shut down.

CHAPTER 32

A slow handclap echoed down the stairwell of the lighthouse. 'Bravo! Quite a performance!'

Jago planted his hands on his hips, causing the trench coat to flare around him. 'I lost track of the animuses you created. Seagulls, eh? Splendid! At least we know how the mirror came into your possession.'

Jack blinked in bewilderment. He was back on the landing next to the lantern room. 'You saw them. How?'

'You left the mirror spinning. I had only to reach out and take it. The pictures it showed us were … well, what can I say? Riveting.'

Jack glared at him.

'Oh come on, cheer up. Your little delivery worked. Or you and I wouldn't be here now!'

'Where is it?'

'Here.' Jago tapped his pocket.

'Give it back.'

'I'm afraid I can't.'

Jack lunged towards the pocket.

'Now then! We'll have none of that.' Jago grabbed his

wrist and pushed him away. 'I'm sorry, Jack, the mirror's mine. Alpha has done his job. He led me to it and you've shown me how it works.'

'Alpha? What do you mean?'

'Let this be a lesson to you. Trust no one. I mean it. This is a hard, unforgiving world.'

'What are you talking about? It's Alpha's magic … he helped me!'

'He didn't.' Jago's eyes drilled holes into Jack's. 'You spoke the command; the mirror followed your will. And when the time comes, it will follow mine.'

'It wasn't like that. We did it together!'

'Nonsense!' stormed Jago. 'Alpha's duty is to serve me. The sooner you understand that, the better.'

Jack shook his head in disbelief. 'Why are you doing this?'

'I have my reasons. The mirror is mine by rights and I've waited a long time to find it – centuries, in fact.'

'Centuries!' In the back of Jack's mind a snake hissed, a bright red one from the Tarot cards. Hadn't Jago said snakes could shed their skins and be reborn? 'Who *are* you?'

'Jago Flyn. I'm an artist.'

'You're lying!'

'No, Jack, I'm not. I haven't lied to you once. In this lifetime, that *is* who I am.'

'But that's only part of it. You're not telling me everything.'

'And why should I? This is *my* business, *my* mirror. I refuse to make excuses for my actions. We all withhold the truth to protect our own interests. Including you, my boy. Take your little story about Indigo.'

'That was different!'

'Was it? You were hiding the truth. You had the mirror all along.'

Jack's eyes blazed. He began to see how completely he'd been duped. 'You knew I had it, didn't you? When you read my palm. Just like you knew there was no keeper. This place is automated. You tricked me to get what *you* want. You couldn't care less about me.'

'Oh, I wouldn't say that. I've enjoyed your company, truly I have. We had fun.'

'Liar! You don't mean anything you say!' Jack hurled himself at Jago and knocked him against the wall, punching and kicking for all he was worth. 'Give – it – back!'

Jago doubled over, moaning, but quickly recovered himself. He grabbed the hood of Jack's fleece, yanked him backwards and hooked a leg behind his knees. Jack landed on his back with a thump and by the time he scrambled up, it was too late. Jago had thrown the mirror high above them.

'Pi!' he bellowed.

A harsh cry cut through the air – tsche, tsche, tsche – and as the mirror tumbled out of view down the stairwell, a flash of black and white swooped past them. Taking advantage of the distraction, Jago seized Jack's arm and twisted it behind his back.

'This is one wrestling match I can't let you win. The fun and games are over.'

248

'Got it!' called a voice from below. 'Hurry up, will ya!'

'Patience,' Jago replied. 'We have a fighter on our hands.'

'What, the kid who can't throw straight? Don't make me laugh! Bring 'im 'ere, I'll sort 'im out!'

Below them, a blond boy leered up from the red sofa. Jack glared back, kicking and struggling as Jago frog-marched him down the stairs. No wonder he'd missed the boy hiding in the lantern room. He was an animus.

'Jack, meet Pi. Be warned, he has no manners of any sort.'

'We've already met. He's bad luck,' snapped Jack, wishing the stone he'd thrown had been a grenade.

'Huh! I like that,' said Pi. 'Worth my weight in gold, ent I, Jago? Brought you a fortune from that big ol' house.'

'That's enough, Pi. Blowing your own trumpet is one of your less appealing habits.'

'But you were proud of me!' Pi leapt up in excitement. 'Go on. Tell him!'

'So it was you!' Jack wriggled free at last and turned to face Jago. '*You* robbed Lady Harington.'

'Not 'im. Me!' said Pi. 'Class job 'n all. Took skill and guts. But you wouldn't know about them things.'

'For the last time, Pi!' roared Jago. 'I'm warning you. If you don't cut it out …'

Pi made a zipping motion across his mouth. The sofa springs gave a twang like a harp as he hastily sat back down.

'Oh, I get it,' said Jack. 'The virus, that was you too, wasn't it? You want the ship to go down … For God's sake, Jago! You're going to kill hundreds of people!'

'Now hold on!' Jago's ears and cheeks went crimson. 'Let's get one thing straight. I'm here to retrieve what's mine. *That* is all.'

He snapped his fingers at Pi, avoiding Jack's horrified gaze. With a knowing smirk, Pi leapt up and handed him the mirror.

'Don't fob me off,' fumed Jack. 'Why steal the money if you only wanted the mirror?'

'Why not? Because it was there!' barked Jago. 'Pi and me, we're opportunists. We make a living where we can.'

'And that creep Lonsdale asked for it,' Pi chipped in. 'Treated him cheap like he's some old fraud.'

'Well, he is!' yelled Jack. 'A fraud, a thief and a cold-blooded killer. He can't even look at me he's so ashamed!'

'Silence!' Jago's hand shot out and though Jack was several feet away, he felt an immense pressure on his chest. A force like an electric shock hurled him back onto the sofa, where he lay gasping for breath.

'Now then.' Jago spoke through gritted teeth. 'That's a warning. Don't make me angry, Jack. Because I do indeed know people – brainiacs who can hack any system, write any code and plant the smartest logic bomb to go off whenever I goddam please.' He put his fists together, then threw them apart explosively. 'That's right. They have their orders. And if you get in my way, it'll be on *your* head, not mine. A few keystrokes is all it takes to activate a neatly hidden program that won't just take out your ship, but every GPS device and lighthouse on its route. Understand? Pi, it's time to leave.'

'But – what we gonna do with him?'

'Nothing. Without the mirror he's powerless.'

Pi looked bitterly disappointed. He eyed the telephone. 'We can't just leave him! He might call someone.'

'Then cut the line!'

'What? And raise the alarm?'

'You have a point.' Jago scowled at Jack. 'We just need a couple of hours to get clear.'

'I know!' Pi leapt eagerly behind the sofa. He re-emerged with the stun gun he'd used on Lonsdale. 'How 'bout this?'

'Not necessary. I have a better idea.'

Jago reached behind Pi's ear and with a flourish of the wrist, produced a small metal object. Jack felt his heart sink. In Jago's cupped hand lay the whistle he'd used to summon Alpha against Blunt and his gang.

'We'll see who he answers to.' With a smile, Jago put the whistle to his lips. The door of the lighthouse banged on its hinges and a low growl came from outside. 'Enter,' he said.

A silence followed. Then, very slowly, a muddy and bedraggled Alpha appeared in the doorway, his head bowed warily between his shoulders. When he saw Jago, his coat twitched like it was infested with fleas and he moved swiftly to heel at his feet.

Jack edged back on the sofa. Alpha's ears immediately flattened and his nose corrugated in a snarl.

'I'd sit very still if I were you,' said Jago. 'You don't want to make him nervous. Alpha will *never* defy me, remember that. He was created by *my* ancestor to defend the Magus line. It's his duty. If he fails, his magic dies. You don't want to end your days a common wolf, do you?'

Alpha tucked his tail between his hind legs.

'There, you see?' Jago pulled the trench coat about him. 'Come, Pi. Alpha will stand guard till we're out of reach. Goodbye, Jack. Our paths won't cross again.'

Jago's heavy boots thumped away down the stone steps but Pi made no attempt to follow. A sneer formed on his face. 'You ent got a clue, have you?' he said, waving the gun at Jack. 'Even now you dunno what you've lost.'

'Archimedes' mirror. I hope it fries him,' said Jack stonily.

Pi pointed the gun at him and pretended to fire it. 'Ent just a weapon. You were right. He only told you half the story.'

Jack glowered at him.

'Oh come on, it's staring you in the face. For crying out loud, your parents were there!'

'Leave them out of it.'

Pi threw back his head and laughed. 'Numbskull. It's part of the ol' Pharos, the centrepiece of the great light. They found it in the ruins – and lost their lives for it.'

'You're lying!'

'Now why would I do that?'

'Because you're a two-faced scumbag like him.'

Pi moved swiftly around the back of the sofa. 'And you can't face the truth,' he whispered. The cold barrel of the gun pressed into Jack's neck. 'At the entrance there was a statue, right? Lost her head, you might say, in the earthquake.'

'I know, moron. They found it … Isis.'

'Shhhh.' The gun dug harder into him. 'Hundreds of years underwater and that head didn't budge. Then along they come and boom! Down she crashes. Next thing we know some fisherman sees a blue light in the water. Bingo!'

'You're making it up.'

'Nope. Ask Alpha. The instant the mirror was free, he knew. Ironic, eh? Isis being the goddess of love 'n that. Ah, don't look so sad. I'm sure you were in their thoughts.'

Jack gazed numbly at Alpha whose eyes were locked on to his. Pi couldn't have dealt a crueller blow. He'd just lost the most tangible thing that connected him to his parents and their dreams. He pictured Charlie holding the library book in the garden, marvelling at the hole burnt in its pages. She'd guessed everything and he'd just ignored her. He wanted to scream at himself. But he couldn't crumble, not in front of Pi.

Flecks of fiery orange danced in Alpha's amber irises, reminding Jack of the rainbow they'd made. 'I'm glad you told me,' he said to Pi. 'My parents did something special. I'm proud of them.'

'Shame you let 'em down, then.'

'I didn't.'

'Come again? You've just lost the mirror – the mirror they wanted you to have!'

Alpha's eyes grew brighter and Jack felt his courage grow. At last he understood. Throwing Indigo into the sea had acted like a signal. The mirror of Pharos had travelled halfway round the world, across oceans and through time to the very moment when he'd not only needed it, but had learned enough to use it. It occurred to him that if he had been in his parents' thoughts, as Pi suggested, that would have been precisely their wish.

He kept looking at the wolf. 'It came to me for a reason,' he said quietly. 'This isn't over.'

There was a long silence.

Jack couldn't see Pi's face, but he knew very well it wasn't the reaction he'd wanted. He heard the click of a safety catch. Alpha's gaze remained steady and Jack knew the wolf was on his side. He felt a sharp pain, then nothing at all.

CHAPTER 33

Charlie woke with a shudder and sat bolt upright. The fish tank burbled quietly on the chest of drawers next to her, emitting a dim glow into the darkness of her bedroom. Nothing stirred except her pet fish, Goldie, who swam goggle-eyed to and fro.

She gathered the blankets under her chin and glanced around the room. Despite the silence, she had the oddest feeling. She could have sworn a voice had just spoken her name.

At the foot of her bed, a shadow shaped like a mountain fell over the carpet and rose up the wall opposite. Charlie bit her lip. She could see the muddy hem of what looked like a long robe. Someone – or something – was sitting in the wicker chair in front of her dressing table.

'I shouldn't be here at all,' said a thin, quavering voice. 'It's against the rules. I'll probably lose my job.'

'Who … who's there?' Charlie clutched the blankets even tighter.

'Interference is forbidden, but, but … how *can* I turn a blind eye? A Seer is meant to see!'

Charlie switched on the bedside light. An old woman with a face wrinkled as a walnut blinked at her. She was small and thin, no bigger than Charlie herself. It was only her coat, a voluminous purple thing, which had made her shadow so alarming.

The light seemed to bring the woman to her senses. 'This visit is hush-hush. No one must know,' she said, rubbing her forehead anxiously.

Charlie noticed a gash over one of her eyes. *She's had an accident, that's it. She's got amnesia and somehow lost her way,* she thought.

'My memory is in perfect working order, thank you very much,' said the woman, sharply. 'Why, I can remember the last millennium as if it was yesterday!'

She's mad, thought Charlie. *There's a mad woman in my bedroom!*

'Depends on what you mean by "mad". I *am* angry, yes. Very angry. But not crazy. I never felt saner in my whole life!'

She knows what I'm thinking! thought Charlie. *You're reading my mind, aren't you?*

'Well, of course I am! That's what Seers do. Look dear, we haven't got time for all this. Jack's in trouble.'

'Jack! What's the matter?' Charlie threw off the covers and scrambled down the bed. 'Where is he?'

The woman placed the tip of her index finger in the centre of her own forehead, near the wound. 'I kept track of him, here, for as long as I could. But then ... he was gone, just like that.'

Charlie stared at her. 'Who are you?' she asked

again. Close up, the woman looked like a tramp. Several dreadlocks hung in her matted grey hair and her brightly painted fingernails were cracked and dirty.

'*I* am Sybil Ayres, custodian of Fenstreet Time Junction,' said the woman. 'At least I am for the moment, if I don't get the sack. Thanks to this business I've been forced to close the place down. No one can go anywhere and now they're all up in arms, blaming me!'

'Time junction? What's that?' said Charlie.

'Everyone has to go through a junction, whichever direction they travel, past or future. That's how it works. It's a bit like a railway station. Only it's not.'

'I see.' *There's a woman in my room who runs a station for time travellers. This is brilliant!* Charlie gave herself a pinch to make sure she wasn't dreaming. 'And why did you close it down?'

'I had no choice!' Sybil's voice grew hysterical. 'That fiend, he has to be stopped! I keep telling them, "We all want to go where we please; it's important to follow our dreams", BUT we can't let *him* get away!'

'Ssshhh,' said Charlie. 'You'll wake Mum. Who's "him"?'

'Jago Flyn,' hissed Sybil.

'No!' *I never liked him.*

'He's not supposed to use any junction. But he breaks rules; he doesn't care. Only yesterday he slipped past me, heaven knows how! It's to do with Jack. He's got some kind of magical device that Flyn wants.'

The disc! thought Charlie.

'What disc?' said Sybil.

257

'It came in a package, in Jack's own handwriting. It made his computer work and Nan's cooker and the street lights! It burned the library book … all except the last chapter. Here, look!' Charlie bounced off the bed and rummaged under a pile of dirty clothes. '*The Seven Wonders of the World*. It's a bit of a mess, I'm afraid.'

'Good lord!' Sybil poked a bony finger through the conical hole in the book and turned to the last chapter. She let out a gasp and sat back down in the chair. 'This explains everything … It's been found. The Pharos mirror!'

'I knew it! His parents died in the ruins. I thought it was too much of a coincidence.'

Sybil shook her head. 'No such thing as coincidence. The time must be right. The light was waiting to be found, waiting for a new Magus.'

'Jack's a Magus?' exclaimed Charlie. She wasn't entirely sure what the title meant, but it sounded impressive.

'Yes. A fledgling, of course. But it's in his blood. Oh dear, this is worse than I thought.'

'Why?'

'He's carrying part of a time junction. The Pharos lighthouse used to be like Fenstreet.'

'No way! This is great!'

'Not, not, not! If Flyn gets his hands on the mirror, he'll have his own portal.' Sybil's shoulders began to shake. 'He must have drawn on the mirror's power to get past me. He's charming, a manipulator. He's gained Jack's trust!'

'It wasn't your fault.'

'It *was*. I should have seen him coming!'

Charlie pressed a fistful of tissues into Sybil's hand, and as the old woman dabbed her tears, she couldn't help noticing how remarkable her eyes were. They looked bright as crystals, glamorous even.

'I *was* quite a catch once,' said Sybil, batting her wet lashes. 'I loved him … but he betrayed me too!' she wailed.

'What! You loved Jago Flyn. Ughh!'

'Nooo! Not him exactly. Oh, it's hard to explain. He was different then,' sobbed Sybil. 'His name was Seth – a fine man, a Magus in his own right. It's the lives he's led since then that are beyond redemption. Flyn is his worst one yet.'

Charlie's mouth fell open. 'Hang on. How old are you?'

'I don't see what my age has got to do with it.'

'How old?'

'Well,' Sybil patted her untidy hair. 'Eons, if you must know.'

'What's an eon?'

'A long time, an eternity … more than two thousand years. There, satisfied?'

'Whoa!' Charlie sat back down on the bed with a thump. 'And Flyn, I mean Seth – whoever – he's really old too, right?'

'As the hills,' sniffed Sybil. 'And meaner than a bucketful of pythons. The punishment only made him worse.'

'What punishment?'

'They wiped his memory of his magic. Most of it anyhow,' said Sybil. 'He could choose to die, of course, but he doesn't. When one existence ends, he moves on to another.'

'What did he do?' asked Charlie, anxiously.

'Killed a man, a genius.' Sybil hung her head. 'The maker of the mirror. Archimedes.'

'That's impossible.' Charlie looked stunned. 'A soldier killed him when his city was invaded. It says so in this book.'

'That's right. He was drawing circles in the sand, working out some great mathematical puzzle. He wouldn't budge, even when the soldier told him to.'

'So what's Seth got to do with it?'

'He was there. He used his magic in the most despicable way. We read thoughts – we're not supposed to plant them. But that's what he did. He channelled every ounce of his rage into that hothead to *make* him cut the old man down.'

'Why?'

'Because of the mirror! Sometimes it was used as a weapon of war. It burnt a ship with his son on it, another soldier.'

'Revenge?'

Sybil nodded sadly. 'His grief turned to anger. Wouldn't surprise me if he thinks the mirror is his, that destiny owes it to him.'

Charlie got up and grabbed her clothes. 'I've got to help Jack.'

'That's why I'm here.' Sybil gave Charlie a searching look. 'Can I trust you to be brave?'

'Of course!'

'I found you because you're the only one thinking of Jack.'

'I can't be. What about Nan?'

Sybil shook her head. 'I should have acted earlier. I lost track of her too. A Seer is not supposed to meddle but … she was right. It's time for me to break the rules.'

Sybil touched Charlie's forehead and then her own. 'Hold tight.'

★★★

Charlie felt her whole body jerk forwards and the next thing she knew, she was standing fully dressed in the driveway outside her house. Above her, the stars twinkled quietly in an ebony sky.

'Sorry,' said Sybil, who seemed to be gasping for breath as much as Charlie herself. 'That was a bit fierce. Go get your bike. Let's make the journey more comfortable.'

Charlie whirled round several times. She couldn't see the old woman anywhere.

'Don't just stand there. I said go!'

Charlie tore off to the garden shed where her bike was chained to a hefty metal post. She fumbled with the padlock.

'Eighteen gears. Very nice,' said Sybil. 'Yes, put that on, you're going to need it.'

'I was just about to!' said Charlie, reaching for her cycle helmet. *Where are you?*

'In your thoughts, silly girl. Now get going! Cycle downhill, fast as you can. I'm on my way to Fenstreet. I'll open the time lock to let you through.'

Charlie skidded out of the drive and pedalled furiously down the street until the houses on either side became a blur. As she approached the T-junction at the bottom, her hand hovered over the brake. 'Left or right?' she asked.

'Straight ahead,' ordered Sybil. 'Two ticks, I'm nearly ready.'

'But there's a house the other side. I'll crash!'

'Nonsense. There, it's unlocked. Where do you want to go?'

'Wakeham!'

'Right. Make the most of this, my dear. It may well be my last piece of magic.'

Ahead, a drunk – the last one to leave The Feathers that night – swaggered across the main road.

'Look out!' yelled Charlie, swerving wildly around him.

'Oi!' he hollered back. 'Bleedin' maniac. What yer doin'?'

'Whoa!' As the bike hit the pavement on the other side, Charlie braced herself, half expecting to plough through the garden wall in front of her. But instead the bike reared up, soared over the house and continued to climb. She changed down a gear, pedalling madly to maintain the upward momentum, hardly able to take in what was happening. Piece by piece, a vast suspension bridge was forming in the night sky. Giant girders that looked like twisted metal rope uncoiled around her, shooting into the distance with a hissing sound.

'A – blimmin – mazing!' she gasped. She not only had a bird's eye view of Morton Muxloe, but the surrounding countryside looked as clear as a night time satellite map studded with the bright lights of the towns and villages beyond. She glanced back at the drunk and waved in excitement. 'Sorry 'bout that!'

He didn't respond. He was too busy pouring the contents of his beer can into the gutter, wondering how on earth a girl on a red bike could disappear into thin air.

CHAPTER 34

Jack half-opened his eyes and groaned. The control room was a blur and a hundred hammers seemed to pound in his head. He tried sitting up, but his arms and legs wouldn't budge. Pi, in his anger, had turned up the voltage on the stun gun, delivering a shock twice as strong as the one he'd inflicted on Lonsdale.

Darkness closed in and Jack slipped back into a strange unconscious state, aware that he was dreaming, yet unable to snap out of it. Above him, the sky was a blameless blue and all around he could hear the gentle slap of waves. He was in Tattoo's boat, anchored in the middle of a turquoise sea.

'Wake up, Jack … Don't let go … You can't forget, I won't let you!' The dream voice was Lily's, but he couldn't respond. The bobbing boat made him drowsy and the hum of faraway traffic sucked him back down.

On the boat's prow, a string of gold letters glistened in the sunlight. Tattoo, it seemed, had come up with a name at last. '*Phantom*,' read Jack. And though fast asleep, he heard himself say it out loud. Why had the thug chosen that? Exactly the same name as his parents' boat?

Before he could figure it out, the sea splashed his face and a flicker of something blue shot under the hull. Without another thought, he got up, planted one foot on the prow and plunged in after it. Dream or no dream, he didn't care. He'd found the Pharos dive site and there, darting away from him, was the mirror.

Kicking furiously, he made a swipe for it. His fist closed around nothing and as he spun round to see where it had gone, a colossal stone head rose through the gloom below him. Somewhere out of the corner of his eye, he saw the disc shoot away like a blue fish. Then with horror he felt himself being sucked down.

Two vast stone eyes drew level with his and his feet gave up kicking.

'Am I dead?' he asked.

The majestic face of Isis seemed to look straight through him. 'No, Jack. Never was a child so loved. They exchanged their lives for yours, so you could find your purpose. It's time to wake up. You're a Magus.'

The tip of his forefinger pulsed fiercely and he felt himself catapult forwards … 'Aaaah-Alpha!'

Heart thumping, he sat bolt upright. The lights on the control panel came sharply into focus. Wide awake at last, he scoured the shadow-filled room. Alpha had gone.

He shook his head, trying to clear the strange images which still seemed to swirl around him. Then, stiff and thirsty, he stumbled to the sink. His stomach rolled alarmingly and with every step the hum of the machinery seemed to grow louder. If he wasn't careful, he'd pass out again. He downed a cup of water and sat for a while rocking and hugging his knees at the bottom of the stairs until, gradually, the nausea wore off and the symphony of noises faded.

A little less shakily this time, he got up to look for his rucksack. It was behind the sofa, tipped upside down with the contents scattered across the floor. *Pi, little creep!* They'd got the mirror. So what else could that lowlife possibly want? The money he'd brought?

Apparently not. Retrieving his wallet and cash, Jack thanked his lucky stars that Indigo was beyond Pi's reach. To think he'd almost given him to Jago. All his belongings appeared to be here except … his fists went up behind his head and he kicked the table. His father's pen had gone.

Outside, the stars blazed brightly and the waves crashed like cymbals on the rocks. Gulping at the fresh air, Jack hurried across the patch of green in front of the lighthouse to the stone steps. Not a trace of Tattoo's boat could be seen in the long beam from the lamp.

He rubbed at his fingers to stop the annoying tingling which had started the moment he'd stepped outside. *They set you up. You should have fought harder!* he fumed. Jago could be anywhere by now, maybe even in another time and place.

In the distance the lights of Wakeham winked silently, dark hills rising on either side. What if Alpha had gone with him? Jack hung his head. Why did he follow that bully when it obviously made him miserable?

He kicked at a stone. Nothing was ever black and white, Nan would say. Maybe Jago hadn't always been so mean and Alpha had served him gladly once … The tie must have been strong to keep him so loyal. But even if it was his duty, as Jago insisted, he must be close to breaking point.

A seagull took off from the landing stage below, clapping its wings together noisily. As it skimmed across the surf, Jack thought of Bill and the magic which had led to his transformation. Jago had got it so wrong. He and Alpha had worked together. It had been the trust between them, not simply his own will, which had made it all possible. *You don't need a whistle to control him,* he thought. *A proper Magus would –*

The tingling in his fingers had grown so strong it interrupted his thoughts. He looked down and his heart gave a thud. If Jago could read his palm now, what would he make of this? A tiny mark, exactly the same size and shape as the symbol on the mirror, was imprinted on the tip of his forefinger.

Bewildered, he stared out at the sea. Had he touched the mirror in his dream? Had Alpha somehow reached him while he'd slept? For a second it seemed the only explanation.

Then, his memory did a sort of somersault and raced back to the extraordinary moment before his last leap, when he'd calmly let go of the mirror. Of course … so much had happened, but now he remembered it clearly: a stinging sensation, like he'd touched a red-hot iron.

A thrill ran through him. It felt as if suddenly he'd

been transformed too. He glanced back at the red and white tower. That place had taught him a hard lesson, yet a strange thought had just occurred to him. If Jago hadn't been there to snatch the mirror, none of this would have happened at all.

He stretched out his forefinger and traced a trembling pattern over the hills around Wakeham. 'I know you're watching,' he whispered. 'We've got to get it back. Whatever it takes. You want to be free of him, don't you?'

As he finished speaking the wind changed direction, flinging white caps of surf into the air. It carried with it an unmistakeable sound: a long, melancholy howl.

CHAPTER 35

'What the heck was that?' Charlie freewheeled off the end of Sybil's bridge and came skidding to a halt. She'd arrived on the quayside at Wakeham. 'Sybil,' she hissed, 'can you hear me? Where's Jack?'

'Close. Very close. But some other magic has taken over, far stronger than mine.' Sybil's disembodied voice sounded frantic. 'Be careful, dear. I'm shutting the time lock down. If anyone catches me, I'm for it. I have to go.'

'Hang on! You can't just leave me here. What am I supposed to do now?' But the bridge had vanished and Charlie's question went unanswered.

Nervously, she wheeled her bike across the bumpy paving stones and propped it against the wall outside the Lock and Quay. Removing her cycle helmet, she looked around. Above the fish and chip shop, the curtains twitched. A middle-aged woman in striped pyjamas stood watching her with one hand clamped to her mouth.

Another spine-chilling howl echoed round the harbour. 'Oo, I don't think I like this at all,' muttered Charlie.

The woman at the window looked terrified too. Following the direction of her gaze, Charlie's eyes settled on the bus shelter on the far side of the quay. From the shadows, two amber eyes met hers. *Man oh man, that's all I need. Bet that's Flyn's dog.*

Alpha emerged. With his eyes fixed on her face, he sniffed at the ground.

'O-kay … that's no dog.' Remembering the gash on Blunt's leg, Charlie slowly put one foot behind the other. 'Easy does it, there's a good boy. You – stay – right – there.'

But Alpha didn't do as he was told. Before she could take another step he sprang forwards and ran flat out, covering the ground between them at lightning speed. Every sensible thought flew from Charlie's mind. She screamed, started to run for her bike, then stopped because the wolf had immediately changed direction to cut her off.

Without any clear idea of where she was going, she fled the other way and, before she knew it, her feet had carried her onto the wooden jetty. 'Help, someone!' she wailed. She'd chosen the worst escape route possible: ahead there was only the sea.

Four paws pounded after her. It was too late to turn back. With a gasp of panic, Charlie flung herself into the nearest boat. 'Come on, come on!' Her fingers felt like sausages rather than parts of her hands, but at last the mooring rope came undone. She tugged at the boat's starter cord. The engine fired, then promptly died.

'Noooo!'

In desperation, Charlie picked up a metal hook which lay at her feet and as Alpha bounded towards her, she hurled it at him.

The wolf stumbled and let out a yelp.

'Serves you right!' she screamed, yanking the starter cord again. The engine only spluttered and the boat drifted aimlessly into the harbour. 'Look what you've done! Oooo, this is hopeless. I'm no use to anyone stuck out here!'

Alpha stood perfectly still, watching her every move, and when the engine failed a third and fourth time, he lifted his nose to sniff at the wind. The rattle of rigging grew louder, the sign at the Lock and Quay swung wildly and Charlie's bike toppled over with a crash.

'Oh, for crying out loud! I s'pose you think that's funny,' she yelled. 'Well, you haven't won yet! Wait till I find Jack. He's a Magus, right, so you better watch out. You and that lowlife Flyn are in for a big –'

Alpha had locked his eyes on the boat. A flash of light ran along the hull, a puff of smoke rose from the prow and the whole thing spun three hundred and sixty degrees, knocking Charlie clean off her feet.

'Whoa, help!' Face down in a pile of stinky fishing nets, Charlie clung on for dear life. A fierce rocking had begun and, for several seconds, it felt as if the boat was about to disintegrate. Then, with a terrifying jolt, it surged forwards, sending her and the fishing nets sliding under one of the benches.

When, eventually, she managed to crawl out, she gazed at the receding figure of Alpha. 'Hey … wait a

271

minute.' Her head whipped round to check where the boat was heading. In front of the Pentland lighthouse, a tiny speck waved at her.

A shriek exploded out of her and she leapt up, waving back madly. 'Jack! Hey Jack, it's me!' *Oh my God, he's never gonna believe this!* 'Guess what, Jack? I got it all wrong. The wolf – he's on our side – he's making the wind blow!'

The boat zipped forwards, forcing her back down with a bump. Beaming from ear to ear, Charlie hung over the edge, playing with the flumes of white spray which rose like wings on either side. And it was only then, when she was hardly looking, that she noticed the row of dark squiggles on the prow. Still smouldering, a name had been scorched into the wood: *Phantom.*

Several more excited shrieks ripped through the night air. Jack was going to love this. He couldn't have come up with a better name if he'd chosen it himself.

★★★

Above the fish and chip shop, the curtains fell gently together as the owner, Mrs Mortimer, went to lie down.

Shutting her eyes very tight, she tried to get her facts straight. A ghost child, who'd appeared out of nowhere on a red racing bike, had just stolen Tattoo's boat … which thanks to a freak wind conjured by … yes, a wolf, was even now carrying her poor tormented soul to the lighthouse.

Mrs Mortimer opened one eye to make sure she

wasn't dreaming. A howling wolf and a shrieking child! She gave a dramatic shudder. Wakeham and its lighthouse was haunted, of that there was no doubt. She couldn't wait to tell her customers.

CHAPTER 36

'So it's a virus that causes all the trouble?' said Charlie.

Jack nodded at her. 'Yep, it affected the ship's GPS as well as the lighthouse.'

'And Flyn's behind it?'

'Uh-huh. At first, he said all he wanted was the mirror. Then he got really mad and …'

'What?'

'I've just thought. I left the mirror spinning …'

'So?'

'It's all my fault. I'm the one who told him about the ship. Then I showed him exactly what to do!'

'Hang on a minute. First of all, it's not your fault there are bad people in the world! And second of all –' Charlie wagged a finger at him '– that whole plan was festering in his nasty rotten mind before he saw the future. Didn't he say he'd got people working on it? Yeah, right. Never underestimate a maniac.'

A smile crept over Jack's face. Nothing could contain his delight at having his straight-talking friend beside him again. They were returning to Wakeham, the boat's engine rumbling noisily at their backs. He'd managed to start it first time, laughing and shrugging at Charlie's raised eyebrows. Her arrival in Tattoo's newly-named boat had made him feel invincible.

From the moment she'd thrown her arms around him, Charlie had been firing non-stop questions, eager to know everything, especially about Alpha, who had earned her undying love. Jack, in turn, had listened spellbound to the details of her encounter with Sybil, turning white at the story of Seth and his son.

Jago had hidden so much of his past he could hardly take it in. Talk about mind games. It was terrifying to think that a murderous thought could be planted in another man's head. Now he understood Jago's black mood on the train and why he'd insisted on calling the mirror a death ray. It *had* destroyed lives.

Jack replayed the journey in his head. 'So Fenstreet's a time junction. No wonder it disappeared from the departure board! We went through it twice. There was an old woman in a purple coat and Jago did this trick –'

'That's her!' interrupted Charlie. 'Sybil! She reckons he tapped into your magic somehow.'

'And they know each other, you say?'

'Yep, apparently she loved him once. Weird, huh?'

'Then why pull a stunt like that? Right in front of her? I don't get it. He could have been caught.'

'He needed to impress you. By showing off his own magic, he got you to trust him, right? Enough to let him see the mirror. And meanwhile Sybil had to close Fenstreet and all the other junctions. She could lose her job over this. So he managed to get at her – and her world. They chucked him out, remember? All the chaos probably suits him fine.'

Jack nodded slowly. 'You should be a detective. You saw through him from the start.'

'Yeah, well … He was hardly gonna get the red carpet treatment. He stole my best friend.'

'Never! You've no idea how often I wished you were there.'

'Really?' Grateful for the darkness, Charlie looked down, blushing. 'I didn't see through the magpie though. Bad mistake letting him go. Nan was furious.'

'How could you have known?'

'I dunno. But Nan was on to him. It's like she already knew.'

They entered the harbour. While Charlie chatted on, Jack scanned the streets leading off the quay, hoping for some sign of a blue Beetle. He couldn't imagine how frantic Nan must be.

'Bet the magic comes from her,' said Charlie, guessing his thoughts and kindly patting his arm. 'Hey, maybe it's like ginger hair – it skips generations. I'm the only carrot top in our family since Grandpa George! Here, show me that mark again.'

Jack turned his palm upwards to reveal the tiny symbol on his finger.

'Sign of a true Magus!'

'I dunno, Charlie …'

'A is for Alpha, right?'

'And Archimedes.'

'And the number one.'

'*Numero uno!*' laughed Jack.

'Exactly. Alpha and the Magus! A and M. Sybil says it's in your blood. I reckon the mirror came to you so you could learn to be one.'

Jack grinned. Until now he'd hardly dared to think about his dream. If Charlie was right, he had a great deal to learn. It was exciting and scary all at the same time.

Charlie looked at him thoughtfully. 'If you ask me, that's why Alpha's stayed with Flyn. To keep you safe. He has to make it *look* like he's on his side – till you're ready.'

'Alpha's not like that. He doesn't pretend,' said Jack. And as soon as he'd said it, he felt a rush of protection for the wolf. He wasn't like any other animus. He'd never been human before, like Pi or Bill. Hermes hadn't borrowed another soul; he'd transformed the wolf with his own generous spirit. For every Magus, not just one. 'He had to give Jago a chance,' he said.

'You're kidding. Why?'

'So he could learn too.'

'Ha! He's gonna learn all right. Big time!' said Charlie. Then, noticing Jack's far-off expression, she added, 'You're not thinking he'll change, are you?'

'Nope.' Jack cut the engine and they floated silently alongside the jetty.

'Good! You've got to get the mirror back. Then we can think about the ship. That's still way in the future and …'

Charlie trailed off. Jack had already leapt out to

secure the boat and didn't seem to be listening. With the same distant look, he said, 'We have to find Jago.'

'Okay. So, now what?'

'Shhh!' Jack's eyes were glued on the hills behind the village. 'I think we've got ourselves a guide. Look!'

Charlie screwed up her nose. 'It's Alpha, isn't it? Where? I can't see him.'

'There! See where the path wiggles uphill? Follow it to the right past that big tree, the one near the green barn. He's in that muddy gateway. Come on! He wants us to hurry.'

Charlie didn't move. 'You must have x-ray vision or something. I can see the path but … there isn't a barn. And how do you know it's muddy?'

'What does it matter? Let's go! If anyone knows where to find Jago, it's him.'

Together they raced across the quay, through a low iron gate and up the footpath which zigzagged along the edge of the cliffs. Jack took one last look at the lighthouse, then, as dawn turned the hills a velvety green, he plunged down a grassy track away from the sea.

'A-mazing!' said Charlie, puffing and panting to keep up. 'You've never done anything like that before.'

'Like what?'

'That thing you did back there. Hey, slow down, will you?'

'What thing?'

'You know.' Charlie tapped the centre of her forehead. 'It's how Sybil found me.'

Jack stopped dead. 'What *are* you on about?'

Doubling over, hands on hips, Charlie nodded at the hills ahead. 'Still no barn,' she said. 'But you saw it like you were there already. You're a Seer, Jack! You tuned into Alpha's mind, looked through his eyes. You knew what he was thinking!'

Jack stared at her dumbfounded. She was right. He'd always been able to sense Alpha's presence, but this was completely different. For the first time he'd been able to tell exactly where the wolf was – and see what he could see.

'I didn't realise I was doing it,' he said.

'That's the whole point! You don't even have to think. It's a gift; you were born with it.'

Charlie nudged Jack in the ribs and barged past him. 'Alpha reads your mind too, of course. The name on the boat – now that was neat. Come on, what are you waiting for?'

CHAPTER 37

Alpha kept well ahead of them, testing Jack's newfound skill to its limit. Several times he thought he'd lost the wolf for good, then a landmark in the distance would rush at him – a tall yew in front of a cottage, a church spire, a bridge over a stream – and for a few seconds, no more, it was like jumping through the lens of a powerful microscope. The details of Alpha's location became so clear Jack could see cobwebs in the grass where he was walking, hear a cockerel crow in a barn, even catch the scent of washing on a line.

A mile or so on, they found themselves looking down on Dunton, where Jack's train journey with Jago had come to such an abrupt end. Normally, the familiar sight of the town's Ferris wheel would have filled him with happiness, but Jack felt his mood darken. Why had Jago retraced his footsteps here?

On the outskirts of the town, they stopped at a petrol station to buy breakfast and while Charlie drifted to the sweet counter in search of chocolate, he tried again to focus on Alpha's whereabouts.

Outside, the early morning traffic thundered past and several people stood chatting at a bus stop. He hoped the wolf was keeping a low profile. The last thing they needed was a scene like the one at the railway station. He replayed the moment the detective had sprinted along the platform, gun in hand. Except this time, instead of watching from the train, he was on the platform too and when Alpha jumped clear, the barrel of the gun seemed to swing and point at him.

Bang. A new image from an entirely different location reared into view – a machine of some kind, an ugly, yellow, rectangular thing with two piston arms and a flat roof lined with giant blades. He felt the mark on his finger prickle. Was Alpha in some kind of danger? He could hear the wolf's heart pounding as if it was his own.

The sound of heavy boots came close and a chain whipped across the ground. Then a raw pain hit the back of his throat. His windpipe tightened until he began to lose focus …

'You all right?' Charlie tugged anxiously at his sleeve.

Instantly, the sensation faded. With a swift nod, Jack grabbed the chocolate bars she'd chosen and walked to the cash desk where a bald man sat reading a newspaper. 'Is there a junkyard near here?' he asked abruptly.

'Auto breakers, you mean? Sure.' The man took his time to fold up the paper and leant across the counter. 'Bit young for car spares, aren't we? What you after?'

'Just some old tyres,' Jack replied. 'To make a swing for her.' He nodded over at Charlie.

'I see. Couple of scavengers, eh?' The man winked at Charlie. 'Well then, Slater's the place.'

'And where's that?' said Jack, trying not to sound impatient.

'Through the industrial estate over there, by the canal. Not far, 'bout ten minutes, I'd say. Watch that main road though. Lunatic drivers this time of day.'

'Thanks.' Jack slammed a fistful of coins on the counter.

'Won't be open yet, mind. Late starters that lot, not like some of us … Oi, hang about, don't forget your change!'

But Jack was already out of the door, dragging Charlie across the forecourt after him.

'What's going on? I don't want a swing!' she protested.

'I know! Shut up, Charlie, and just walk, will you!' Steering her in and out of the traffic, Jack turned left down a wide road lined with factories and offices.

'It's Alpha, isn't it? You looked like you were being half throttled back there. What's the matter? Is he okay? Jack? Talk to me.'

'I don't know!' exploded Jack.

'Sorry! I only –'

'Honestly, Charlie. You've no idea how hard this stuff is! It comes in such short bursts. I get flashes – bits and pieces – then "bam!" it's all gone and I wonder if I'm right or not.'

'Okay, okay, calm down! You're doing just fine.'

'Yeah, right!'

'I mean it. Look, you got us this far!'

'On a road to a junkyard! Not much of a Seer.'

'You are! It takes practice, that's all. You're picking it up fast and you're doing it *without* the mirror. Who knows, maybe it's a good thing it was taken away.'

Jack stared at her, speechless. Of all the crazy, stupid things … he pulled himself up short. Hadn't he had a similar thought at the lighthouse?

'I'm not saying what Flyn did was right,' Charlie said hastily. 'All I mean is you've discovered something – something you didn't know you had.' She stuck her fist in the air, superman style.

Something right under my nose, thought Jack. He glanced down at Alpha's seal on his finger and smiled at Charlie's cleverness. Even though they were the same age, sometimes she seemed a lot wiser. Then again, sometimes she didn't. She was now beating off imaginary attackers with a kung fu manoeuvre. He gave her a shove.

'Come on,' he said. 'Alpha's chained up near some big machine. We've got to find him. Fast.'

CHAPTER 38

At the end of the industrial estate, they reached a rough road running alongside the canal. It led to a square of wasteland surrounded by a high wooden fence on which a blue sign announced: 'Slater's Auto Breakers. Quality parts for all makes and models. Welcome to car heaven!'

Two heavy iron gates at the entrance hung ajar and on the ground nearby lay the pieces of a broken padlock and chain. Jack and Charlie exchanged glances. Taking care not to disturb the rusting hinges, Jack eased himself through the gap and motioned at Charlie to follow.

Inside, a hush hung over everything. Even the birds seemed to have forgotten their early morning chatter. Hundreds of dead and broken-down cars were strewn everywhere, some rusting among the grass and weeds, others stacked on top of each other in tottering heaps. Jack couldn't help thinking it was more like a graveyard than heaven.

A twig crunched explosively under Charlie's foot. She froze, mouthed an apology and they took cover behind an old bus filled with batteries and bits of exhaust pipe.

In the centre of the yard, behind a Portakabin sales office, stood three semi-circular buildings made of corrugated iron: Nissen huts from the second world war which now served as workshops. Jack scanned the windows for signs of life. All were dark and empty. Nevertheless, something about the furthest building held his attention. He shut his eyes and the mark on his forefinger smarted. Alpha felt very close indeed.

He whispered this to Charlie and she nodded. Then her face fell. 'Over there, Jack, look!'

Beyond the buildings, surrounded by more piles of wrecked vehicles, was an ancient, yellow car crusher – the same machine Jack had glimpsed earlier. A flattened slab that had once been a pickup truck lay spewed out of one side, and on the platform that led into its gaping mouth sat its next victim. The car's wheels were missing and the entire front end had been burnt out, but Jack would have recognised the make anywhere. It was a Beetle. A blue one.

He was vaguely aware of Charlie saying something and trying to hold him back, but it felt like a switch had flicked in his brain. He couldn't stop himself. He got up, wriggled free of her grasp and tore down the muddy track.

Coincidence, that's all it is, he told himself. There were plenty of old classics that colour … hundreds probably. It couldn't be –

No such thing as coincidence, my dear.

As Nan's words played through his mind, he slowed to a shuffling sort of run, went a few more paces, then stopped. Two black and white dice dangled from the Beetle's rearview mirror.

'Noooo!' he screamed.

His legs buckled beneath him and he sank to his knees. 'What have I done?' he muttered. Was this why Alpha had brought him here? To show him the consequences of his actions? The mangled wreckage wouldn't be here if he hadn't gone and left her.

'Nan!' he cried, and suddenly he was seeing the world through a prism of tears.

In the long silence that followed, a shadow fell across him. 'Now then,' said a familiar voice, 'we'll have none of this.'

Too numb to move, Jack went on staring at the dice. They looked so fragile and foolish hanging there. Why weren't they burnt too? He dug his fingers in the mud. 'Where is she?' he muttered.

'How should I know? This has nothing to do with me. For heaven's sake, get up!'

Two hands grasped Jack from behind and the next thing he knew, he was being hoisted to his feet. He wrinkled his nose, overpowered by the stench of whisky. 'Lemme go!'

Jago did as he was asked, turning Jack to face him. He looked haggard and grey and his eyes had sunk deep in their sockets. 'Only a coward would tamper with an old woman's car. And whatever else I may be, I'm *not* a coward. Your school bully did this.'

'Blunt?' exclaimed Jack.

Jago nodded. Half drunk, he looked as if he'd aged

by a hundred years. 'Pi saw him go into the garage. Schoolboy revenge, I'm afraid. Way of the world.'

'Revenge? Ha! Well, you'd know all about that!'

Jago looked taken aback. 'You're referring to Archimedes, I assume. I wonder how you came by that little tale.'

Jack said nothing. Jago could assume whatever he liked. He hoped Charlie was keeping her head down.

'Well, I don't deny it,' said Jago, swaying slightly. 'I told you the mirror was destructive. It killed my son.'

'So? People die! I know how that feels. I lost my parents, remember? But I didn't take it out on everyone else.'

'Oh, is that right? Then what was the storm about, hmm? You should be careful how you direct your energy. It has consequences.'

'I didn't cause the storm!'

'Not entirely, no. I gave the instruction, of course. But you – you doubled its strength, caused havoc beyond anything I ever intended.' Jago raised an eyebrow. 'I'd say we make a good team.'

Jack was speechless. Jago was twisting everything, behaving as if he'd done nothing wrong at all. Why was he even here? What did he want?

In the cracked wing mirror of an old Mercedes truck, he caught a glimpse of ginger hair beneath a black beanie. Charlie had just disappeared via a side door into the farthest workshop.

'You see, I've been dealt a bad hand,' Jago continued. 'I can't change the past and I'm sick to death of this present. If you'd seen the things I've seen, led the lives I've led, you'd understand. I want a different future, a new beginning.

'I have a confession to make, Jack. I too overlooked something right under my nose. My old self lost a son, but I think fate has sent someone in his place.'

Jago's yellowing fingers unfurled. In the middle of his palm lay Jack's silver pen. 'If I could rewrite the last twenty-four hours, I would. Here, this is yours.'

Jack gazed down in astonishment. Jago's hand, he noticed, shook ever so slightly. Did he really mean he was sorry? 'You can't undo what happened,' he said. 'No one can erase time.'

'Ah, but you're wrong,' cried Jago. 'You're a Magus, my boy. It's within your power to do exactly that.'

'Tsche, tsche, tsche.'

Overhead, an insane screeching broke out. A pair of black and white wings swooped down and suddenly the pen was gone.

'Pi!' roared Jago, balling his empty hand into a fist. 'Damn it, Pi! Bring it back. NOW!'

Pi's boyish form materialised on top of the tallest heap of cars. 'It's mine!' he shrieked. 'You said I could have it!'

'Thundering idiot …'

'I did everything you wanted,' wailed Pi. 'Everything!'

'I don't have time for this. Get down at once!'

Pi shook his head furiously. 'So it's a new beginning, is it? You said you'd get us out of here. You and me!'

'I'm warning you.'

Pi stamped his foot and the pile of cars teetered below him. 'Just cos the mirror won't work! That's why you need him. He's not a Magus.'

'Shut up, Pi.'

'He's not your son either! He's just a … a puppet!' Pi began dancing a crazy jig like a marionette.

Jago lifted his hand.

'No! Don't!' Pi flung himself down.

A groan of metal erupted from the base of the tower and the topmost car tipped forwards. Pi slid across its roof and down over the bonnet. With acrobatic skill, he managed to grab hold of the car's bumper.

'Little fool. Use your wings!' bellowed Jago.

But Pi didn't bother to transform. He simply clung on, his feet dangling uselessly. Jack could see he was crying.

Jago raised his hand again, his fingers trembling with rage. 'You had your chance. You bring this on yourself.'

'Nooo!' wailed Pi.

'Anima …' began Jago.

'Stop. Please! Don't unmake me. Not now, I –'

'Animus …'

'I'll be good.'

'Animal!' Jago snatched back his hand as if tugging an invisible rope.

'Aaaaa!' Arching his spine in pain, Pi let out a bloodcurdling scream. As the noise echoed round the yard, he clutched at his throat. A ball of bright orange vapour had erupted from his mouth.

Jago inhaled deeply and the ball sped towards him,

illuminating his face like a grisly waxwork. For one horrible moment Jack thought he was actually going to swallow the thing, but before it touched him he breathed out sharply. The orange ball sank to the ground, turning the soil black where it landed.

'Tsche, tsche, tsche …'

Jack looked up to see the magpie racing towards him, claws outstretched. He ducked and felt Jago's sleeve sweep over him. 'Out of my sight!' roared Jago, and a white light exploded from his hand.

The magpie careered into the sky, spinning and shrieking. Jack watched as it fought in vain to recover itself. When finally it disappeared beyond the ridges of clouds, he shuddered. 'You – you took away his soul,' he said.

'What of it?' Jago stood doubled over, panting. 'Oh come on, don't tell me you're sorry. He was jealous and spiteful. We're better off without him.'

He straightened up, gripping Jack's shoulder for support. 'Now then,' he said, raking his long hair off his temples. 'Let me fetch the mirror. That *is* why you're here, isn't it? We met for a reason, Jack. I think we can be of assistance to each other. Partners. After all, a new Magus needs instruction, does he not?'

He began walking towards the workshop.

'Wait!' Jack's heart thumped. Charlie was still in there.

'Well?' As Jago turned on his heels, a slight breeze stirred his trench coat and a wisp of dust rose up from the blackened soil between them.

'I, er …'

'What is it? Spit it out.'

'Alpha,' said Jack. 'Where is he?'

'Why, here in the yard, of course. But you know that; he led you here.'

'I need to see him.'

'All in good time. He'll come when I call.'

'No. I need to see him *now*.'

Jago regarded him coolly, and the moment seemed to last an eternity before he said, 'Very well, if you insist.' With a flick of the wrist, he produced the whistle.

A vision flashed into Jack's mind – a pit of some kind, small and suffocating. It was followed immediately by an insane high-pitched buzzing. The whistle sounded like a giant mosquito locked inside his skull.

A chain rattled behind him and he spun round.

'Alpha!'

The wolf stood barely a yard away, tethered to the corner of the crusher. He'd been hiding beneath the machine all along. His great head drooped with exhaustion and long skeins of saliva hung from his jowls. He tried to move forwards, but the chain was already at full stretch and jerked him back.

Jack was at his side in an instant. 'Easy, boy, it's okay. I'm here.' *I made it, thanks to you,* he added silently.

As he touched the ruff of fur on Alpha's neck, the amber eyes closed and before Jack knew what he was doing his arm had stolen over Alpha's shoulder. To his surprise, the full weight of the wolf's body fell against him. Something was very wrong. His coat felt sticky as if

291

covered in oil. Jack caught sight of his own fingers. They were red with blood.

'What have you done to him?' he cried. A deep cut extended several inches across the base of Alpha's neck, and where the chain bit into it, the open wound oozed blood.

'Alpha must know his place,' said Jago. 'I called him last night and he didn't come.'

'So you beat him!'

'I will *not* be ignored, Jack. It was a lesson – three lashes of the strap, no more. Now move away. He isn't a pet.'

As if to prove his point, Jago blew into the whistle again and Alpha cringed down on his belly, whining.

Jack's eardrums buzzed painfully. *This has gone far enough,* he told the wolf. *You did your best. He's not going to change. I won't let him hurt you any more.*

The mark on his forefinger stung like never before. Without pausing to think, he reached out his hand and a white light flashed in front of him. The whistle flew from Jago's grasp and he staggered backwards.

'What the hell are you playing at?'

'Let him go! You don't own him. He wasn't made for this and you know it!'

Alpha was on his feet once more, every muscle in his body quivering, his ears pricked towards the workshop door. Adrenalin pumping, Jack held his breath.

Right on cue, Charlie emerged.

'Run!' he yelled. 'Charlie, get out of here!'

But Charlie didn't appear to hear him. Either that

or she had plans of her own, because she was hurrying between the mountains of cars towards them, her face alight with excitement.

'How the devil –' spluttered Jago. 'Pah! Is this the best you can do, Jack? A slip of a girl …'

'One true friend is all it takes,' said Charlie. Jack saw the hint of a wink in her eye. 'Tut, tut. Bin drinking, have we? Looks like world war three back there. What's wrong? Run out of tricks? Guess you won't be needing this, then.'

With a cheeky grin, Charlie produced the mirror from the back pocket of her jeans.

'Why, you little –' Jago's rage exploded and he stormed towards her.

Charlie reacted quickly, dodging first one way, then the other. She managed to wrong-foot him and in the split second it took him to recover, she threw the mirror low and hard.

Alpha, who had been watching her every move, flung himself against the chain, eyes flashing. A rush of wind rumbled through the yard and the mirror soared upwards, turning over and over in the light. Jack's mouth curled upwards too. The mixture of Charlie's audacity and Alpha's magic had produced the perfect result, delivering the mirror neatly into his outstretched hand.

'Thanks!' he called.

'No problem!' yelled Charlie who'd clambered onto the crusher and was tugging at the door of the Beetle. 'Watch out!'

A blast of light zipped past Jack's cheek and boomed against the side of a van. On turning, he saw Jago thundering towards him, his hand outstretched as if he meant to pluck out his heart. He hit the ground fast, rolling to one side. There was another ear-splitting crash and glass shattered over his head.

Covered in pieces of windscreen, he scrambled up.

'Too slow, much too slow,' roared Jago, raising his hand to deliver another blast.

This time he struck Jack squarely on the shoulder. First one foot, then the other left the ground, then his whole body twisted in the air. He crashed down, sprawling headlong into a pile of rusting hub caps.

For a moment he lay still, all the breath knocked out of him, conscious only of a splintering pain tearing down his right arm. He gripped the mirror tight, willing himself not to pass out. Its warmth radiated through his hand and he flexed his fingers. With a roar of effort, he sat up and met Jago's next blow with one of his own.

The collision of wills produced an explosion that knocked them both sideways. Jago slammed into an oil drum, tipping it over, and Jack landed face down in the mud. Alpha lunged and turned desperate circles as a shower of sparks rained down.

'That's more like it!' Blood streamed from Jago's nose. 'No point in being afraid, eh? I know the worst and, believe me, death is *not* the worst.' He moved quickly to the crusher. 'The worst is having to live when you have no family … or friends.'

He clapped his hands and the door of the Beetle

slammed shut. A muffled cry came from inside as Charlie clambered across the front seats and yanked helplessly at the handle.

'Now then,' said Jago, swaying slightly. 'Like I said before we were so rudely interrupted, there's a reason we met. We were meant to share the mirror – and its secrets. So why don't you bring it here, hmm?'

His fist hovered over the button on the crusher's control panel. 'Well? What's it to be, Jack? You have a choice. It's quite straightforward. We can be partners … or enemies.'

Jack stared at him in dismay. Jago's mouth twisted in a strange kind of smile, as if he was actually pleased with the turn of events. He obviously expected to get his way. But what terrified Jack even more was that, in some dark corner of his mind, Jago still seemed to think he was in the right.

Nan's dice swung furiously over Charlie who hammered on the window, shouting something he couldn't hear. Why she'd got in the car was beyond him, but he had to get her out.

Thinking fast, his eyes flicked to Alpha. The wolf kept thrashing his head from side to side, snarling and pulling at the chain for all he was worth. 'All right,' he said abruptly. Suddenly there was no doubt about what he had to do. 'You win. I'll show you how it works.'

Jago's eyes narrowed. 'No games now. I want the truth. Or your precious ship goes down too, you hear me? Our little caper has made me a very rich man. And

Pi's nasty hacker friends have your virus ticking like a time bomb. If I vanish, who's to stop them?'

Jack nodded slowly. It wasn't a drunken threat. Jago had not only set in motion events that would cause untold misery, but he was also using them to cover his own back. His revenge was like a virus itself, spreading down the years and poisoning everyone – most of all, Jago himself.

'You want the truth?' The heat from the mirror intensified in Jack's hand and a wind gathered about him, making the cars rattle. 'The truth is, I'm still learning. But I know one thing. The magic is about trust. If you want it to work, you can't force Alpha. You have to work with him. Let me show you.'

Kneeling down, he turned the mirror towards Alpha who instantly went quiet.

It's time, Jack told him silently.

The wolf's eyes flashed and a white hot beam poured out of the disc, hitting the chain close to his neck. As the metal links began to soften and stretch, he threw his body forward, clawing at the ground.

'Why you lying little –' All the confidence drained from Jago's face. His fist smashed down on the control panel and, like a waking monster, the crusher screeched into action. The huge jaws yawned open, black diesel fumes billowed out and a terrified Charlie scuttled to the rear of the Beetle.

'Alpha! Quick!' screamed Jack. In less than a minute the car, with Charlie in it, would be pulverised beyond recognition. Snarling and tearing at the earth, the wolf pulled forwards with all his might. *Go on*, urged Jack, *you can do it!*

And then everything seemed to happen at once. As the chain broke, a bang like a gunshot reverberated around the yard. The car windscreen had exploded as one hundred tons of pressure closed down on the bonnet.

While Alpha bolted free, Jack sprinted for the machine. He saw Jago raise his hand and thought he meant to prevent him, then realised it was a defensive gesture. Glancing over his shoulder, he saw Alpha crouched and ready to attack, teeth bared, ears laid flat.

'Stay!' roared Jago, backing away.

But he may as well have commanded the earth to stop turning. Alpha gave a low growl, the wind blew stronger and the tower of cars where Pi had made his stand rocked to and fro. No whistle, no chain, no fearful allegiance could hold Alpha now. He bounded forwards.

The noise of the crusher died.

Having stopped the machine, Jack raced from the control panel and hauled himself onto the platform. And that was when the dreadful yelling began. He wished he could plug his ears, because amidst the frenzy of snapping and snarling, he could hear Jago repeatedly calling his name. 'Jack! Jaaaack!' There was nothing he could do, even if he'd wanted to. He had Charlie to think about and Jago's cruelty had pushed Alpha beyond the point of no return.

A metallic groaning thundered overhead and suddenly the sky seemed larger and the wind wilder.

The tower of cars had begun to topple. As Jack circled the Beetle, frantically searching for a way in, the Seer in him flew fleetingly to Alpha. *Run*, he told him, *run!* Through a film of red, he caught a last glimpse of Jago as Alpha must be seeing him. His mouth hung oddly ajar and one eye stared up like a cloudy yellow marble.

There was a violent crash and the yard became a whirlwind of dust and flying debris.

'Charlie!' Jack screamed. He thumped the car in desperation. Its roof was crumpled like a paper bag, leaving no space in the seats below. The only part that remained intact was the tiny boot which contained the engine.

Yet it was from there that a faint thudding came. He hurriedly flipped the handle. As the lid sprang open, he saw that the engine had gone, every last bit of it removed for spares.

'Charlie? Are you okay?'

Curled up in a tiny space with her arms cradling what looked like Nan's two dice, Charlie whimpered, 'No, I'm bloody not. Help!'

Jack leant further in. To his astonishment, the black and white fur in her arms moved. 'I don't believe it – you nutcase!'

'Well, someone had to save him,' said Charlie, handing over the wriggling ball of fur. 'Come on, let's get out of here!'

Blinking up at them both, Odin dug his claws into Jack's shoulder and yowled his agreement.

CHAPTER 39

The lift bell gave a loud ding and several bright-faced nurses jumped smartly aside as Jack and Charlie stepped onto the third floor of Dunton General Hospital, a big glass-fronted building in the town centre. Tongues clucked around them. Feet shuffled past. Then seconds later the departing lift whisked upwards, filled with girlish laughter. Heads bowed together, Jack and Charlie walked briskly on, so engrossed in conversation they hadn't noticed a soul.

Shadows flickered on the white walls and ceiling. No sooner had the merriment faded than another sort of clamouring began. Barely audible through the thick glass windows, a flock of seagulls dipped and dived, their calls quickening with excitement …

A full week had passed since the events at the scrapyard, during which time Jack and Charlie had only managed a few hurried phone calls. 'Typical adults,' Charlie had grumbled. Nothing was straightforward when they got involved. Being separated, after all they'd been through, had felt like the worst kind of punishment.

Desperate to trace Nan, they'd gone straight from Slater's to Dunton police station, only to find themselves at the centre of a missing persons hunt. Mrs Day, Charlie's mum, had wasted no time reporting her disappearance. And after dozens of unreturned calls to Nan, she'd given Jack's details too. When the police finally realised his description matched the boy seen with Jago Flyn, all hell had broken loose. 'Who is this stranger?' Mrs Day had screamed. 'What if the children have been abducted?'

Jack and Charlie couldn't believe the fuss. Endless interviews followed until eventually Charlie was packed off home. Jack, meanwhile, went to stay with an elderly relative who lived a short bus ride from the hospital. Nan, to his immense relief, was alive, though seriously ill with a head injury.

It was Charlie's first visit. At the sight of another red sign directing them to intensive care, she gave a little shudder. 'So –' she said quickly. 'What about Osmaston Hall? Have they finished grilling you yet?'

'Hard to say. I really hope so.' Jack steered her clear of an oncoming trolley. 'They're tearing their hair out, but I don't see how I can help any more.'

With no leads on the stolen millions, the police had questioned him long and hard. They knew he'd gone with Jago to sell the painting and met him later on the train. And he'd told them what he could about the boat trip and Charlie's rescue mission. But his statement had been jumbled and when he'd tried to warn them about the hackers, they hardly wrote anything down.

He knew they suspected it was only half the story. And they were right, of course. He'd said nothing about the mirror. Or Jago's magical past. Or their fight at Slater's. And he hadn't even mentioned Pi, the real thief. What was the point? Pi had gone, Jago was dead and no one would have believed a single word. Especially when they hadn't found the body.

Big squares of sunshine slanted along the corridor, making a pattern on the floor like a giant game of hopscotch. Avoiding the lines as usual, Jack bounced across them. 'It's weird,' he said, pausing on one foot. 'It comes and goes but I keep getting this funny feeling ...'

'Like what?'

Jack moved sideways and hopped two squares forward. 'Dunno ... it's hard to explain.'

His shoulders hunched up. It was like a dark cloud had passed out of him. Somehow the emptiness he'd associated with losing his parents had gone and in its place something else had taken over. 'It's like ...' He struggled to find a word big enough. 'Electricity. Sort of.'

'That figures.' Charlie stretched out her arms, walking along like Frankenstein. 'Definitely a loose wire.' She watched the black gym shoes make another manoeuvre. 'People don't run on electricity, donut. It's hope. You're getting on with life.'

'Yeah, I guess. Except –'

The sunny squares on the floor flickered and danced.

Without warning, the sensation Jack had been trying to describe grew ten times stronger and he looked up.

301

Above him, three seagulls fussed and squabbled at the windows, clipping the glass with their wings.

As he turned, they fell silent. Six beady eyes drew level with his, staring at him with such intensity that when the wind finally carried them off he was left with the strangest impression: it was like they wanted something.

'You okay?' Charlie gave him a nudge.

'Uh-huh.' Jack gazed after the birds, which had disappeared over the hospital roof.

'Friends of yours?'

He burst out laughing. Good question! Three seagulls – maybe it was a good sign. The mirror hadn't been working for days, not since the fight with Jago. Yet something strange was happening to him. Despite all the worry over Nan, he *had* to stay positive – be prepared for the unexpected.

He rang the security buzzer outside the ward doors.

'This is it. Ready?'

Charlie stuck out her bottom lip. She hated hospitals and anything to do with people being sick. The winking lights, the steady beeps of the monitors, the unnatural silences, all of it unsettled her. The mere thought of seeing Nan wired up to those machines made her insides turn to water.

Jack led her along the row of beds to Nan's corner of the ward where a nurse was filling in records. 'Two visitors – how lovely. Temperature's up a bit, but nothing to be concerned about,' she said breezily.

Nan lay motionless on her back with her thin arms straight down by her sides. She had a tube in her mouth

302

and a thick crepe bandage around her head which made her look like she was wearing a crown.

'Guess who's here!' Jack announced, giving her a hug.

Charlie tried to smile, and failed. The mechanical ventilator next to the bed was making horrible little clicking sounds. 'Nan, it's me,' she began. 'I would have come sooner but … well, only Jack was allowed.'

She put a card she'd made on the windowsill and pulled a face at Jack who nodded encouragingly. They both knew Nan was unlikely to respond – she'd been unconscious since the accident – but the doctors had said there was a chance she could still hear them.

'I'm sorry about the magpie,' Charlie resumed. 'Nasty, mean little … Oh Nan, I got so much wrong! Alpha wasn't that man's dog after all. He helped me. I wish you could have seen him. He – I …' Words deserted her and she flopped into a chair.

'It's okay, she knows. I told her the whole story,' said Jack.

'I expect she's proud then.' A big tear rolled down Charlie's cheek.

Jack stared glumly at the wave patterns on Nan's heart monitor. The tiny upward spikes looked more like mountains really, but at least they were regular. On impulse, he grabbed the mirror from his rucksack and placed it in his grandmother's hand.

'What are you playing at?' hissed Charlie. She glanced round the ward.

He didn't really know. But he was glad she'd stopped crying. 'I'd give anything to get her back.'

'I know.'

'I mean it. Anything. Even the mirror.' He thought he saw a blip on the monitor.

'Don't be daft. What about being a Magus?'

'I'd give that up too.'

'You can't!'

'Why not?'

'Well, for starters, what if Flyn comes back?' Charlie's voice dropped to a whisper. 'You know, in another life.'

'He's dead, Charlie.' Jack kept watching the screen. 'Punishing Alpha was the last straw. You saw for yourself.'

'I s'pose.' Charlie sniffed again. 'Sybil said you'd stop him.'

'I couldn't have done it alone. You were amazing.'

'You reckon? Ha. Nearly messed up though, didn't I? All for a stupid cat!'

A definite blip, like Mount Everest, appeared on the monitor. Jack's eyebrows arched too. 'No, you did exactly the right thing. And Odin's not stupid. He survived, didn't he?'

Another mountain, even larger this time, made his own heart leap. He leant across the bed. 'Take your time,' he whispered. 'I meant to tell you, he's fine. He's having fish every day!'

He gently removed the mirror from Nan's hand.

Charlie leant closer. 'Anything?'

'Stone cold.' The disc had been unresponsive ever since he'd freed Alpha. It was as if its store of energy had been completely exhausted by that one act. Maybe he *was* meant to pass it on, let someone else take a turn.

'What about Alpha? Have you "seen" him?'

He shook his head.

'What if –?'

'He's alive,' Jack cut in.

'How do you know?'

'I just do. Stop worrying, will you?'

'I can't help it. It's this place!' Charlie got up, scraping her chair back, and marched over to the window where she stood with her arms crossed, staring out.

A nurse came and went, smiling kindly at them.

Jack forced a smile back. Then, pursing his lips at Charlie, he slumped into the chair she'd vacated and, for the umpteenth time that week, tried to home in on Alpha.

To his surprise, the air around him grew instantly chilly and a vile smell hit the back of his throat. Yuk! He could even taste it. The stink was like rubbish at a dump, only a hundred times worse.

Covering his nose, he quickly willed himself back. He wished he could stop up his ears too, because apart from the hideous droning of flies, another sound had made him almost vomit: the crackle and crunch of bones being chewed.

He leant back in the chair, relieved to breathe in the smell of hospital disinfectant. *Phew!* No wonder Alpha had been elusive. It didn't take a genius to figure out whose rotten remains he was digesting.

He shot a glance at Charlie who was still gazing at the horizon, making no effort to talk. She hadn't even noticed. With a sigh, he stretched out his legs and let his own thoughts unravel.

Four leaps ... His eyes rested on the mirror which lay dully on the bed. Was that it? Surely the magic hadn't run out for good? Something else had to be going on. Maybe now he'd freed Alpha it had some other purpose.

He turned the disc over, peering at the ring of tiny Ms around the edge. Without Jago's magnifying glass they were almost impossible to see. M for myriad: Archimedes' number for calculating an insane amount of sand. How many were here? Myriads of myriads, probably. Certainly enough to make him go cross-eyed.

Feeling none the wiser, he gave Nan's hand a squeeze and wondered again if he should pass the mirror on. But who to? And what about *The Empress*? Defeating Jago hadn't changed that bit of destiny. How could he ever hope to stop a virus?

As the questions gathered, scraps of paper covered in crayoned fish blew up from his subconscious and his finger twitched. He rubbed at it thoughtfully and a rush of other memories pressed in: three tumbling birds above a bus shelter, a rolling pram, two tiny fists reaching up ...

And then it hit him.

Of course. In that crazy moment when Alpha had brought him and Lily together, the mirror had found a way to show him exactly where it belonged. He'd already seen the place on his computer but it hadn't meant anything. Then Lily, with her funny watch dial design, had reproduced it. Pharos. That was its home. It had come from the ruins of the old lighthouse and she was going to be the architect of a new one ...

As the pieces of the puzzle fell into place, his heart beat faster. No wonder the mirror had taken him to the ship. It carried a precious cargo – a small girl with a big plan that somehow involved the disc itself.

'Jack.' Charlie spoke his name sharply.

He didn't respond. The seal on his finger was burning madly and he needed to concentrate. *M for myriad,* he mused. His imagination seemed to flex and expand as a powerful idea began to form.

'Jack!'

'Hmm?'

'I think you should take a look at this.'

'Hang on.'

'No, I mean it. Will you please –'

There was a thud.

Charlie stifled a shriek and Jack swivelled round. On the other side of the hospital window, suspended in the air like model aeroplanes, were the three seagulls. Behind them, dozens of others turned in the air as if spinning in a whirlpool.

Charlie pointed at the biggest bird, which hovered inches from the glass. 'That one, it flew right at me!'

Hurrying over, Jack placed his palm on the window. The seagull immediately swooped around it.

'Ee-ee-lectricity!' Charlie squeaked. 'That feeling you described … it's Magus magic. Did you call this lot?'

Jack gazed up at the gull. It kept charging forwards, then swerving away at the last moment as if it wanted to get in.

'Bill?' he murmured. The gull reminded him of the

one in Wakeham who'd landed on the bollard, pestering him for sandwiches. His mouth fell open. 'I should've realised. He was bound to try and find me. The others must have travelled back too. They're from the ship!'

'Ghosts!' Charlie took several steps back.

'No.' Jack drew a circle on the window and watched the gull fly in a big loop. 'He's an animus actually. Mine. They all are!'

'But the wreck – it hasn't happened yet. What do they want?'

'A different future. I have to make sure it never happens. They want their lives back. I left them in a kind of limbo; they can't stay like that.' He went over to the bed and picked up his rucksack.

'Where are you going?'

'To find Lily. I have to give her the mirror.'

'But she's just a baby!'

'Not where I'm heading.' Jack bent over to kiss Nan's forehead. 'I'm going to fix things,' he whispered. 'Once and for all. And this time the mirror's going with me.'

'W-wait! You're coming back, aren't you?' Charlie looked at him in dismay.

'Course! Only not to this present. It won't exist.'

'What! Jack, slow down. Look at me, please! Why won't it? For God's sake – I'm here, so are you – this *is* happening!'

There was another thud at the window, as if the birds were reminding Jack of their existence too.

He put his hands on Charlie's shoulders. 'I'm not saying this isn't real.' And suddenly he was hugging her.

'We've had such an adventure. You won't forget it, will you?'

'How could I? Jack, you're frightening me. What are you going to do?'

'Something Jago showed me.'

'No!'

Jack picked up the mirror. 'That trick on the train – it's no wonder Sybil got so upset. He didn't just replay time, he sort of switched tracks. To a new reality. Similar but different. Oh, I know he was trying to impress me, but the point is Alpha let him. He'd never have managed it otherwise. Don't you see? I was meant to learn, Charlie, so I can use it too!'

'I – I don't get it. You went through the same station twice …'

'That's right.' Jack hopped sideways from one line of tiles on the floor to a parallel line. 'There are lots of paths – myriads, in fact. And when I deliver this to Lily's future, everything will change.'

There was no more time to explain. The magic was under way. He had to get going or miss the opportunity completely. He went to the window where the seagulls were circling higher and higher, calling noisily to each other.

'Alpha's here,' he said.

'Where?' Charlie rushed to his side. There were buses and cars parked all along the street below and children pouring out of a nearby school. She half expected them to scatter, screaming, but they carried on shouting happily.

'Keep away from the glass,' warned Jack.

She edged back, looking around. Nothing in the ward appeared to have changed, yet she could hear the swish of grass and the drumming of feet getting closer. She crouched down by Nan's bed. From the expression on Jack's face, it was clear he could see what she could only hear: Alpha approaching at incredible speed.

There was a sliding sound, an avalanche of rocks and debris tumbling down some distant slope, then silence. A long shivering silence. Charlie kept her eyes on Jack, hardly daring to breathe. He stretched out his hand and when the mirror burst into light, she braced herself.

A bang like a cannon blast rang out and the air around them seemed to explode. The wind tore at Charlie's clothes, the ocean roared in her ears and she heard faraway voices calling. Shattered glass rained down and, one after another, the seagulls stormed in, circling over her in a tornado of pounding wings which beat as fast as her heart.

Amidst their shrieks, the voices grew louder and faces began to stream everywhere, disappearing in and out of the light that poured from the mirror. Though Charlie didn't recognise any of them, they seemed to know her, because several came close, whispering her name, and tried to pull her along with them.

In the ward itself, nothing moved. Everyone and everything appeared frozen, as if ordinary time had ground to a halt. She clung to Nan's bed, the only thing that felt solid, narrowing her eyes into slits. The light around Jack was so intense she could only see his silhouette. He was standing at the place where the window had been, as if on the edge of a precipice. And he wasn't alone. Another shape had joined him, a great hulk of a man with a mass of thick, shaggy hair: Bill. Throwing his arm around Jack's shoulder, he stooped to say something. Charlie wondered what it could be that made Jack shake his head so fiercely. But after a few more words, Bill seemed to accept it and with a friendly thump on Jack's arm, he was gone.

Then Jack stepped forwards too and the light around him shimmered into a kind of arch. Charlie crossed her fingers. She hoped he knew what he was doing. The road below was a long way down. What if he fell? What if –

Claws rattled on the tiled floor.

She bobbed her head up, peering over the top of the bed like a soldier in a trench. Her lips curled into a smile. No security door could keep Alpha out: he was here!

When the wolf appeared, all that existed around her seemed to melt away. She only saw him for a split second before he flung himself headlong after Jack, but it was long enough to marvel at his transformation. He was magnificent. No longer the bedraggled creature from the scrapyard, his coat glistened and rippled with every stride. And his amber eyes, set deep within his broad face, shone with all the things they loved him for – his loyalty and endurance, his strength and wildness.

The light flared even brighter till Charlie couldn't look any more. Reaching for Nan's hand, she felt small and terrified. But as her mind emptied of thought, she knew one thing for certain: she wouldn't have missed Alpha's return for the world.

CHAPTER 40

Being in that wild place between one reality and the next took all Jack's courage and concentration. As the adrenalin pumped he kept his eyes firmly shut, willing the magic to do its work. *Come on, wolf,* he urged. *What's keeping you?*

The falling seemed endless. His heart hammered in his throat and his stomach flipped and churned like he was riding a rollercoaster. But it was his fifth leap, he could handle that. What made the experience unnerving wasn't so much the physical stuff, it was the 'not knowing'.

An infinite number of presents lay before him, yet for the right one to take hold, he had to remain open. The mirror belonged to Lily now: she must draw it to her. All he could do was stay calm, trust his intuition and hope Alpha would be quick, because without him the exchange was impossible.

He clutched the disc to his heart, listening as the shrieks of the seagulls rose to a crescendo, then faded quickly to nothing. *Dear, brave Bill.* His offer to stay had been hard to refuse. But he could never keep an animus trailing after him, not like Jago. Bill deserved better. Unmaking the gulls had been as important as freeing Alpha.

A great shuddering breath escaped him. The plummeting sensation had stopped.

His eyes flicked open. In the nothingness that surrounded him a soft thumping could be heard, as if the silence had a heartbeat.

'Hey, how long have you been there?'

Two amber eyes glinted up at him. *For ever*, they seemed to say. *Where have you been?*

Jack's throat tightened and for an instant he stood rigid, his fingers curling into fists. But fighting off the emotion was beyond him. When Alpha's head bowed to lick his knuckles, he sank down with a sob, burying his face in the wolf's gleaming coat.

It was a moment he would never forget. While the embrace went on, Alpha kept perfectly still. He didn't even seem to mind when Jack gently parted the ruff of fur on his neck. The gash had gone and in its place tufts of soft new hair were growing.

'So. That's decided then,' said Jack, finding his voice at last. 'We're friends, you hear me? No more running away. I can give up the mirror, but never you.'

Alpha's rough tongue licked away a tear from his chin, tickling slightly. Then he nudged at the disc which lay between them, exactly as he had on the jetty.

'I know. Lily's the keeper now. It's her future that matters. Come on then, I'm ready.'

But Alpha seemed in no rush. He let out a small whine, which turned into a yawn, and sat down on his haunches as if coolly biding his time.

'What's got into you?' Jack laughed. The same soft thump he'd heard a moment before came from the wolf's tail.

And then he saw it. In the middle of the mirror, a hazy picture had begun to form – the curved outline of a man's back and shoulders hunched over some task. As Jack leant closer, the folds of a robe appeared, followed by an arm, a hand and a stick, grasped firmly like a baton. It was slowly drawing a circle in the sand.

'Archimedes!'

Jack couldn't see a face, only the wisps of grey hair and the ancient hand as it carefully brought the circle to a close.

The stick hovered a second, before moving swiftly to the centre where it pressed down, making a tiny symbol.

α

'It's the mirror ...'

But even as he said it, Jack knew Alpha was trying to show him something much more mysterious. There they sat in between the doors of time, in a strange kind of nowhere-nowhen. It was an exceptional place, timeless and infinite, full of light, love and magic. That was what Alpha had wanted him to see – the space which a Magus, young or old, could reach in a heartbeat.

The picture faded and the mirror began to glow. Jack picked it up, nodding at the wolf to show he understood.

Alpha would never leave him; he'd always be here.

The amber eyes gazed back, seeing all there was to see. Then they blinked. A million rings of light – myriad upon myriad – spread out like ripples around them.

Chapter 41

Lily paused in the doorway to her office, a plastic coffee cup in hand. She'd worked most of the night, a delegation of ministers was arriving in less than three hours – and now this. An intruder, in the shape of a scruffy boy, sat sprawled at her desk, a filthy rucksack at his feet.

Her mouth twisted to one side. How had he got past security? And what did he think he was playing at? His head was so close to the 3D hologram she'd been preparing for her boss he was practically inside it. Hadn't he seen an Imagepad before?

'Oi! Leave that alone. Who gave you permission to be here?'

Her favourite black chair swung round, the coffee cup left her hand and a dark stain spread out on the carpet below.

'Oops. Sorry. Hang on, let me get that,' said Jack, scrambling after the cup.

Through a window next to a tall bookcase, a patch of pink sky blossomed around the dome of St Paul's cathedral. Lily's eyes flicked towards the building, before returning to his.

'I'm dreaming, right?'

'No, that's real out there. So am I,' said Jack gently. 'Here, sit down. This stuff takes some getting used to.'

Lily sank slowly into the chair, blinking at him through owlish brown glasses. Everyone, even the workaholics at Abelwhite Design, had told her she was overdoing it. Could lack of sleep make you hallucinate? A boy – no, a ghost – from her childhood had come to haunt her.

She glanced at his black gym shoes. 'Jack?'

A smile spread across Jack's face. He put the cup on the desk, slowly so as not to make her jump, and nodded. Despite the fierce chin and angular cheekbones, he could still see hints of the baby face he knew. Lily, he guessed, must be in her twenties.

'Don't worry. You're not going mad. Look, it's 5.49, an ordinary Friday morning.'

The digital clock on Lily's computer clicked to 5.50.

She continued staring at him as if he'd grown another head.

'Okay, maybe not that ordinary!' said Jack. He turned slowly in a circle. 'Wow, you really made it! What an office. This is brilliant, by the way. I like the spire. How will a building that size manage to float?'

Lily transferred her bewildered gaze to the hologram. A soaring architectural model of the Pharos lighthouse, a perfect replica of Jack's screensaver, rose from the Imagepad embedded in her desk and bobbed across a virtual sea.

'Um, Archimedes' principle, I guess,' she mumbled.

'No kidding! What's that?'

'It's to do with water displacement … But you're not here for a maths lesson, I take it?'

'Not likely! Archimedes comes into it though.' He beamed at her, glad the shock of his appearance was wearing off. 'You're stuck, aren't you? Something's missing. A piece of genius, perhaps?'

Lily nodded mutely. Then before he could say any more, she opened a desk drawer, produced a tatty looking scrapbook and began turning its pages. Dozens of sketches, similar to the one she'd drawn for him in Wakeham, flipped through her fingers, all child-like prototypes of the hologram in front of him.

She glanced up uncertainly. 'We met on the quay, right?'

'Yes.'

'I remember because you were kind and …' She trailed off, frowning at the book. 'You gave me the name. You wrote it down: Pharos. I've searched high and low over the years. I don't know where I put that sketch.'

Jack shrugged. 'You were small. Things get lost.'

'Maybe.' Lily smoothed out the curling pages and chewed her lip. 'How on earth – I mean – did I *do* something to bring you here?'

Jack's eyes rested on the fish shapes which covered the scrapbook. 'I expect you made a wish. That's how it starts.'

'I see.'

It was obvious she didn't, but he kept quiet.

'If I did, I don't remember. To be honest, I can't even think straight. I'm that close to giving up.'

'Why?'

'A hundred reasons. It's complicated.'

'You mean I'm too young to get it?'

'No! Nothing like that. It's just –' Lily removed her glasses to rub her eyes, leaving dark make-up smudges on her cheeks. 'Everyone has their own big ideas: the investors, the government in Egypt, the partners here … especially them.'

She pulled a grumpy face and copied the deep, plummy voice of her boss. 'Pharos has to be an "icon", Ms Harington. A landmark for the next century. A symbol of peace between east and west.' She sighed.

'There's a snag?'

'Yes! Don't get me wrong, that stuff's important. But honestly? No one realises the technical problems. This is our fourth attempt. It's meant to be a lightship, an observatory *and* a communications tower. Only we can't do it all. Frankly, it's a mess.'

Jack frowned. The model looked amazing to him. Inside the blue dome, tiny figures sat at café tables in a huge glass atrium. And below the waterline, in a tunnel which ran like a watch dial around the edge, others strolled about admiring the ruins. He knew it was only a trick of light, but he couldn't resist. He reached in to watch the figures walk across his hand.

A faint smile flickered over Lily's face. She gave the computer screen a smart tap and the image tripled in size.

Jack leapt back as if electrocuted.

'You know, I should really be thanking you, not complaining,' she laughed. 'Just imagine if we'd never met. There'd be no Pharos. Not even in a hologram!'

Blues and greens swirled about Jack's head, making patterns on the floor and walls. Half of the lighthouse spire had disappeared through the ceiling and from the waist up, he was standing in an illusion of sea water. His mind reeled with memories of the shipwreck.

'Can I ask something?' he blurted.

'Fire away.'

'In Wakeham you mentioned a holiday, a cruise.' He drew in his breath slowly. 'Did you go?'

'On *The Empress*? Yes. Its maiden voyage.'

'Past the Pentland lighthouse?'

'All the way to the Med!'

'With your grandmother and Mr Lonsdale – '

'And my parents, of course. It was incredible, like a film set. People loved the furniture. Very retro: shades of the Titanic! They were in every magazine.'

'Who?'

'My parents! That's what they do. Look, they made me this.' Laughing, she spun round in the chair.

Jack stared at her. He could hardly take it in. Lady Harington had built her ship. There'd been no virus …

As the chair turned, a chain of minute events seemed to rewrite themselves. He pictured Herbert Lonsdale snoring soundly in his cabin, undisturbed by a twelve-year-old stowaway, his glasses unbroken, the engine pounding, while outside his door the steward passed quietly by, brushing at his uniform to remove a handprint: a greeting left by a certain bearded engineer before he bounded up the stairs to peer at a distant winking light ...

You're a piece of bloomin' magic.

A tingle of electricity shot through him. He'd done it! He'd sent events down another track. It was Fenstreet all over again, except on a much grander scale. Grinning, he gave the chair a nudge so it spun faster. The irony was priceless. Jago had given him the whole idea!

'Whoa, hang on.' Lily got up, slipping her foot into a stray shoe. Her fingers flicked over the computer screen, pinching at various folders and stretching them open. 'Give me a minute. There's something I want you to see.'

A piece of bloomin' magic!

From a past that no longer existed, Bill's ghostly words replayed in Jack's mind. He quickly undid the rucksack. *No shipwreck means no seagull,* he told himself. It was time to go home and start over, back to a life in which the mirror would never arrive.

Outside, the clouds had grown luminous, fanning out like spidery hair in the reddening sky. A quiet swish, like a curtain grazing the floor, made him start. Out of the corner of his eye, he saw the hem of a purple coat next to the bookcase.

Sybil! He nearly said the name out loud. But the old woman raised a finger to her lips and nodded in Lily's direction.

'You've led me a merry dance, Jack Tideswell,' she

said, in a breathless voice only he could hear. 'It's a pleasure to meet you at last.'

The brilliant eyes twinkled. 'Fenstreet has never seen such mayhem. All journeys on hold, people stranded in different centuries; complete madness. However, you've done well. Extremely well. Thanks to you, the junction has reopened. You may pass through on your way home.'

Jack gaped at her.

'That's right. You can travel light; you're a Magus now. The ability was always there, I might add. No more need for the mirror. Speaking of which –' she pulled her coat about her '– better make haste. Let's not push our luck.'

She glanced at the crimson sky in which the clouds, Jack noticed, were moving surprisingly fast.

His heart thumped. *Jago. Is he –?*

'Don't even say his name,' Sybil snapped. She touched the scar over her right eye. 'Wounds inflicted by magic don't heal that easily. Your wolf picked his bones clean and blew his soul to kingdom come. He's gone. Kaput! In this timeframe and every other.' She glanced at the racing clouds. 'Even so, until this exchange happens things in the ordinary world are – how can I put it? – a tad unstable. Hurry along; finish what you came to do.'

She nodded at Lily who was busy typing a long string of code. 'She doesn't know it, of course, but she's building a new junction. You're about to deliver the main component.'

Jack's jaw dropped.

'Ah, here we go,' said Lily.

A large cylindrical object, like a bass drum, rotated on her computer screen. She flipped it upright and entered some co-ordinates. The hologram returned to its original size and the cylinder appeared inside it.

'So that's the data centre,' she said. 'I've managed to reduce it to three floors, but see how it's crowding the observation deck? Apart from the light transmission, we've got all sorts of communication systems on board: internet servers, TV, radio, satellite. That's a load of hot electronics. And with all the cooling equipment, there isn't enough room. It's like you said, I'm stuck, and unless –'

'You need more space, right?' Jack placed the mirror on the Imagepad.

'I … yes!' The disc had begun to glow, turning his hand a translucent blue. Lily's eyes bulged. 'What – is – that?'

'A mirror. The centrepiece of the old Pharos lighthouse. It has Archimedes' initials on it.'

'Archi-m-medes!' she stammered. 'Where did you –?'

'My parents found it in the ruins.' Jack wanted to tell her all about them, but already the seal on his finger had begun to sting. Once he let go, his time would be up. 'It connects the past with the future, a kind of superconductor.'

He removed his hand and the mirror rose off the pad, glowing like a huge blue coin. For several seconds it revolved inside the hologram before attaching itself to the underside of the cylinder. Equations poured down

323

the computer screen, the data centre flickered and slowly began to shrink.

'You won't need cooling equipment. There's niobium in it,' said Jack. 'It conducts electricity without overheating.'

He thought of Charlie and the fun they'd had with the street lights and suddenly his head swam. The sounds of another place were filtering in, the everyday noises of a train station.

'Jack, what's happening?' Lily's voice sounded muffled. 'Where are you? Come back ...'

'You're standing in front of the turnstile,' said Sybil. 'Speak your name and destination.'

Jack's mouth opened but nothing came out. All he could see was the brightness of the mirror.

'We *have* to go. The arrival hall is through here. What are you waiting for?'

'Jack!' called Lily faintly.

'I can hear you,' he shouted.

'What do I do?'

'She'll be fine,' Sybil cut in.

'Sybil says you'll be FINE!' he yelled. When no response came, he hung his head.

'Oh cheer up. She's hardly going to forget you. I've never seen anyone with such strong shadow memories.'

'What do you mean?'

Sybil's eyes rolled. 'Must I spell it out?' she huffed. 'There's a reason she can't find that sketch. It's because it doesn't exist. You never met her on the quay. Not this time round at any rate ... Oh Jack, do keep up. In cases like this, the subconscious holds on to what no longer exists. All she's remembering is –'

'Pharos!' shouted Lily. 'Not far, but fair …'

'There. Satisfied? She's thought of her wish. That one memory and the confidence you gave her has made a new time junction possible. Now, give yourself a pat on the back and move along, please. There's a lady with a small dog and a large suitcase right behind you … Dear lord, this isn't doing my blood pressure any good. Say your name and destination. The turnstile opens automatically.'

The brightness faded and Jack became aware of something sniffing at his ankles. But his own name and where he was going were the last things on his mind. The tiny dog looked up at him, then scuttled away in terror as he filled his lungs one last time.

'LILY!' he bellowed across the years. 'We made it. I kept my promise!'

CHAPTER 42

FULL CIRCLE HOME

In the kitchen of number 12 Hill Rise, three rashers of bacon sizzled under the grill, sending tiny puffs of smoke uncoiling towards the ceiling below Jack's room.

On the radio, a voice jabbered excitedly. The great-grandson of William Godley himself had abandoned his usual 'Thought for the Day' to announce a competition. The sight of the town's ancient chestnut tree, on his way to the studio, had put him in an oddly reckless mood. He'd half expected the tree to be gone, the family statue too. And so, even though he'd meant to say something grand – about roots and tradition – he found himself advising everyone to find a nut and aim for glory in the town's first conker festival.

His audience at the kitchen sink was miles away. Despite the smoke creeping over her shoulder, it took several explosive pops from the grill to break Nan's reverie.

'Oh, for crying out loud.' A flurry of soapsuds floated

down from her yellow gloves. 'Watch what you're doing, woman!' With a groan of despair, she grabbed the grill pan and threw open the window.

Outside, the wind chimes on the apple tree tinkled like a sweet shop bell. A breeze blew in, bringing with it the scent of wet grass, and the fumes evaporated.

Pink-faced, Nan looked down at the pan. The bacon was extremely crispy, but fortunately not cremated. In fact, the crunchy rinds were just how Jack liked them. She tightened the belt of her dressing gown and set about cutting the bread.

That's it, she told herself, sawing furiously. *Absolutely, positively The Last Time.* Brandy Brainstorms were a great invention – possibly her most delicious recipe ever – but from now on, they were for medicinal purposes only. Not a treat and certainly not a nightcap. Never in all her life had she woken up feeling so peculiar.

It wasn't a hangover exactly. It felt more like permanent déjà vu. She kept getting flashbacks of strangely familiar events, as if this particular morning had already happened, but under very different circumstances.

For the hundredth time she checked the sky outside. Not a storm cloud in sight, nor a single white seagull to bring whispering voices she didn't want to hear. Instead, the sun glinted off the chrome bumper of her blue Beetle, which stood by the garage awaiting its weekly wash and polish.

Dreams and premonitions: it was just as well half of hers meant nothing whatsoever. She glanced at the black and white dice which hung motionless over the steering wheel. Thank goodness her magic was so fallible. If last night's wild imaginings had any substance …

She turned down the radio, fading out the weather forecast. The barometer had already told her what she needed to know. It was going to be a cold day, so whether he liked it or not, Jack would need a coat.

'Time to get up! Bacon sandwich on the table – twenty minutes and counting!' she bellowed.

There was a thud on the ceiling.

Nan's eyes shot upwards. She'd never known Jack get out of bed so fast. Footsteps thundered overhead, accompanied by a volley of bangs from the study. Odin tore in like a missile, skidded to a halt and proceeded to twine himself around her ankles, yowling in a rusty voice and looking up at her with moonstruck eyes.

'Hey, what's all this?'

Odin rolled over on his back, waggled his legs in the air and purred his loudest tractor purr.

'You daft thing!' Nan bent down to rub his tummy. 'Anyone would think you'd been starved for a month.'

A pair of black plimsolls appeared in front of her.

'He missed you,' said Jack.

Nan straightened up slowly. There it was again: that déjà vu feeling. Why was Jack wearing those grubby old gym shoes when he had a perfectly good pair of trainers in the hall cupboard? And why had he brought Indigo downstairs?

Jack put the blue horse in her hand. Without another word, he threw his arms around her, squeezing so tight she could barely breathe. 'Everything I ever wanted was right here under my nose.'

Nan's eyes grew round as saucers. Seagull or no seagull, something peculiar *was* going on. She looked from her grandson to Odin, who nervously licked his paw, then back again to Jack.

'Wait a second. Show me your hand,' she ordered.

With a grin, Jack unfurled his fingers.

'Oh good lord, oh my …'

'It's not a tattoo, if that's what you're thinking.'

'I know, I know.'

Nan covered her mouth. There it was, large as life, a name represented by a single letter: Alpha. $\bigcirc$ It was the wolf's seal transferred via the mirror the moment before Jago Flyn had stolen it. But how did she know all that? A chill ran through her. In hospital, after the accident … Jack had told her everything. The memories weren't déjà vu at all, but the truth.

'Apparently, I get it from you,' said Jack brightly.

'What?'

'The magic! It bypassed Dad, skipped a generation. Sybil says you're in denial. She says hiding from your own gift isn't good for you.'

'Oh she does, does she?' A vision of a cantankerous old woman on a rainswept road came back to Nan.

'Yes! That's why it only half works. Why on earth didn't you tell me? She says you're welcome at Fenstreet any time. When you're ready, that is.'

'Fenstreet?'

'Why not?'

'Oh heavens …'

And now Nan was hugging Jack, a big tear rolling down her cheek. It wasn't so much Sybil's extraordinary invitation that overwhelmed her. It was the fact that her own grandson (who had made it home with the seal of a Magus on his hand!) was taking everything in his stride.

Odin gave a plaintive mew. Uncertain what all the fuss was about, he leapt up on the counter where the bacon sandwich was going cold. With one ear pricked towards the open window, he nosed the bread onto the floor and tucked into the meat, gulping down as much as he could while Nan's back was turned.

The wind chimes tinkled again. A breeze delicately combed his fur, delivering a sound which only his finely-tuned hearing could detect. It came from more than a hundred metres away: the whirr of a bicycle labouring uphill.

A few minutes later, the noise of screeching brakes and the crunch of gravel caused Nan to dry her eyes. The bell pull creaked and the house filled with impatient ringing. Odin hopped down, following his two humans into the hall.

When Jack opened the door, the first thing he noticed about Charlie was that she wasn't wearing the black beanie. Her ginger hair fell in a tangle on her shoulders and her school shirt was buttoned up all wrong.

'I got here as fast I could,' she wheezed, clinging to the bell pull. 'Well? Go on then …'

Jack and Nan stared at her.

'Tell me!'

'What?' said Jack.

'Tell me it happened!'

'It happened,' said Jack and Nan together.

Charlie let out a banshee shriek, sending Odin scurrying through Nan's legs into the study.

'Honestly, Charlie, the whole town heard that,' said Jack, who was being half throttled in a bear hug.

Charlie planted a kiss on his cheek. 'So you saw her. Did you hand over the mirror? Was she pleased?'

'Yes,' he said, his face burning.

'And she's going to build it, right?'

'She'd already started. It's going to be a time junction, like the old Pharos.'

'No way. A-mazing!' Charlie grabbed Nan and danced her round in a circle. 'We're home! Feels weird, doesn't it? Like being on a different planet or something!'

'Yes, dear. Please slow down, you're making me giddy.'

'Sorry. Hey, guess what? On the way here I passed this guy and when he saw me, he tipped his can of drink in the gutter. That's the second time! He remembers, you know.'

'What?' said Nan.

'The bridge! It went for miles and miles and miles … He saw me cycle over it.'

Nan shook her head. She couldn't take much more excitement.

'Hey, let's cycle to school!' continued Charlie.

There was a resounding silence.

Jack looked at his grandmother.

'I don't know ...' In vain, Nan tried to ignore the pleading eyes. 'Oh, all right then.'

'Yee-ha!' Charlie made Nan dance some more.

'Promise me you'll watch the main road. And the junction by The Feathers. It's rush hour, remember,' said Nan as she spun round. 'And Jack – take a coat, will you?'

'Got it,' called Jack from the depths of the hall cupboard.

Grabbing his trainers, he went to sit on the stairs to change into them. But as he pulled off the plimsolls, he couldn't help feeling wistful. He'd learned a lot in these beaten-up old shoes. And, by rights, they should have been in the school lost property box. Yet here they were – like Alpha's seal – defying time, the only items to have travelled the entire journey.

He noticed Charlie had gone quiet too. It wasn't hard to guess what she was thinking. What kind of mood would Blunt be in today? Jack put on the trainers, tying the white laces tight. *Man or mouse?* Whatever, he was ready. Besides, Blunt would have his own memories, some of which wouldn't be too pleasant.

'Okay, let's go,' he said.

'Oh no you don't!' said Nan. 'Not on an empty stomach. Back up and turn around.'

Odin, who had just reappeared at the study door, hung his head and fled. Nan clicked her tongue at him. 'Right, you two,' she ordered. 'Follow me. All this coming and going is making my head spin.'

★★★

When they finally set off for school, Jack and Charlie were laughing so hard they could barely cycle straight. Cursing Odin for his greed, Nan had hastily prepared a second breakfast during which time yet another visitor had arrived. Its high-pitched shrieks had startled them all and before they could stop her, Nan had rushed into the garden banging two saucepan lids together like cymbals.

A very frightened peacock – Percy from Osmaston Hall – had taken refuge on the garage roof. He looked almost as shocked as Nan herself, and no amount of coaxing with kind words and pieces of toast would tempt him down. So, after fixing Nan a strong black coffee (to which she later added a shot of her favourite remedy), they left Percy to it. There he would remain for the rest of the day, rattling his feathers and shrieking in disdain at every passing car.

Even now, they could hear his cries as they rumbled across the cobbles towards the market square. The wind plucked at the canopies of the traders' stalls where a noisy crowd had gathered, stamping and cheering. Two grown men were engaged in a conker game which had become so serious the fishmonger was taking bets.

'See that?' yelled Charlie. 'The guy in the apron had a fistful of tenners!'

Steering between the shoppers, Jack grinned and looked away at the sky. A certain I.O.U. written in the sand had come to mind. High above him, the cirrus clouds spread out like white feathers … He was going to miss Bill. In the blink of an eye, a million extraordinary incidents seemed to have taken place. And now, here they were, back at the beginning: A for Alpha. The wolf had transformed everything.

'So,' said Charlie, noticing his faraway gaze. 'Was she beautiful?'

'Who?'

'Lily! Who else?'

'Oh … yes, I suppose so. Very.'

'You liked her?'

'Obviously.'

'Think you'll see her again?'

'Charlie?'

'Yeah?'

'Shut up.'

'I was only asking. I thought –'

'Hey, look at that!'

They'd reached Elmwood Crescent, a downhill stretch of road which ran past St Mark's Church. There wasn't much traffic and, with the exception of a man mowing the grass in the cemetery, hardly anyone was about.

'What is it?' Charlie wrinkled her nose.

'Nothing. Race you!' And before she could even find the right gear, Jack was off, freewheeling down the hill with his legs in the air.

'Oh very funny!' Charlie steamed after him. She knew he'd wait until she was dead level, then pedal like a maniac. That was their rule.

On this occasion, however, Jack seemed to have forgotten the rules. Either that or he was being far too casual, because when she drew level, he let her speed straight past.

'Yee-ha!' she yelled, seizing the advantage. Head down, she pedalled furiously, not bothering to look back.

If she had, she might have noticed Jack smiling. What he liked about Charlie, apart from the way she always spoke her mind (even when you wished she wouldn't), was that she couldn't resist a challenge. He'd managed to distract her. But if he didn't catch up, he'd never hear the end of it.

In the market square another raucous cheer broke out. Jack gripped the handlebars tight and kicked down.

Behind him, an unseen pair of amber eyes blinked. The wind gusted at his back and the trees along the crescent bowed their branches, shedding leaves like orange and yellow ticker tape. With Alpha's blessing, Jack sped on.

ACKNOWLEDGEMENTS

Many people have helped me during the writing of this novel, giving unstintingly of their time. Without their generosity, it would have been impossible to bring the story into the world.

Special thanks must go to those who read the book in draft form and provided invaluable feedback. They include the exceptional team of editors at Electrik Inc, Janine Amos, Kay Leitch and Kim Donovan, proofreader Jude White, Becky Bagnell at The Lindsay Literary Agency, and Julia Green, who helped me find my voice on the Writing for Young People MA at Bath Spa University.

Heartfelt thanks also to my dear writing pals Victoria Rothwell, Daniel Goodleff and Terry Ellen, whose enduring faith and good humour kept me going on the long journey to publication. Last but not least, my love and thanks to my two sons, Rob and Ben, who grew up with the story. Two muses with big imaginations, they always had brilliant answers whenever I got stuck.

For character illustrations and stories about the
inspiration behind *The Mirror of Pharos* visit:
www.jslandor.com